I Will Remember You

By Lisa Cardiff

I Will Remember You

Copyright © 2021 by Lisa Cardiff.
All rights reserved.
First Print Edition: February 2021

Limitless Publishing, LLC
Kailua, HI 96734
www.limitlesspublishing.com

Formatting: Book Pages By Design
Cover Design: Deranged Doctor Design

ISBN-13: 978-1-954194-07-6

Dedication

A special thanks to my family, without whom I'd be lost.

Chapter One

"Ten, nine, eight..." The hushed chant reached my ears, and I clutched my mother-in-law's frail hand tighter.

Nora's faded blue eyes held mine. A silent tear streamed down her lightly lined face. Her normally meticulously groomed hair had fallen out of her smooth chignon and wispy pieces framed the side of her jaw.

I glanced down at my husband and a bolt of panic shot through me. I swallowed hard over the tightness in my throat, begging my courage not to fail me now. I hadn't deserted him before and I wouldn't now.

"Seven, six, five, four..." The countdown continued.

Time inexorably moved forward despite the fact that my life as I'd known it was coming to a hasty end. I closed my eyes, wishing the moment away. Wishing to be anywhere other than here, but not wanting to be anywhere else except here. I couldn't believe this was the end of the story.

"Three, two, one. Happy New Year!" The last three words were slightly louder followed by muted laughter and a few shushes.

My chest burned with an unrelenting grief and my bones ached, making me feel eighty rather than twenty-six. The irony of losing the one person who saved me from destitution and absolute misery wasn't entirely lost on me. While the entire world made plans and promises, gulped champagne, and counted down the minutes until they could ring in a new year, I counted down the minutes of my husband's life.

Andrew's labored, raspy breath drew my attention back to him. His eyes were closed as they had been for nearly two days. His jaw was slack and his familiar lips were parted. Over the last hour, his inhalations had become louder and further apart. My gut told me the end was near. I stood as still as a deer in headlights, waiting for his next one. When the celebration faded from down the hall and the slow even tick of the wall clock continued for one too many seconds, I knew it was over.

I couldn't hold back any longer. Tears flooded my eyes, and every cell in my body begged me to run as far away from here as possible. I scanned the dingy white walls, the worn overstuffed chairs on either side of a window overlooking the brightly lit parking lot of the hospice care facility.

Instead of running, I released Nora's hand, sunk down onto one of the navy chairs, and let the sobs escape. I sounded deranged, almost like a wounded animal, which made sense because I'd been bottling them up for years now. I hadn't cried, really cried,

2

since my husband was diagnosed, and now that I had opened the floodgates, I wasn't entirely certain I could stop.

Misery squeezed at my heart until I was certain it would stop beating. Longing and despair tore at my insides. I pressed my lips together and wrapped my arms around my body, desperate to stifle the noise coming from a deep primal place inside of me. Desperate to bring warmth back into my body. Desperate to hold onto reality when nothing made sense.

Andrew was young. Andrew was strong. Andrew was brilliant. This didn't happen to men like him. I blinked repeatedly in a half-hearted attempt to convince myself this was all a dream. It didn't work. Nothing did. The tears kept coming. The pressure inside my head increased until I couldn't think, and Andrew never took another breath no matter how long I stared at his chest.

When I finally ran out of tears, Nora pulled me into an embrace for the first time in our acquaintance. As I'd gotten to know her, I realized she was formal, not cold, and that realization explained a lot about Andrew too.

"Emma, sweetie, we need to talk about a few things. I—" her voice trailed off and she shook her head. "Now's not the time. Do you want me to get the staff?"

"No. I'll do it. I need a few minutes. You can go. I know you're tired."

She nodded in understanding and then slipped out of the room that had become a second home to both of us over span of the last two weeks.

Chapter Two

Seven Months Later

"Yo, Em, where does shit like this go?" My brother, Brock, lifted two crystal champagne flutes over his head, dangling them from his meaty fingertips as if they hadn't cost one of my wedding guests three hundred dollars for the pair.

I pushed a strand of tangled blonde hair away from my face with my forearm. I couldn't remember the last time I had brushed it. Much less bothered with makeup. What was the point? While I was only twenty-six, I felt ancient, and it was only my brother and me here. He had seen me so much worse, so he wouldn't comment or even notice for that matter.

"I don't know. Just set them in the kitchen. I think there's a glass cabinet. That might be a nice place to put that stuff." If they didn't have sentimental value, I would have left them for Andrew's sister along with the mountain of china. Hosting a dinner party didn't seem like it was in the

4

cards for quite a while.

Exhausted, I stretched out like a starfish on the dusty hardwood floors. I glanced at the hem of my oversized sweatshirt. It was faded, tattered, and I'd spilled coffee down the front a few days ago. I sucked in a deep breath and the musty scent of old furniture and floor polish surrounded me. I could leave all the doors and windows open for a week and this place would still have the distinct smell of age and disuse.

Moving into a home that hadn't been occupied on a regular basis for over a decade was a lot harder than I'd envisioned. While Nora had someone clean the home quarterly, no one had thrown away anything in the last hundred years. Maybe longer. Every closet, cabinet, and drawer held innumerable objects, most of which needed to be dumped in the trash. I'd peeked into the attic yesterday and nearly had a heart attack. Except for a few small aisles for walking, boxes reaching to the sloped ceiling covered every inch.

Brock set the fragile flutes on top of a box and ran a hand through his shaggy light brown hair. "Why did you decide to move here again?"

"Ah, because I have nowhere else to go. Remember, Andrew gave our house to his sister."

The day the attorney read my husband's will, I learned my house was no longer my house, and my car was no longer my car. Basically, I was entitled to the money in our joint bank accounts and all personal property in our home. It amounted to $20,000. Granted, that was $20,000 more than I came into our marriage with, but I had no idea he planned to leave everything to his mom except our house. That went to his sister, Leah, who hadn't even bothered to attend his funeral.

In an attempt to make things right, Nora had given me this home along with trust for upkeep. It came with some restrictions and strings, but it was better than being homeless.

"Yeah, that's messed up," he mused. "You could sell this place."

"That could take years and in the meantime, I don't have much cash or a job."

He shook his head. "But the trust—"

"Reverts back to Nora if I sell this place within the next five years. I'm stuck."

"Your husband was a jackass."

I turned my head to the side to avoid his hot glare. My brother's dislike of Andrew wasn't new. It was hate at first sight. Andrew thought he was a dirty coal miner and he hadn't done much to hide his disdain. Brock, on the other hand, told Andrew exactly what he thought of him. I think his exact words were pompous dick. Needless to say, it drove a huge wedge between my brother and me. He refused to step foot in my home, and Andrew refused to accompany me when I visited Brock in West Virginia.

While it hurt that Andrew wouldn't come with me, I kind of understood his reasoning. Going back to West Virginia meant dealing with my mama, and that was something I wouldn't wish on my worst enemy. From a young age, I had made excuses for her. Brock did the same. In the beginning, it was understandable. Pa had died in a mining accident and Mama deserved time to grieve and sort out her life. Unfortunately, rather than helping her heal, time turned her into a person I didn't recognize. She screamed. She hit. She drank, and that was just the tip of the iceberg. She was a certifiable train wreck.

"Yeah, well, he's no longer around to defend himself, so let's not get into it. In the end, everything worked out. I have this house."

"Right. I'm not sure it's much of a consolation prize." Brock rolled his eyes. "What the hell are you gonna do out here in the middle of nowhere? It's at least an hour to Macon from here. Longer to Atlanta."

I scanned the grand parlor with its dark wood-paneled walls, floral furniture, and oil paintings of Andrew's ancestors. To my right was a grand staircase, a narrow corridor leading to the kitchen at the rear of the house, and a formal dining room with a crystal chandelier with scrolling brass accents and large supporting pendeloques. At some point, someone had converted it to electricity. The whole place made me question what century I was living in. It boggled my mind that I somehow ended up with the Clayton family ancestral home.

When I'd seen the black and white photo of this place in Andrew's office not too long after we'd married, I'd fallen in love. Something about it called to me. It'd inspired me to focus my studies on the Antebellum period. Andrew promised to take me here more than once, but it never came to fruition. He'd spent all of his Christmas holidays here growing up and he'd claimed that was more than enough for him. To him, this place was a drafty, rambling home with nothing to recommend it.

"Maybe I'll turn it into a bed and breakfast. I think people like those."

Andrew and I had spent a couple weeks staying in bed and breakfasts throughout the south. We had a good time, but I wasn't entirely certain I could deal with having non-stop company and being forced to make conversation. Conversation was hard these days, and inevitably I'd have to explain how I ended up running this place alone.

A bark of laughter flipped his perpetual frown. "Who's gonna come here? This place is like a creepy time capsule. It's probably haunted, or at the very least it has a shitload of bad karma."

I shrugged. "Well, I don't know. People interested in the Civil War, a romantic weekend, or just some time away from the city. There's a cute historic town not too far from here. And haunted houses aren't real. Stop trying to freak me out."

Turning this place into a bed and breakfast was a stretch. I might get a trickle of people, but not enough to make a career out of it. I'd have to farm the acres surrounding the property and that didn't seem realistic. I didn't know anything about agriculture and truthfully, I didn't have any interest in overseeing a working farm. Maybe someday that would change, but not in my current state of mind. I still had days when getting out of bed felt like an accomplishment.

"You'd know more about that than me, but in the meantime, you're gonna die of loneliness out here."

"A little time alone won't hurt me. I need to

process everything that happened. I spent the last two years taking care of Andrew." Brock snarled, and I held up my hand to stop him from bitching about Andrew. He'd made his opinion crystal clear. "Besides, I wouldn't be lonely if you agreed to stay here and help me fix up the place. I'd pay you more than you're making in the mine, and I wouldn't have to worry about you."

He was already shaking his head by the time I finished my plea. "You know I can't do that. What would happen to Ma?"

It was my turn to snarl. "Here's a novel idea. She could start taking care of herself. I'd say it's about time. You don't owe her anything. It's not like she ever worried about us."

"You and I both know it's not that simple," he snapped. "Stop bringing it up."

"Yeah. Yeah. I'm sorry." I came to my feet, dusted off my pants, and inched toward the foyer with its carved wooden staircase. I brushed away the strings of a lingering cobweb. "I don't want to make you mad. It's just that after spending the last two weeks with you, I don't want you to leave. I miss us. It used to be us against the world."

"You can thank your dearly departed husband for alienating you from your old life."

Instead of picking another fight, I chuckled. "I'm going to ignore that comment and unpack the boxes in the study. I need to find some room on the shelf for Andrew's books."

"I'll finish these last two boxes, and then I need to get on the road. I told my boss I'd be back on Monday."

My chest squeezed. The enormity of what I'd gone through over the last few months—no years—hit me with the force of a semi-truck. I had watched my husband die, buried him, and exchanged my familiar home and circle of friends for a long-retired former farm in the middle of the boonies where I didn't know a soul. Until this instant, I hadn't given it a second thought. In fact, I had the distinct attitude of "good riddance." Now, I felt noticeably queasy. I was homesick for the comfort of the University, the grocery store five blocks away, and the friends who I knew would welcome me back into their life if I put a little effort into rebuilding the flagging relationships, particularly Lainey.

She married one of Andrew's best friends, Noah, right around the time I married Andrew. We'd taken a couple trips and enjoyed many joint date nights. Granted, they faded from our life like everyone else at the end, but Lainey had been texting and leaving messages weekly since the funeral, asking to meet up. I didn't even tell her I'd left town. Just thinking about the way I'd ghosted her made me feel like a giant asshole. It hurt to see her and it hurt even more to see Lainey and her husband together. It reminded me of what I'd lost.

Brock threw a crumpled-up piece of packing paper in my direction. "Hey, Earth to Emma. Where'd you go?"

"Sorry. I just got lost in my thoughts. Don't leave without saying goodbye, 'kay?"

"As if, li'l sis."

The second I entered the study, the pining for my

old life vanished. Other than my bedroom, it was my favorite room in the house. It had sage-colored paneled walls and ebony oak bookshelves that smelled of lemon oil and old paper. The best part, though, was the fireplace surrounded by floor to ceiling windows, overlooking a large live oak tree. With the way its limbs stretched out for fifty or so feet, it had to be a century or so old. I'd read somewhere that they could live for over a thousand years.

My thoughts came to an abrupt halt when I spotted something moving in the distance. I stepped closer toward the window, pressing my palms against the cool panes of glass. Staring into the fading light, I saw a man in a long dark coat staring back at me. What was he doing here? According to the deed, I owned nearly a hundred acres surrounding the home. I squinted, trying to bring him into focus. He lifted a long rifle and pointed it in my direction. A scream exploded from deep in my chest and I swiveled around, pressing my back flat against the wall.

Footsteps echoed down the hall. "Em? Em!"

Brock grabbed me by the shoulders, his serious blue eyes studying me. "What happened?"

My heartbeat echoed in my ears and my hands shook as I pointed at the window. "There's a man out there with a gun. He was aiming it at me." It sounded dumb when I said it, but I knew what I'd seen…or at least I thought I did.

He stalked to the window, and slid it open. "What man? I don't see anyone."

Gathering my courage, I joined him by the

window. "Right there. Underneath that big tree." I blinked my eyes a few times when I didn't see him. "Huh, maybe he left or maybe I'm tired and seeing things."

"Are you sure you're going to be okay out here by yourself? I don't think living here is a good idea. This house wasn't meant for one person. Not to mention it's haunted because of all the evil shit that probably happened here. How many slaves did the Claytons own back in the day?"

"Stop it. I already told you I don't believe in haunted houses. It was probably a trick of the light, and as far as I know, the Claytons didn't own slaves."

"Riiight. Because most southern plantations of this size had paid employees," he derided.

"It wasn't always this big. They bought the neighboring property after the war." I rubbed my eyes. "Or at least I think they did. Maybe it was the other way around and the Claytons bought this property after the war because their house burned down. Jesus, Brock, please stop trying to freak me out. I don't exactly have many alternatives right now."

"I know." His lips curled into a sneer, and I suspected he was thinking about Andrew giving our house to his sister. I held up my hand in protest and he rolled his eyes, knowing I wasn't receptive to his criticism on this point. I'd silently and not so silently cursed Andrew hundreds of times since he had died, but none of my cursing gave me the answers I needed. Fortunately, he changed the subject. "You're not getting enough sleep. I heard you downstairs late last night."

"Don't know what you're talking about," I lied. "I went straight to bed, but I did have a bunch of crazy dreams."

"What sort of dreams?" His eyebrows scrunched together. "Are you having nightmares?"

"Stop it. We're not analyzing my dreams, my husband's will, or my state of mind. I'm grieving, but otherwise I'm perfectly fine." I pulled my phone out of the back pocket of my distressed jeans, ignoring yet another text from Lainey before checking the time. "And you need to get on the road."

He groaned. "You're impossible."

"Impossibly perfect," I quipped, trying to lighten the mood.

After I walked Brock out, I made my way back to the study with a glass and a bottle of white wine in hand. For reasons I couldn't explain, I stared out the window, willing the man to return. When trees swaying in the orange and purple drenched sky were the only thing I could see for miles, I gave up. I sat on the tiger oak hardwood floors next to the stack of boxes and continued unpacking Andrew's books until I couldn't keep my eyes open.

Chapter Three

In the three nights since Brock left, I'd only slept a combined total of twelve and a half hours. Yes, I counted. Every day I worked until my body was dog-tired. Unfortunately, the minute I climbed into bed my mind raced with thoughts of the man I'd seen outside the study windows the night Brock left. Hours passed as my ears chased every creak of the hardwood floors, pop of the radiator, and brush of a branch against the side of the house. Only when the sun broke across the sky did I finally feel safe enough to fall asleep.

Needing to break the cycle of monotony, I decided to get out of the house to clear my head and join the living. Even more than that, I needed food and some supplies. The town my brother and I passed through on the way here wasn't more than twenty minutes away. If I was lucky, I might even meet a few people. It wouldn't hurt to have some friends if I actually planned to make a life here.

As I drove along Main Street, I took in the tree-lined herringbone patterned sidewalks and the painted brick buildings. Evenly spaced shiny black lamp posts displayed banners announcing an upcoming Civil War reenactment. I couldn't believe people actually participated in those. A few blocks in, I spotted a little diner on the corner and pulled into one of many open parking spaces. Breakfast and coffee made by someone other than me sounded too good to be true.

The second I entered the diner, the scent of bacon and maple syrup hit me, and my stomach grumbled. I'd been living on health bars, apples, sandwiches, and chips for the last week. While the space was cramped and dark, even a little shabby, it felt cozy. The old wide plank flooring showed its age with too many nicks and scratches to count. Civil War memorabilia covered the red brick walls. Some of the pictures were a little gory, but I knew the town depended on the income of history buffs, so it made sense.

Apart from a group of gray-haired women gathered around a circular booth with red vinyl cushions playing some sort of card game, I was the only other customer. Behind a long counter with barstools stood a woman wearing an apron with a cell phone pressed to her ear. I took a seat on a barstool and studied the chalkboard menu on the wall.

Within a few minutes, the woman approached me. She couldn't have been more than twenty-one or two, with long dark brown hair, soft gray eyes, and warm golden skin. "What can I get ya?"

I shrugged. "I don't know. What's the town favorite?"

She tapped her pen on her thigh. "Biscuits and gravy. Hands down."

"I think I'll try the pancakes and a cup of coffee."

She laughed with unaffected amusement as she jotted down my order on a pad of paper. "Good choice. The biscuits and gravy will hit you like a ton of bricks and you'll want to go back to bed until dinner time."

"If I didn't have so much stuff to get done, I'd change my order. I haven't had a good night's sleep for nearly a week."

"Are you staying in the B&B in town? I heard Glenna needs some new beds, but between you and me, she's too cheap to do anything about it. Luckily for her, there's not a lot of competition around here. It's her place or a motel in the town twenty minutes east of here."

"No. No. I'm living at the Clayton Estate outside of town."

She quirked an eyebrow. "Are you the new caretaker? Because I must say I'm disappointed if Caleb Anderson's gone for good. He's not too friendly, but he's easy on the eyes."

My heartrate sped up. Maybe that explained the man with the gun. I was starting to think I had imagined the whole thing and that wasn't a comforting thought. "No, the house is mine as of last week."

"No way." She grabbed an ivory mug from a shelf behind her, filled it with coffee, and placed it front of me. "The Claytons sold the house? I didn't even know it was on the market."

"It wasn't." I shifted on the barstool, feeling a little conspicuous. "My husband passed away and he was a Clayton. The family gave me the house, and I decided I needed a change of scenery. Atlanta held too many memories."

"Oh, wow. I'm sorry to hear that. I didn't know any of them personally because they don't come around much anymore, but I've heard they're nice people." She tore the top piece of paper off the pad and clipped it to a wire hanging above the opening to the kitchen in a practiced motion. "I'm Addison, by the way."

"Well, nice to officially meet you. I'm Emma. So, tell me, what do people do in this town for fun?"

She scrunched up her face. "Not a lot. There's a bar at the end of the block. It gets pretty rowdy on Friday and Saturday. There's a movie theater around the corner, but it mostly plays old movies. About twenty minutes away, you can find a few big box stores along with that motel I mentioned. Other than the Civil War reenactments and the gossip that spreads like wildfire, I think you'll find this place rather boring, especially compared to Atlanta."

"I'm not worried about it. Like I said, I needed a change, and the house needs some work, so I'll have plenty to keep me occupied."

"Yeah. Caleb mentioned that a few times."

I took a sip of my coffee. "What's his deal, anyway? Does he work in town? My mother-in-law didn't mention anything about a caretaker, and now I'm a little nervous that I've been living at the house for a week and haven't seen anyone."

That wasn't entirely true. I'd seen that man, but something kept me from saying anything about him.

"No, he's an artist. From what I've gathered, he goes to Savannah a couple times a month to sell his art, so maybe that explains his absence. Other than that, I don't know much about him. He's more good-looking than any one male has a right to be, and he's slicker than snot on a doorknob to boot. You know the type. Shot out of his mother's womb, caught a glimpse of his reflection in the doctor's forceps and pumped his fist in the air because he'd won the genetic lottery. His bad attitude doesn't stop the girls in town from drooling all over him. Full of himself, that one." She muttered the last sentence, and I suspected she'd been one of the girls drooling over him at some point in time.

I took a sip of my coffee. I should save my questions for Nora, but it'd been days since I'd talked to anyone in person and I had a good feeling about Addison. "I take it he didn't grow up around here."

"You got that right. He's from somewhere up North. I don't know why he picked this town. There are lots of more interesting places to live closer Savannah than here, but what do I know?"

"Sounds like you're itching to get out of this town." I could sympathize with her. I felt like a prisoner where I grew up. All of my dreams centered on getting out of there and away from my mom. Except for Brock refusing to come with me, I counted getting the hell out of there as one of my successes in life. Staying meant getting married and popping out as many kids as possible and commencing the cycle of poverty all over again.

I shivered just thinking about where I'd be if I hadn't met Andrew or God forbid, Evelyn hadn't called in sick to work that day and he fell for her instead of me. Even though I hated how things ended, I wouldn't change the course of my life for anything. Less than a decade with Andrew was better than never having him in my life.

"Yeah." She lifted and dropped one shoulder. "I'm stuck here, though. This is my dad's restaurant. He'd chain me to the counter if I ever tried to leave."

"Addie, I heard that," a man yelled from the kitchen.

She hiked a thumb over her shoulder. "That's my dad. He's the cook."

"Chef," he countered.

"Sure Dad." She rolled her eyes. "Whatever you say."

I chuckled. Being here lifted my spirits and I definitely needed that right now. "Is the hardware store in that town you mentioned earlier?"

"You got it. There's a general store at the end of this block, and you'll find a few random things, but for anything major, you'll need to go to Bettington. Do you have any plans for the ol' Clayton Place?" She mock shivered and leaned closer. "I heard the place is haunted. You should start with one of those house cleansings. Maybe sage the place."

"Haunted?" First Brock and now Addison. My heart started pounding with enough velocity to launch itself right out of my chest. The irony of uprooting my life only to be saddled with a creepy home people whispered was haunted didn't escape me.

"Yep. It's a known fact around here. Even Caleb—" A summons from the group of ladies in the booth interrupted us. "Hold on."

While Addison attended to them, her dad came out from the kitchen with a stack of steaming pancakes and a dollop of melting butter. He placed them on the shiny dark wood counter. "I'm Pete."

"Nice to meet you. I'm Emma, and apparently I live in a haunted house."

I chugged a giant mouthful of coffee, wishing it were something stronger. Contradictory emotions roared through me. I certainly didn't need any additional drama in my life. I moved here to reflect and start over.

"Hey." Pete patted my hand. "Don't listen to Addie's crazy stories about the Clayton house. As far as I can tell, it's a bunch of nonsense. One of their ancestors died in the house almost two centuries ago. Reckon the people around here like to invent stories to make the town sound more interesting than it is. They even put the home on a haunted tour about five years ago, but the whole idea was dumb as one oar in the water. It was too far out of town and the tourists complained that they couldn't see anything except the exterior."

I forced a smile. "You're probably right." I wouldn't lie. Learning the town thought someone who died over a hundred years ago haunted my house freaked me out. Any sane single woman living in the middle of nowhere alone would concur.

Addison came back and shoved her dad playfully. "Get back to work, Daddy, and stop flirting with our customers. I know how much you like blondes, but she's half your age. Besides, Emma and I are gonna be best friends, so she's officially off limits."

My pale skin heated. "We were just talking."

Pete let out a deep belly laugh. "See you later, Miss Emma. Watch out for my daughter. She could start an argument in an empty house."

"So, I have a brilliant idea." The corners of Addison's mouth turned up and her eyes danced with mischief. I could see what Pete meant. "You're coming with me to the bar on Friday night. I'll pick you up around eight."

A thread of unease rippled through me. I'd never been an extrovert, and going to a bar where I only knew one person didn't sound appealing on any level. On top of that, I still had the habit of bursting into tears at unfortunate times. "Oh, I don't think I could do that. I haven't finished unpacking and that's not really my scene."

She rolled her eyes. "Lord, girl, it ain't a big city club or anything. We'll grab a beer and I'll introduce you to some people our age. Think of it this way. If you're planning to live here, you need to meet people. Besides, everybody's gonna be talkin' about you nonstop the minute you walk out of here. You might as well get the introductions over with before the townsfolk start knocking on your door with casseroles, flowers, and knitted socks you don't need."

I shot her a heated, sideways glance. "Are you

planning on running out and announcing my presence to everyone within hearing distance?"

"Nope. They will." She pointed to the group of women in the booth. On cue, all six women waved, and I groaned internally. "They called me over to ask if you were single. They're already arguing about who they're gonna set you up with first. Trust me. Going out and making your own introductions and connections will be kinder than having them meddling in your life. They're all itchin' to get their grandsons and sons married off and you're prime pickin's with your own house not too far out of town."

"All right." My shoulders sagged. "I'll go with you on one condition."

"What's that?"

"I drive my own car so I can leave whenever I want. I'm still not over everything that happened with my husband, and I don't always make the best company."

She narrowed her eyes and tapped her long red fingernails on the counter. "Deal. But you have to stay at least an hour. Anything less and everyone will think you're as bad as Caleb."

"Fine."

She pulled her pad from the pocket of her apron. "This is the address of the bar and my phone number. Meet me out front at eight."

"I'll be there."

Chapter Four

"I was just thinking about you," I said in greeting to Nora when I answered her call.

"Funny because I was starting to think you'd forgotten about me."

"I know. I know." I put her call on speaker so I could continue to organize the kitchen cabinets while we talked. "I'm sorry I didn't call earlier. My brother stayed for a couple of days to help and then I've been busy unpacking and organizing."

"That couldn't have taken long. You left most of the stuff at the house."

"I took what mattered." I shifted my gaze to the window over the sink. A heavy canopy of waxy vines covered this side of the house blocking my view. I'd have to cut those down before they corroded the wood siding on the house.

"Leah will never spend a day in that house. She's already hired a realtor to list it." She sighed like she had the weight of the world on her shoulders. "She'll go through that money within a year or two. I don't know what to do with her. Andrew was the one I thought would care for me as I got older. He was the one who was supposed to give me grandchildren. Now, who knows what will happen to the Clayton name? Leah will squander all of my money. She already told me she has no intention of having kids, and at thirty-nine she's running out of time. Tell me why you and Andrew didn't have kids again."

I placed a stack of plates on the counter, guilt and regret twisting in my gut. My knees wobbled, and I let them give way. Crouching, I leaned my elbows on my thighs, cupping the sides of my head through the sudden wave of grief. Memories of the choices we'd made still troubled me. I couldn't think about them without breaking my heart over and over again.

"We ran out of time."

It wasn't entirely the truth. I was twenty-one when we married, and I wanted to prove to him and his family that I could make something of myself. I hated people thinking I was a gold-digger with nothing going for her other than snagging an older successful man.

If Andrew had pressed, Lord knows I would have given in. That was the pattern of our relationship, which wasn't surprising given our age and socio-economic differences. Needless to say, he never acted very eager to start a family and when I brought it up, he always said we had plenty of time. Sadly, that turned out to be the only thing we didn't have. Maybe if I had pushed, Nora and I would still have a little piece of Andrew with us.

"I know." She sniffed, then continued in a more

upbeat tone. "Tell me what you think of the place. Don't you love it?"

I scanned the white kitchen, which while charming definitely needed some updates if I ever got my act together and tried to market this place as a bed and breakfast or decided to sell it.

"It's beautiful. I have so many ideas for this place, I don't know where to start. Thank you for giving me the opportunity to—"

"Oh hush, Emma. You deserve the house and more. Now tell me, have you met any of the locals? I could make some calls for you. I used to live there in the summers growing up."

"I went into town this morning and I met some people. I even have plans for Friday night."

"A date?" Her voice was carefully neutral, but I knew she wouldn't approve.

"Yep." I forced out a laugh. "A date with a girl name Addison. Her family owns the diner and she blackmailed me into going out on Friday."

"Oh, the Hayden Family. They're good people."

"I thought so." I sneezed a few times, my eyes watering. As the day had progressed, I'd been feeling worse and worse. It started with a sore throat this morning. Initially, I had attributed it to living in a dusty home that hadn't been occupied in years. For the last hour, I'd been chilled like I was getting a fever so I suspected I was coming down with something. Dammit, a cold was the last thing I needed right now.

"Are you okay?"

"Of course. It's just allergies from all this dust, nothing to worry about," I lied. I didn't want to alarm Nora. She'd been so protective of me in the last couple of months, almost as if she expected another shoe to drop at any moment, spinning her life into another tragedy.

"Oh, I almost forgot. Brian told me he's planning to be in the area tomorrow. He wanted to stop by and see you and maybe stay a night or two to help you out. I told him you'd be happy to see him."

I scraped a few errant hairs away from my face. Brian had checked on Andrew regularly until the bitter end. We'd never spent any time alone and he was divorced so we didn't do the couple dating thing. I never would have guessed he'd want to keep in contact with me. Sure, we had a few heart-wrenching conversations as Andrew's illness progressed. None of those seemed like the basis for a lasting friendship, more like a moment of shared grief over losing someone we both loved.

"Sure. I'll keep an eye out for him."

"Good. Good. Andrew asked him to look out for you after he was gone. I'm glad he's taking that promise seriously."

That was news to me. While I generally liked Brian, I didn't know how much of my former life I wanted to take with me into this new chapter. I loved Nora. Somehow over the last six months of Andrew's life, she evolved into a mother figure. However, Brian was in a different category. Because his and Andrew's dads were twins, they looked more like brothers than cousins. And while that might bring comfort to me sometime in the future, being around him reminded me of what I had lost. Some of his facial expressions were achingly familiar, and their voices were so similar it pained me to talk to him.

"My house is always open to you and your family."

"You're such a sweet, generous soul. I can see why Andrew fell head over heels in love with you the minute he saw you."

A sudden overwhelming sadness gathered like a thunderstorm beneath my sternum and I didn't know if there was enough air in the world to push it away. I couldn't believe I'd found and lost the love of my life by the age of twenty-six. It seemed like a sick joke. I willed the increasingly familiar state of comfortable numbness to wash over me. It was the only way I'd get through the next year.

"Well, I'll let you get back to work. I have a facial in an hour. Keep in touch."

"Wait." As I stood, my elbow bumped a glass on the counter and it exploded on the gray stone tile beneath my feet.

"Are you okay?"

"Yeah. Just a broken glass. Addison told me there's a caretaker looking after the property. I haven't seen anyone around. Do you know anything about him? Does he live in the house?"

The thought made me uncomfortable. I had combed every square inch of the house with Brock and again when I got home from the diner. I didn't see any evidence of someone living here. Granted, the closets and drawers were packed with clothes and other random personal effects. None of them seemed like recent purchases, indicating a current inhabitant.

27

"Oh, right. I forgot about that. Andrew hired some artist a few years back, Caleb something or other. I can't remember his last name off the top of my head. He lives in the barn on the south side of the property."

Her response didn't surprise me. Nora's husband had amassed a rather large real estate portfolio over his lifetime. There probably wasn't enough time in the day to keep up with all of the details.

"Does he have a lease?"

"Not that I'm aware of. If my memory serves me, he lives in the barn rent free in exchange for checking in on the house, overseeing maintenance, that sort of thing. I'm sure you could give him notice now that he's not needed, though it wouldn't be a bad idea to have someone around. I hate thinking of you rambling around in that big home all by yourself." I heard a drawer open and the shuffling of papers. "I think I have his phone number somewhere."

"No." I grabbed a broom and dustpan from the pantry. "Don't worry about it. You're on your way out. Just tell me how to get to the barn and I'll drop by or leave a note on the door. I think I saw more than one."

"There's a trail on the south side of the house near the study. Follow it and you won't have any problems. Let me know how it goes. I've never met him. We had a conversation after Andrew got sick and I put him in contact with Andrew's attorney. That's it. I didn't even inform him I no longer own the house. I'm sorry I didn't tell you about him. It slipped my mind with the chaos of everything else."

Her voice trailed off and her breathing became heavier.

"No, worries, Nora. I completely understand. I'll take care of it."

I nodded even though she couldn't see me. "I will. Enjoy your facial."

I hung up the phone, and braced my elbows on the long, rectangular kitchen table. Talking to Nora was hard. Not for the first time I wondered whether I should sever all ties to the Clayton family. Would that help me move on? Or would it make it worse? Like I'd cut out a chunk of my heart. Groaning, I rubbed my temples. All I knew for certain was that wound from losing Andrew might never heal. Funny, I hadn't even made it to the third decade of my life and I already felt exhausted.

I wished I could go back to the time before our lives fell apart and wrap my arms around Andrew. I'd tell him how much I loved him. I'd convince him to have a baby. I'd ask him how I was supposed to go on living without him. But then again, I'd been wishing for a lot of things when it came to Andrew. My monotonous prayers had worn me out over the past two or so years. Especially because none of them had done a damn thing to change fate.

Chapter Five

Before I lost the nerve to introduce myself to the elusive and apparently ill-mannered Caleb, I brushed my hair and changed out of my yoga pants and oversized t-shirt and into something professional yet casual. After one last glance in the gilded mirror in the foyer, I stepped onto the front porch. The wood creaked under my weight, reminding me I needed to hire someone to check out the soundness of the structure. Brock warned me that some of the beams underneath had rotted.

With little effort, I found the dirt path leading to the barn. Strolling slowly with my face turned toward the sun, I basked in the humid, clean air that was so different from that in the city. It reminded me of trudging along the trails with Brock on the mountainside where we grew up. We'd wander around for hours so we didn't have to face *her* and whatever hell she planned to rain down on us on any given day. During the last six years in the city, I'd almost forgotten how nature fed my soul. Maybe I made the right choice in coming here after all.

Maybe this place could heal me and point me in the right direction for the next chapter in my life.

My footsteps sounded inexplicably loud as I crunched over pine needles and twigs outside the weathered barn; almost akin to an unnatural disturbance into the surreal setting in front of me. The barn had a peaked center with two winged extensions on each side. The sunlight peeked through the puffy white clouds, creating a burst of shimmering light around the structure. Immediately, I understood why an artist would want to set up shop in this location. It felt more like a home than the house I settled into last week.

Inching forward, I knocked on the large barn door. Shifting from foot to foot, I waited for someone to answer. When no one came, I opened the planked door. Inside was a vaulted space with high windows, blanketing the space in a warm glow. One wing contained a kitchen with a lofted area above it, accessible by a winding black iron staircase. The other wing accommodated a bed and sofa, more utilitarian than I would have expected for an artist. The vaulted room in the middle stole my breath, though, making up for the sparseness of the rest of the space. Huge painted canvases decorated every surface.

One wall in particular, though, caught my attention. Every painting was of the same woman in the countryside, either facing away from her audience or in profile. Her long blonde hair shimmered like a halo. She dressed in a different variation of the same style—long hoop skirts complete with elaborate bows and lace. And from what I could see of her face, she always looked so happy. Like my feet had a mind of their own, I crept forward and traced my finger over the detailed swirls of paint.

An ache ignited beneath my breastbone. I rubbed the spot with my fist to soothe the growing discomfort. An overwhelming sense of loss came over me, and I swallowed back a whimper. Whether he was an asshole remained to be seen, but I couldn't overlook his gift, not that I could count art critique as one of my talents. Even I knew not every artist could evoke so much emotion.

I leaned closer. "She needs a magnolia in her hair," I whispered, not even understanding why I said it.

A half-growl, half-shout snapped me out of the trance I had drifted into. I swiveled around and lifted my head, my heart lurching wildly in fright. The moment my eyes locked onto the stranger's brown ones, the past three sleepless nights, the long hours of getting settled into an unfamiliar home, and the cold I'd been fighting caught up with me. Trembling hijacked my arms and legs. My chest tightened. He drew closer, and I couldn't bring myself to speak. I stood rooted to the floorboards, making no effort to explain my intrusion into his space or run.

"Are you listening? I'll ask you again. Who are you and what the fuck are you doing in my home?" The sharp angles of his face were etched with menace. His eyes glowed with anger, yet they somehow looked entirely too familiar for comfort. Vestiges of self-preservation begged me to flee while frissons of inquisitiveness urged me to stay. Rather than acknowledge or investigate my uneasiness, I lifted my hand, intending to wave or shake his hand. I wasn't certain. It didn't matter, though, because my vision dimmed and I fainted at his feet instead.

As I sat on the edge of this stranger's rumpled bed with my head between my thighs, trying to regain my equilibrium, I wondered if I had ever made a worse first impression. Maybe with Nora. She hated me at first sight, although it likely had nothing to do with anything I said or did. Whatever I had hoped to gain by invading his space, I certainly hadn't accomplished it. I couldn't imagine what he thought of me. Nothing good, I decided.

"Here's a bottle of water," he said, kneeling down in front of me.

Rather than accept his offering, I pressed my hands into the mattress, intending to get the hell of there as fast of humanly possible.

"Don't be an idiot," he persisted, pressing the bottle into my hands. "You're not going anywhere yet. You're lucky I caught you. You could've hit your head."

I groaned. "Thanks for pointing out the obvious."

I cracked open the bottle and brought it to my lips while discreetly looking at him again from beneath my lashes. Addison had mentioned he was attractive, but I didn't even know where to begin. He had a face that implored you to keep looking at him. Thick, dark hair brushed the top of his shoulders. His tawny eyes were framed by long dark lashes and perfectly masculine brows. His stubble-covered cheekbones were as razor sharp as I suspected before I fainted, and he had a faint dimple in his chin. And that was just his face. He was over six feet tall, broad shouldered, with an otherwise slim athletic build.

"Thank you," I muttered, avoiding looking directly at him. While I couldn't have been out for more than a few minutes, it was long enough to eternally embarrass me in his presence. I had a shadowy memory of him catching me and carrying me to the bed, and then absolutely nil until I sat up.

Rather than responding, he grunted like he didn't want to waste his words on me. After a couple more sips of water, I set the bottle on the floor and came to my feet. "I've taken up enough of your time. I wanted to come and—"

He grabbed my forearm. "You're not leaving until you tell me what you're doing in my house. My work is private. I don't like anyone looking at it before it's ready."

I ripped my arm out of his grasp. "I was getting to that part. No need to manhandle me."

"I already made it clear to everyone in town, I didn't want them stopping by my house uninvited. Apparently, you missed the memo."

"First of all, you're the one who missed the memo, because as of last week, I'm the owner of this house, your place included, and the only reason I stopped by was to give you notice to vacate the premises. You're no longer needed."

"No."

"Excuse me?"

He moved closer. His body heat was noticeable in the drafty barn. "No."

"What? Why?"

"Because I had a deal with Andrew Clayton."

His imposing size made me hyperaware of him. Clamping down on my nerves, I lifted my chin. "Well, Andrew passed away." The words hit my tongue like a pile of ash, and I wanted to take them back. They felt so final. Too final. "So, unless you had something in writing, you're out of luck."

Chapter Six

He smiled and took another step forward, invading my personal space. His teeth were perfectly straight and white, a striking contrast to the dark scruff of his beard. "I don't think so, Emma Clayton."

"Wait. You know my name?"

The emotion swirling in his eyes intensified. He pushed his untamed, dark hair away from his face. His strong Roman nose flared and his mouth curled up at the corners. Wow, those lips. They were plush and glistening, almost indulgent, when everything else about him screamed with viciousness.

I edged back, silently cursing myself for the tremble in my limbs. I wanted to blame it on panic and fear, yet my gut screamed a different truth. I felt a spark of attraction to him and it scared the shit out of me. I had no clue how to deal with this uncomfortable sensation. My husband hadn't been gone more than seven months. I shouldn't feel a thing. What did this say about me?

That I was a bad person.

That I had betrayed Andrew.

Guilt bubbled around in my chest, and I wanted to faint again to escape further self-reflection. I shook my head. No, the strain of the last few days and the fever were addling my brain, and inventing things that weren't real. I didn't feel anything for him.

"The last time Andrew came to visit, he made an offer on one of my paintings. He said his wife, Emma, would want one. If you're here claiming Andrew is dead, I naturally assumed you're his wife."

I glanced at his paintings again. They enchanted me the instant I spotted them. Something about Andrew wanting to buy one for me settled my nerves and my heartrate returned to normal.

"Did you sell one to him?"

He leaned against the wall and folded his arms against his chest, drawing attention to his body and the way his black long sleeved thermal molded around the contours of his chest and his thighs shaped his form-fitting joggers.

"No," he answered curtly.

My spirits deflated. Logically, I would have seen the painting if Andrew had purchased one, but this man had unknowingly raised my hopes. For a fleeting second, I thought I'd get one more tangible gift from Andrew, something new to remind me of him.

"Oh, well, yeah," I stammered, not sure what to say. "That makes sense." And it did. Andrew hadn't exactly been himself in the year prior to his death. Maybe longer.

He ran the tip of his tongue along his bottom lip, his curious gaze locked on me like he had more to say. "He commissioned me to paint something original."

"He did?" My voice dropped to a whisper, tension leaking from my shoulders. "Is it done?"

"No."

"Can I see it?"

He scrubbed his face, highlighting a streak of black paint near his temple I hadn't noticed before. He glanced at the floor, uncertainty rolling off him. "Look, I haven't started it yet. Andrew never approved the final concept. When he stopped responding a year or so ago, I thought he changed his mind. That you two broke up or something. The only contact I've had since then was with some woman named Nora who directed me to the Clayton family attorney. He made it clear I could keep living here as long as I looked after the house."

"Well, you were wrong. Andrew died. We didn't break up."

His shoulders crept up, his cocky attitude returning with a vengeance. "Can't blame me for thinking it. From the picture, you looked a lot younger than him. It seemed like the natural order of things. You know, young girl meets older, wealthy man, soaks him dry, then moves on to the next guy."

I flinched. Wow, that stung. The room evaporated. Blood red clouded my vision. My lungs iced over inside of my ribcage. His assumption shouldn't have shocked me. Nora hinted at the same thing the first time she met me, and I was sure more than a few of Andrew's friends shared the sentiment until they'd gotten to know me.

"What did you just say?" I asked slowly, keeping the 'you fucking asshole' part to myself.

"You heard me."

Maybe if he had backtracked, I could've been the bigger person and ignored the jab, but fuck it. "And yet you're the one living rent free. Remind me, what is that saying about glass houses?"

"I'm not living here rent free. Like I said, I supervise any maintenance on the house and watch over the place."

"Sure, whatever you need to tell yourself. The fact remains, though, that you don't have a lease. Consider this your thirty days' notice, Caleb."

"Ah, you do know my name, then."

"Unfortunately. Goodbye. I suspect we'll talk soon."

"Wait." He grabbed my hand, and his body heat hummed through me. "I need at least six months to find an alternate location. Maybe longer. It's not easy to find a place to live that can double as a studio."

"Not my problem. You should have thought of that before you insulted me."

"I'll pay you."

I flashed a smile that wasn't really a smile and raised my eyebrows. "As you insinuated, I don't want or need your damn money." It wasn't entirely true. I had enough to keep the property afloat, but I was by no means set for life.

His jaw clenched and his eyes narrowed. "What do you want then? There has to be something."

39

I shook my head, irritated. I didn't want anything. I didn't need anything. At least not from him. I opened my mouth to refuse him, except something entirely unanticipated came out of my mouth. "The painting you promised Andrew." I didn't know where those words came from. It's not as if a new painting would replace the one Andrew had planned to give me.

"What?" He stumbled backward, releasing his grip on me.

"Finish the painting Andrew commissioned based on the last conversation you had with him, and you can stay here until it's done. Granted, it can't take more than a year, and it has to be something similar to the quality you have hanging up in here."

He glanced away as if he couldn't stand looking at me. Then he cleared his throat and his eyes locked on mine with authority. "I can't do that."

"Then you have thirty days."

"You can take one of the paintings above the bed."

I glanced at the paintings, but they didn't resemble the ones that had enchanted me earlier. They were landscapes of cities around the world. While they were beautiful, they lacked the heart and emotion of the others. "Not interested."

His gaze glided over me, his thoughts impermeable, and a jawline so severe it would split the tip of my finger if I ever rallied enough courage to touch him. "I'll even frame it for you. Don't answer now. Just think about it."

I clenched my teeth and didn't reply. A snooty

glare would have to do because I didn't trust myself not to punch him in the face. Then he'd probably call the police just to screw with me, and somehow I'd be stuck with him on my property for eternity or at least until he decided to move on. I peeked at his paintings one more time. Addison had summarized Caleb accurately. It was a crime against humanity that such a jerk could look like that and have the ability to craft such beauty.

Not daring to make eye contact with him another time, I marched out of the barn as proper and authoritatively as I could manage, yet some feminine part of me put a little swagger in my hips. My own body betrayed me, wanting to show him that I wasn't another woman chasing after him and I could be attractive if I put in any effort. In reality, I shouldn't give a damn. No, I *couldn't* give a damn for too many reasons to name.

Chapter Seven

Aggravated from my encounter with Caleb, I curled up on the front porch swing with a glass of wine, hoping to unwind and catch the sunset. I'd read online that there was going to be a strawberry moon tonight. I wanted someone to camp out on a blanket with me, but it didn't look like that would happen. Addison had to work late, and Caleb was the only other person I knew nearby. Given that I'd rather chew off my arm than talk to him again, I was stuck by myself.

By the time darkness blanketed the sky, my head felt peculiarly woozy, whether from the wine or a lack of sleep, I didn't know. The katydids increased in volume, filling the air with their hypnotic chant-like sound. I closed my eyes and let sleep claim me.

"Elizabeth, what in the Sam Hill are you doing out here?"

I pointed up at the sky. "Have you seen it?"

Henry looked up and I kind of wished it were lighter outside so I could see the expression on his face. "The strawberry moon."

"I've never seen anything so beautiful in all my born days," I uttered.

He crouched beside me on the blanket and clipped the end of his cigar. "I don't know about that."

"Do tell. What's more beautiful?"

He scooped up a magnolia that had fallen from a nearby tree and tucked it behind my ear. "You."

I sighed. "I don't know why you must tease me so." I had worshipped the ground Henry walked on for as long as I could remember, but I didn't know if he felt the same. Just last month at my debutante ball, he danced with nearly four girls before asking me to dance.

When I mentioned it to him, he had chuckled and claimed he was only there for me, but he didn't want the other girls to feel slighted. He stuck close to my side after that, giving me hope there was some truth in his words.

He struck his thumb against the tip of a sulfur match and brought the orange flame to the end of the cheroot. "Do your parents realize you're out here?"

"I slipped out the back door when the men started playing cards." My eyes flared, and I hastened to get up, my heart pounding crazily. Mama would have a fit if she discovered I'd snuck outside unaccompanied. She was always ranting to Pa about my antics. "Is the game already over?"

He reached out and squeezed my hand. "No. I'm taking a break. They won't be done for a couple of hours."

43

"You won't tell?" I said quickly. "That is, Pa..."

"...shall never learn of your little escapade from me," Henry completed the sentence for me. He patted the top of the blanket I had pulled from my bed and stretched out on the grass. *"Lay next to me while I finish my cigar."*

Hesitantly, I leaned back beside him, and fixed my gaze on the sky. I was glad I had changed into the pants and shirt my Pa had brought back from his last visit to Athens. Mama called them an affront to society, but he argued several of the women were wearing the fashion around town. To appease Mama, he strictly forbade me from wearing them outside of the privacy of our home. Truth be told, I preferred them over the elaborate gown Mama had forced me to wear to dinner. The bodice was rimmed in a coarse lace, and I had to sit on my hands several times so I wasn't tempted to rip it off and forever shame my family.

The sounds of tree frogs and chirping crickets mixed with the masculine laughter trickling from the windows lining the parlor. A warm, almost dream-like breeze swayed the limbs of the magnolia trees overhead, rustling their thick, waxen leaves and filling the air with a sweet, lemony scent.

When I angled my head to look at Henry, he was peering up at the sky. His forgotten cigar rested on a patch of dirt next to the blanket. A trail of smoke curled upward, twirling above us, then evaporated into the darkness. The soft, rosy glow of the moonlit night highlighted the sharp angles of Henry's handsome face. I adored everything about this man, from his thick dark hair to the proud jut of his chin *and jaw. Most of all, I loved how he always indulged me even when I was doing ridiculous things.*

After a while, he turned his face toward mine. His golden eyes were so achingly familiar, they jolted my heart. There was something possessive and raw in his countenance as he lay there looking at me. His body was entirely motionless, and I didn't dare breathe for fear the moment would come to an end.

Overhead the trill of a nightingale floated through the air, and his gaze stayed fixed on mine. My belly flipped and my body hummed with an indescribable pleasure. While our parents had openly plotted our marriage for as long as I could remember, I couldn't be sure if he felt anything other than a brotherly affection for me.

I offered him a cautious smile and brushed my hand along his jaw, my fingertips prickling with awareness. He pressed his lips to the tip of my nose, just like he'd been doing since we were kids. He lingered there for a second, and my body swayed closer to his like we were two magnets.

His deep voice broke the spell he'd cast on me. "I have to get back before they notice I'm gone and they come looking for me." He pushed to his feet, straightened his puffy cravat, and dusted off his jacket. "Don't stay out here too long, little Lizzy. I would hate for your mama to forbid you from going riding with me on the morrow. I have something to show you."

My head slumped forward, I blinked my eyes

repeatedly, waking up slowly. The cool air caused the skin on my arms to pebble, alerting me to the fact that I was no longer dreaming. I glanced up and the strawberry moon was high in the sky. The details of my dream came rushing back to me. While my dreams generally featured people I knew, on occasion I'd had one about other people or where I was another person. They'd never been so vivid, though.

I could've sworn it took place right here in the antebellum south, which made sense. While writing papers for my master's degree, I had scoured the libraries for obscure sources on that time period. I'd read firsthand slave accounts, editorials of the partisan press in antebellum America, and relevant literature. Apparently, my unconscious mind took that information and refashioned it for my dream.

I was struck with the thought that I should write down the details. If I didn't make a record of it, all the information would be lost by morning, and for some reason I sensed the story was important. A shiver and a yawn simultaneously rolled through my body, and I decided getting inside and going to sleep was the more pressing matter. Brian would be here early in the morning and it wouldn't be polite if I slept in and left him sitting in the car until mid-morning.

Chapter Eight

"Do you want me to talk to him?" Brian asked in response to my long-winded story about my encounter with Caleb.

Tempting as his offer was, I wouldn't accept it. Growing up, I lived with my mom and brother in absolute chaos. During that time, Brock shielded me from many of the horrors of our life. Then I'd met Andrew and he took care of everything until he couldn't. At first, I was scared out of my mind that I'd make a mess of everything. Gradually, I realized I didn't need someone to fix everything in my life. I didn't want to slip into old habits because it would be easier. I really did need to resolve my problems with Caleb like an adult.

I yanked the threadbare green blanket tighter around my shoulders, shivering despite taking two Ibuprofen an hour ago. "No. If I'm going to live out here by myself, I need to figure out how to take care of things on my own, including dealing with rude tenants."

While I'd been dreading Brian's visit ever since

the phone call with Nora, having him here had offered a welcome break from the unending cycle of loneliness that had permeated my life since Brock had left. I even put on normal clothes today rather than another pair of yoga pants with one of Andrew's button-down shirts. If it weren't for this nagging cold, I'd almost feel human.

"I don't like this, Emma. You don't know anything about this guy and you're so isolated out here. Who knows what could happen?"

I shrugged. "He's probably harmless and he'll be gone in less than a month."

He rubbed his thumb idly along the piping on the arm of his chair. "Probably is the operative word."

"You're trying to scare me, and it's not going to work. Andrew met him, you know, and he must have trusted him to some extent if he allowed him to stay here. Besides, I did barge into his place uninvited, so his behavior wasn't exactly unjustified."

"Trusting someone with an empty house is different from trusting someone with your loved ones."

"Well, there's nothing I can do about it right this second, and it's not like I'm alone with him. He lives in the converted barn."

He leaned back in his chair, shifting the position of his torso. "Does he have keys to the house?"

"I'm sure he does." He opened his mouth to interject what was likely another warning, and I held up my hand. "Don't start. I already called a locksmith."

"Good. You know, I could stay around for a

couple of weeks until you get settled. I don't have anywhere to be."

Brian owned quite a few apartment buildings in Atlanta and he had a property manager. As far as I could tell, he didn't have a job other than collecting rental income. He'd invested in a few businesses here and there. I think he even owned half of one of Lainey's restaurants, but to my knowledge he wasn't involved in the day to day management or finances.

I frowned. "I thought you were on the way to Savannah to visit friends."

"I was, but I can delay the trip. They won't mind."

"I know what you're doing." I shook my head in sudden comprehension. "Nora told me about the promise you made to Andrew, and while I appreciate it, you don't have to stop your life to look after me. I'm fine. I don't need a keeper."

He scanned me. "You don't look fine."

The last time I checked, my skin was unnaturally pale. In fact, there wasn't much difference in color between my skin and my white-blonde hair. I'd put on some mascara and blush, hoping I looked more human than vampire. Apparently, it hadn't worked.

"Ouch. It's not very gentlemanly of you to point out how crappy I look. I do have a little cold and I've been working my ass off for weeks. This place needed a lot more work than I suspected."

Brian leaned forward, tucked a strand of hair behind my ear, and I froze. In my opinion, we didn't have that sort of friendship. "I didn't mean it that way and you know it. You always look

49

beautiful, Emma, even when you're not feeling great. Andrew was a lucky man. When he first introduced you to me, I think I was a little jealous. You know, I was supposed to go on that trip with him to the Appalachians. Who knows how things would've turned out if I hadn't canceled?"

His comment was awkward on too many levels to count. Not many people would call a man struck down in his prime by a devastating illness lucky. As for the rest of his remark, well, I couldn't bring myself to think about it too much. Thank God, he planned to leave tomorrow.

I laughed disingenuously. "I'm going to take a walk."

Brian stood up. "I'll come with you."

"No. I'm good. I need some fresh air, and you mentioned you wanted to shower before dinner."

Brian smiled a little too adoringly for my comfort. "Okay, but don't be gone too long. It's going to get dark in about an hour."

"Thanks."

With long strides, I circled around the back of the house. Busy making the interior of the house comfortable, I hadn't explored much of surrounding land, and now seemed like a good time to do exactly that. Based on the survey of the property that Nora had included in my paperwork, there was a creek about a quarter mile behind the house.

Truthfully, I wasn't in a hurry to get back. As sweet as Brian was, I kind of suspected he believed he had feelings for me that went beyond friendship, and I'd rather stick a hot poker in my eye than have him confess his interest in me. Especially when I was pretty sure his feelings had more to do with missing Andrew than me anyway, and he'd realize that himself soon enough.

I stopped now and then to smell a flower or take in the view. It really was a picturesque piece of property. I glanced at the sky and a ripple of unease went through me. Sometime during the last half hour, heavy thunderclouds had crowded out the blue sky, and I still hadn't made any progress locating the creek.

Reaching for my phone in my jacket pocket, I came up empty.

"Shit," I mumbled, realizing I'd left it on the coffee table.

The search for the creek had to wait for another day. I'd explored more than I should have given my fever and my state of perpetual exhaustion.

Chapter Nine

As I retraced my path to the house, the sky continued to darken and thunder rumbled overhead, shaking the ground beneath my feet. I folded my arms across my chest to keep warm and picked up my pace until I was jogging. Unsteady and shivering, I tripped over a tree root and tumbled to all fours. Rocks dug sharply into my knees and palms, making me gasp with pain. A pounding noise echoed in my ears. My limbs vibrated deep in my bones. A bright light flashed and my vision went black for a second.

Jumping up, I pushed myself to keep going. Long grasses tangled around my ankles, and shrubs lashed my legs. The farther I ran, the more unfamiliar everything looked. I was lost. The realization made my stomach constrict in alarm. The trees looked different somehow. The path resembled trodden down underbrush rather than the dirt I remembered from earlier. Drops of rain pelleted my body and the vibrating in my limbs grew into a full body tremor. Then the house came into view, except it looked different. The shutters were black instead of green. A woman stood in front of the door, yet nothing seemed out of order.

"Elizabeth," Mama yelled from the front porch. "Come back here right now."

I ignored her, running away from the house, my fingers clutching the front of my white muslin dress, and lifting the hem. With every passing minute my lungs burned more. My leather soled ankle boots did little to protect my feet from rocks, and pain ricocheted up my calves.

A low branch snared my bonnet, and it slid off and dangled from a small ribbon wrapped around my neck. Rather than stop to fix it, I forced my legs to move quicker, away from the depressing reality of my life. To hell with the cussed fools, my family included, who carelessly predicted "only" a ninety- day conflict. It'd been years of suffering, heartbreak, and sacrifice.

My God, Henry was injured or dead. His parents repeated over and over the reasons we had to be hopeful. The survivors of the battle had been transported to a field hospital and then on to the Confederate general hospital in Richmond, Virginia.

The letter from a friend of Henry's in the same regiment claimed Henry was injured, but he didn't know his fate. I knew, though. Something in my gut told me he was gone, or maybe all the death had conditioned me to expect the worst.

Before Pa died, he told me to be strong, but my resolve was nonexistent these days. The people of

Georgia went into this war expecting the best and they were wrong. I didn't understand how any of this was worth fighting for. I never did. Life in the South was changing and there was nothing we could do to stop it. Henry realized this. Unfortunately, that didn't stop him from being sent off to fight a lost cause that likely took his life.

As I fled deeper into the woods, the trees blocked most of the sunlight. While Mama had repeatedly warned me not to venture too far with the Yankees bombarding Atlanta, I didn't care about that, the stitches in my side, or the spasms racking my lungs. I had never been so dratted mad at everything and nothing. I kept going. Kept putting one leg in front of the other without any destination in mind; death and despair chasing my every step. I darted through a creek, rolling my ankle on the slippery rocks hidden beneath the surface, and I fell. Chilly water swirled around my white dress and ruffled petticoat.

"Sakes alive." Mama would surely lose her mind over this given the shortage of fabric due to the blockade. The women of Georgia were sadly in want of all the trimmings to make pretty dresses these days.

By the time I dragged myself to the opposite bank, my legs quivered and my lungs screamed with fatigue. Defeated, I waited for my breathing to normalize and my teeth to stop chattering.

After a few minutes, I summoned all of my strength to stand. I had to get back. Mama would be wild with worry, and she was right, it wasn't safe around here anymore. I scanned my surroundings. I hadn't been this far out on our land in nearly six *months.*

A faint groan echoed in my ears, and I froze in place. A lump of fear lodged in my throat, preventing me from screaming. Not that screaming would do me any good this far from the house. The groan came again, and I looked around for some sort of weapon. I plucked a stick from the ground and crept closer.

A man in dirty grey pants and a belted navy jacket was sprawled out beneath the bushes. Dark shadows circled his closed eyes. Rusty colored blood stained the lower half of his right pant leg. He was a Union solider. An injured Union soldier. Every cell in my body demanded I run.

I took a couple steps backward, my stick raised above my head prepared to smack him with it if he so much as twitched in my direction. Then an image of Henry came to mind. My chest ached at the thought of someone abandoning a wounded Henry because he was a Confederate soldier. The divisions of war shouldn't run so deep that common decency disappeared. Life was fragile. It should be respected and protected.

I tossed my stick on the ground and leaned down to get a closer look at the man. His chest rose and fell, so I knew he was alive. Even with his eyes closed and hurt, a jolt of fear squeezed my lungs.

"What should I do with you?" I whispered.

The man cracked open his eyelids and grabbed hold of my arm. "Water. I need water."

I studied the ruthless angles of his face, the sandy brown hair covering his jaw, and the fire in his gaze. Anger radiated from him. Part of me already regretted my rash decision to help him. I gritted my teeth and pushed away my unruly thoughts, silently chanting Matthew 7:12: *"Therefore all things whatsoever ye would that men should do to you: do ye even so to them: for this is the law and the prophets."* I would do this for Henry, in hopes that someone would be equally kind to him wherever he was and then, perhaps he would come home to me soon.

"There's a creek right there. Put your arm around my shoulder and I'll help you get there."

He did as I requested, cursing and grimacing with every step, his scabbard swinging wildly. When we reached the bank, he dropped to his knees, pulling me down with him. He cupped the water and brought it to his mouth over and over. When he finished, he rolled on to his side.

"Mighty good of you to help me," he mumbled after few minutes, raking his piercing eyes over me as if he were trying to read my thoughts.

"It's no trouble at all. I need to get back, though. My family will be worried about me." I didn't dare say it was only Mama and me living in the house with a handful of house servants. Even in his weakened condition, he could cause problems, and while I wanted to do good, I didn't want my actions to bring harm to us.

Before I could stand, he pushed me onto my back and straddled me, immobilizing me with more strength than a man of his condition should have. He smelled of earth, gun powder, and dried blood.

"We're not done yet," he said.

Panic took hold of me, and I couldn't get my

body to move. I knew I'd made the biggest mistake of my life by helping this man. Mama had likely already locked herself in her room with some of Pa's whiskey. She'd been doing that a lot lately, so it was highly unlikely she'd send anyone after me.

"Please, please, let me go."

"I can't let you go back. You could send out an alarm that I'm here."

"They'll come looking for me." I swallowed the lump in my throat, breaking eye contact for the lie I was about to tell. "I'd be surprised if they haven't already sent out a search party."

"I'll take my chances."

"What do you want?" I squirmed beneath him, and he winced. My chin dipped, and I saw the blood seeping from his wound onto my already ruined dress.

Completely lacking emotion, he glanced at his leg. "The way I see it, you have two alternatives."

I nodded like a lunatic, willing to do anything this ornery man wanted if he'd let me go home unharmed. I had enough problems without adding this into the mix. Silently, I promised God I'd be more attentive during Reverend Bryant's sermons and I'd never wander away from home again if he let me live.

"Help me find shelter until I'm better. Do that, and you'll never see me again. Otherwise, I'm taking you with me as leverage. It's up to you."

My eyes widened. "You want me to give you a place to stay?"

He jerked his head in the affirmative. "Just until my leg heals. Then I'll disappear. It'll be our secret."

Scenarios raced through my head. I couldn't hide him anywhere in the big house. The barn wouldn't work either. We didn't have much livestock, but we still went in there regularly. Then it came to me. The old slave cabins had been abandoned when Mama sold all except for the three slaves after Pa died, claiming we needed the money. Axie worked in the house and Sam and his son managed the livestock and what was left of the fields. They lived in a makeshift room in the cotton gin house.

"Do we have a deal?"

His voice snapped me back into the present moment. *"Do I really have a choice?"*

He lifted one shoulder. *"Like I said, I could take you with me, although I'd rather not. So, yes, you have a choice."*

God Almighty, I wanted to tell him no and take my chances. Maybe he'd let me go anyway. Dragging an unwilling woman across the country wouldn't do him much good. Then again, he could just kill me and toss my body under a bush. Did I really want to risk inciting his anger when he could easily overpower me even in his condition?

Definitely not. Mama wouldn't survive another loss.

"Fine." I pushed against his shoulders and he stood up, releasing me. *"You can't stay more than a week, though. It's not safe for you or my family."*

"That should be more than enough time."

"Sit on that rock by the stream and let me see that wound before you bleed out."

After he sat, I crouched next to him and carefully rolled up his pant leg. A long diagonal cut ran from beneath his knee to his ankle. I tore off the strip of fabric binding the hem of my dress and divided it in half. I dipped one half in the water and dabbed the wound softly, trying to remove any dirt and dried blood.

"This cut needs stitches." I wrapped the other half of the fabric around and around his calf, securing it with a double knot. "I'll come by with a needle and thread later tonight. Now, follow me. I'll show you where you'll be staying. It's not pretty, but it's better than sleeping outdoors." I held out my hand. "By the way, my name is Elizabeth."

"I'm Charles," he said, taking my hand in his.

Chapter Ten

"Emma. Emma. Wake up, sweetheart." The words were slushy, nearly unintelligible. I curled tighter into a ball, willing the darkness to pull me under again. I didn't want to face reality.

"This is bullshit. She could be hurt. I'll carry her back to the house," another man said.

"Don't touch her," the first man growled. "We don't need your help."

"If you didn't need my help, then you shouldn't have banged on my door in the middle of the night."

"I found her, so you can go now."

"You mean I found her," the other man grumbled. "You couldn't find your ass if it wasn't attached to your body."

"Fuck off."

I blinked slowly, trying to bring my surroundings into focus. I was lying on a wood floor, moonlight peeked through the roof, and I was so cold. I rubbed my temples.

"Where am I?"

Brian bent down, his concerned face hovering

over mine. "In an old sharecropper cabin not too far from the house."

I bolted upright, jumbled memories coming back to me. "Where'd he go?"

Brian's brows bunched together. "Who?"

"You can question her later. She needs to get home," the second man said.

My eyes snapped in his direction. He paced back and forth in the shadows. Something about him struck me as oddly familiar. Then my thoughts scrambled, confusing the present with my dream, and I mumbled, "I was wondering where you went."

"What the hell is going on? You said you hadn't seen her tonight. Did you hurt her?" Brian barked out, his cheeks red.

The man stepped out of the shadows. "Jesus. Look at her. She's clearly delirious. She doesn't know what she's talking about."

I recognized his sharp jawline and imposing height immediately. "Caleb?"

Brian's gaze jumped from me to Caleb. "What were you doing out here with *him*?"

I scrubbed my hands over my face and flinched. My palms were tender. Then it came back to me. Falling in the woods. Getting lost. My heartrate sped up at the memory of what came after. It didn't make sense.

I shook my head, trying to clear my thoughts. While it felt real, it must have been a dream, though having reoccurring dreams about the same woman seemed odd. No. I'd think about that later. Much later when I wasn't laying on the dirty floor confused, sore, and tired, feeling like my world had

61

been turned upside down.

"No. I wasn't talking about Caleb. I'm confused. I think you caught me mid-dream." I glanced at Caleb again, studying his harsh features and hostile scowl. "It was raining. I guess I came across this place and fell asleep."

Caleb kept his face adverted so I couldn't see him. "Let's get out of here before it starts raining again."

"I don't think I should move her." Brian pressed a hand to my forehead. "Take the ATV. Get some blankets, and pain killers."

Caleb pulled his phone out of his pocket, crouched in front of me, and directed the flashlight in my eyes. He smelled like paint, pine, and soap, and for some reason his nearness made my heart skip a beat. It was disconcerting to say the least.

He switched off the flashlight and pocketed it. "She doesn't have a concussion."

Feeling the heated blush working its way up my cheeks, I ducked my head and distracted myself with retying my sneakers.

"You're an artist, not a doctor. What the hell do you know?" Brian countered.

"No." I cleared my throat and stood. "He's right. I want to go home. Other than being cold and tired, I'm perfectly fine."

"Here." Brian slipped an around my shoulders. "Lean on me."

"Thanks," I mumbled. As much as I wanted to refuse his help, I didn't. The strangeness of the night left me shaky, and my knees wobbled with every step.

Caleb tossed keys to Brian. "Only two people can fit on the ATV. I'll walk back." He turned and disappeared into the darkness. Only then did I realize he hadn't uttered a single word to me. After our confrontation, his behavior didn't surprise me. What did surprise me, though, was that he agreed to help Brian in the first place.

I climbed onto the ATV behind Brian, wrapping my arms around his waist, hoping to borrow some of his body heat. The engine roared in my ears and each bump jarred my stiff, aching body.

By the time we arrived at my house, humiliation had replaced my aches and pains. What in the hell was I thinking, wandering around at dark by myself? Worst of all, when Brian hadn't been able to get ahold of me, he'd sought out Caleb. How mortifying. Our short acquaintance involved me fainting, fighting with him, and getting hopelessly lost on my own property.

"I think I'll take a shower and go to bed," I said, making my way to the stairs.

Brian closed and locked the front door behind him. "I saved you some food if you're still hungry. I can bring it up to your room after you shower."

"I think I'm going to call it a night. I feel a little out of sorts. What time are you leaving tomorrow?"

"Around ten, but I can stay for a few more days if you need me. I wouldn't mind. I feel kind of bad, leaving you here by yourself in your condition."

I winced. I hadn't done much to prove I could take care of myself. If anything, I demonstrated my complete lack of common sense. "I'll be okay. After today, I think I'll limit myself to short walks during

63

the day."

"That's probably a good idea." He shifted on his feet. "Well, goodnight, Emma."

My name triggered a memory from the dream. I had introduced myself as Elizabeth. "Brian?" I called. "Did anyone named Elizabeth ever live here?"

"Elizabeth," he repeated slowly. "Not that I can recall, but my family didn't spend as much time here as Andrew's family. As the older child, his dad inherited this place. You could ask Nora or the townspeople. They'd know better than me. Why? Did you find something around the house?"

I hesitated, considering sharing my experience with him, then immediately dismissed the idea. "Yeah. I thought I saw the name somewhere when I was cleaning out the drawers in my room."

"I could take a look at it if makes you feel better."

As soon as he made the offer, I regretted mentioning it. I didn't have anything with the name Elizabeth on it to show him, and the experience was most likely the result of a dream, the fever, or a combination of both. Either way, the likelihood that some woman named Elizabeth inhabited this home or a neighboring one was remote. At least, I desperately hoped so. Because if Elizabeth really existed, then that would mean...nope. I refused to go there. It was a dream. End of story.

"The papers are long gone." I flashed a sheepish smile. "I threw them away to make room for some of my stuff."

"Then Nora would be the person to ask. She's

the family genealogy expert. I think she still belongs to that United Daughters of the Confederacy Group." He shook his head. "I have no clue what for."

I glanced at my watch. It was nine thirty. I had disappeared for over three hours. Reckless wouldn't begin to describe my actions.

"Maybe I'll ask her. It's not urgent." I climbed up a few steps before turning around. "By the way, thanks for coming after me. I don't know what I was thinking."

"Of course I'd go looking for you, Emma. I'm not cruel. By the way, I see what you mean about Caleb. I have no clue why Andrew hired him as the caretaker. He's a real piece of work and not in a good way. Don't let him talk you into letting him stay."

I shrugged, feeling oddly protective of Caleb. "I don't know. It's possible I misjudged him. He could have told you to get lost. We didn't exactly hit it off when we met. I basically kicked him out with thirty days' notice. And yet, he helped you search the property for me."

"Yeah." His shoulders relaxed. "Maybe you're right. He did seem concerned about you even though he was an asshole to me."

Chapter Eleven

I rested my hands on the open driver's side window of Brian's car. "Thanks for coming."

He smiled. "I'll stop by on my way back from Savannah. I won't stay long. I know you're busy."

"That sounds nice." And it did. After everything that happened last night, I dreaded being left here alone.

"By the way, I was thinking about your question about someone named Elizabeth."

A thread of unease ghosted down my spine. "Oh, what about her?"

"Andrew and I used to play down by the creek. There's a small family graveyard not far from there. It's not big, maybe ten to twenty gravestones. You might find something relevant there, though it's not in the best condition. Not all of the names were legible. We used to drag the Ouija board out there and mess around." He waved his hand as if he hadn't freaked me out more than I already was. "Anyway, it's surrounded by a low wrought iron fence. You could poke around out there."

"Did anything ever happen? I mean with the Ouija board."

He chuckled. "No. Nothing. We even tried it in the middle of the night, thinking we'd have better luck."

"Nora never mentioned the cemetery."

"It's not uncommon for these old estates to have one, so she probably didn't think it was worth mentioning. If you go looking for the graveyard, bring the survey of the property. It should be noted on there somehow. Maybe a cross. And for God's sake, take your phone and go while there's plenty of daylight left."

"Yes, sir. I promise not to act like a complete imbecile again."

He studied my face for a second. "All right. Call me if you need anything."

"I will."

Once his car faded into the distance, I didn't waste a second. I ran inside, grabbed a bottle of water, and took a picture of the survey with my phone if I needed to reference it. It didn't have a cross anywhere, but there was a small square fenced-in area near the creek. Based on the location of the sharecropper cabin, I realized how I got turned around yesterday. I needed to head east instead of west when the path forked.

Just like the day before, I made way to the rear of the house. The instant I stepped outside, I tipped my head up and went stock-still, gawking at the unusual color of the sky. It wasn't a limp baby blue or an intense cobalt. It was something between lavender and azure, almost cornflower.

Uncontaminated and dramatic, standing there felt surreal as if I stepped onto a movie set.

When I finally dragged my gaze back to the scenery in front of me, I plodded along until I found the bifurcated path depicted on the survey. Once I veered east, something about my surroundings bothered me. Not the trail in particular—it was mostly flat without much overgrowth—but the creeping awareness of familiarity.

Like most people, I'd had bursts of déjà vu. They lasted for a second, then faded away almost immediately and were totally forgotten not too long after. This sensation was different. Every tree, every bend of the path felt intimately familiar. Most likely, I'd somehow wound up around here yesterday and my subconscious mind registered it.

Buzzing cicadas increased in volume as I closed in on my destination. Then the throbbing deep inside of me started, and it was so similar to the sensation I had last night before everything went topsy-turvy. My steps slowed, uncertainty brewing through me. A gnawing sensation burrowed beneath my breastbone, urging me to turn around.

I ignored my intuition and kept putting one foot in front of the other. As I came around the corner, the edges of my vision blurred until a square, rusty wrought iron fence in front of me was the only thing I could see. I edged closer until I stood in front of an ornate gate enclosing the space. The sound of someone weeping caused me to freeze mid-stride.

"Elizabeth, is that you?" A woman crouched in front of a stone marker.

"Yes, Mama," I responded. "Sorry to sneak up on you."

"No. No. It's fine." She dusted off her dreary gray hoop skirt and matching jacket. "I was just visiting with your father."

Pa had been gone for over two years and Mama still insisted on visiting his grave every couple of days. "I don't think he can hear you."

Mama smiled but there was no friendliness in her eyes, only displeasure undoubtedly inspired by her constant annoyance with me. "Don't sass me, and where's your parasol? No man is going to want a woman browned by the sun. You're always gallivanting around the woods these days. Not proper. Not proper at all."

I glanced over my shoulder, searching for Charles. I thought I had caught a flash of his gray pants. I increased the volume of my voice to warn him away. "That's where we'll have to agree to disagree, I reckon. If a man really loved me, he wouldn't care about a few freckles."

"Hm. Speaking of men, I spoke with the Cadwells last night. Brett's back."

"Good for them. I know they were awaiting his arrival with great eagerness—nay, excitement."

"You should pay them a visit."

"I'm not ready to visit yet." I swallowed hard. "Maybe in a few weeks. We should let him settle in first."

We strolled along the creek, and I took a few minutes to really study my surroundings. The bugs were usually fierce down here, but they weren't so bad in the last days of autumn. Though I hadn't

69

traveled much, I still believed Clayton Plantation had to rival other places for the title of most charming place in the world. The soft rolling fields filled with snowy puffs of cotton, the expansive woods, and the undulating pastures for horses, though we didn't have many of those anymore. And with all of the slaves gone except a handful, I doubted the cotton would be harvested this year.

"Elizabeth, Brett agreed to honor his brother's promise and marry you. I don't think we should delay too long," Mama said, interrupting my ruminations. "Men are in short supply."

My mood switched from serene to exasperated. Henry held a dear place in my heart. We'd been friends since childhood and I'm pretty sure I'd loved him as long as I could remember. Brett was another story. Where Henry was kind, Brett was cruel. A life with him would crush me, and even if war had changed him for the better, I couldn't marry him. My heart had died with Henry. I wasn't capable of loving anyone else.

I couldn't share any of that with her. She wouldn't understand. I needed to placate her until I figured out how to change her mind. Because God knew, even if she let the subject drop right now, it wouldn't be long before she brought it up again. "I don't know, Mama. I need time. Henry's only been gone for a short while. It's all so distasteful."

My mama grabbed my arm and threaded it through hers as we strolled. "We don't have time, Elizabeth. With your dad gone and your brother in Europe, we need help. We can't run this place alone."

"Perhaps, but until the war ends, we don't need to make any decisions. Jordan might come home."

"Pshaw. Don't be foolish. He married that girl and he'll never come back."

I didn't disagree. On the last trip he and Pa took to London, Jordon met and married Olivia Cunningham, and he stayed with her. When Pa wrote him to come back to join the war effort, he refused to leave her because she was with child. It'd been three years since that letter and we hadn't heard much of anything from him because of the embargo, but I suspected he was lost to us.

"Brett might have to return to the battle," I hedged.

"Not with his injuries."

I halted mid-step beneath the shade of a large pine tree shuddering from the wind. "Injuries?"

"He lost his left hand and something happened to his knee, but I understand it will recover in time."

I shivered and tightened my shawl around my shoulders. Tears clogged my throat. How many more people had to suffer before this war ended? "Oh, Mama. I didn't realize that was why they sent him home."

The vibrating in my body returned, and a bright white light flashed. Squinting, I lifted a hand to shield my face. When the light dimmed, the woman next to me had disappeared, and the neat rows of cotton were nowhere to be found. In its place, I saw a rolling field covered with tangled green weeds and vines.

A cold sweat broke out on my skin and my ribcage heaved with every inhalation. My mind locked down, instinctually smothering any and all questions. Rather than exploring the cemetery as I initially intended, I took off in a sprint, not stopping until I reached the rear service door of my house.

Winded and shaky, I clutched on the door handle and bent at the waist. "What the hell was that?" I whispered to myself.

Chapter Twelve

Addison knocked on the window of my truck. She'd told me to meet her here at eight. Loathing the thought of being alone in my house for another second, I left thirty minutes earlier than necessary.

I lowered the window. "Hey, Addison."

She flashed a big smile, then frowned. "You look like you're in desperate need of a drink."

A drink wouldn't come close to settling my nerves. I had slept poorly the last two nights. Even more so than normal if that were possible. A large chunk of both nights entailed me staring unseeing into the darkness, afraid if I blinked I'd fall back into the rabbit hole of Elizabeth's life. Whoever she was…or wasn't.

Maybe years of stress, losing Andrew, and trying to start of new life had finally pushed me over the cliff of sanity and firmly into the realm of madness; hallucinations included free of charge. The more I thought about Elizabeth, the more confused I became. Nothing made sense. First, the dream of her with Henry, then the encounter with the Union

73

solider, and now her mother wanted her to marry someone else. I couldn't keep track. I pushed the unsettling thoughts so far away I couldn't see them, hear them, or taste them.

To avoid ruminating on her or my sanity, I'd spent the better half of the afternoon getting ready for my night out. My blonde hair was perfectly straightened, my eye makeup expertly applied, and I had on my favorite pair of flare cropped jeans with a black silky top and low snakeskin booties. Eyeing Addison's black t-shirt that said, "I say what everyone else is thinking," I wondered if I looked like I was trying too hard.

"You could say that." I opened the door of my truck and slammed it behind me. "Unfortunately, I have a long drive home so I can't have more than a one. Two if I stay long enough."

"Nah, you need to let your hair down. I'll be the designated driver. Drink all you want."

"I can't leave my car here."

She bumped her shoulder into mine as we strolled to the entrance of the local bar. "I'll stay over at your place. That is if you're up for havin' company."

Relief flooded through me. I really didn't want to spend another night alone in the house. I needed a break from whatever was going on with me, and I hoped Addison would be the magic bullet to keep my unwanted visions at bay. "Girls' slumber party?"

"Sounds like fun to me." She flung open the heavy wooden door leading to the bar, and we were greeted with the whine of a country ballad about lost love.

A blast of muggy heat molded my black blouse to my torso. I smelled the remnants of decades of greasy food and stale beer. At the bar, a group of guys wearing a mixture of cowboy and trucker hats with worn jeans sat drinking beer. Since it was still somewhat early, half of the tables were vacant, or maybe it was always like this given the small population of this town. Yellowed flyers and random bumper stickers dotted the walls haphazardly.

Addison steered me to the bar even though I would have preferred to hide out at one of the dimly lit corner tables.

"What'll you have?" A lanky man with dirty blond hair and a plaid shirt asked from behind the bar.

"A glass of white wine, preferably Chardonnay."

"Bless your heart." The man laughed and patted me on the shoulder. "Where'd ya find this one, Addie?"

"Hey, Josh." She balled up a cocktail napkin and tossed it at his face. "Don't go and make the new girl in town feel uncomfortable or this'll be the last time we'll see her."

His gaze snapped back to me. "You're Emma? The new owner of the Clayton place."

"In the flesh."

"In that case, I'll check around in the storage room to see if we have any wine. We don't normally stock it unless it's tourist season."

I held up my hand. "No, it's fine. I'll have a beer. Whatever's on tap." I preferred beer anyway, but

I'd become accustomed to ordering wine instead. In Andrew's social circle, most women ordered white wine or vodka so I fell in line, not wanting to be the oddball. I stayed clear of the hard stuff, though, because I had no desire to follow in my mom's footsteps.

"I'll have the same," Addison added. "No, give us a pitcher to share."

A few minutes later, Josh slapped two glasses and an overflowing pitcher down in front of us. He filled each glass. "So, has Addison been filling your head full of spooky stories about that home of yours?"

I curled a hand around my glass, and took a swig of my drink before answering. "Lord have mercy. Why does everyone keep saying that? I live there alone. Are you guys trying to run me out of town?"

"No, but seriously. Have you heard or seen anything?" Josh persisted, leaning closer to us.

"Like what? A white sheet floating down the hallway? Flickering lights? Howling?" I forced myself to make a joke about it because what was actually happening was far stranger than I could explain. Not that I had any intention of sharing my hallucinations. I'd be the official town nut job by the end of the weekend.

Addison leaned over the bar and shoved Josh's shoulder. "Get back to work. I can hear the Hanson twins complaining from here. Somethin' about you being slow as molasses."

Josh smirked, bringing out a dimple in his left cheek. It made him far cuter than I gave him credit for after my first glance. "Addie, you sure have a way of sucking the fun out of things."

"And you like to gossip too much for a man."

"And on that note, I'm out." Josh made his way down the bar, talking to a couple of men at the other end.

"All right," Addison said when Josh was out of earshot. "What's happened that has you lookin' like you're scared of your shadow?'

I finished my first beer and filled my glass again. I wasn't a big drinker. In fact, I hadn't overindulged since before I met Andrew. Public drunkenness wasn't acceptable in Andrew's high society world. "I don't have any clue what you're talking about."

"I could hardly get you to agree to come out with me," she said, "then you show up early and invite me to stay over to your house. And now you're already on your second beer. Not," she added, with an impish grin, "that I'm judging, but based on my first impression of you, this doesn't seem like your thing."

I pointed at my glass. "Can't a girl drink in peace without spilling all of her secrets?"

She swiveled to face me on her stool and crossed her legs. "Did I freak you out with the ghost story or are you worried about being harassed by the locals?" She waved her hand. "'Cause I warned them to give you some space so they wouldn't overwhelm you."

I surveyed everyone in the bar and it did seem like they were really trying to mind their own business. With the exception of Josh, they hadn't acknowledged Addison, and in a town this size they all had to know her.

"I want to drink and forget about the rest of the madness going on in my life."

"You sure?"

"I'm sure, and when I'm done with this one," I tapped the rim of my glass, "I want to dance."

A slow smile slid across her face. "You got it. Josh," she yelled, "turn up the music. Emma wants to dance."

He laughed. "Ah hell, this is gonna get ugly."

Time passed quickly as Addison and I sang along to the lyrics booming from the bar's speakers while dancing like we didn't have a care in the world. We only stopped long enough to refill our drinks or make a trip to the bathroom.

Tonight was exactly what I needed. I'd went from being an insecure twenty-year-old, not really knowing who I was or what I wanted, to a wife of a man living a life far out of my realm of experience, and finally to a widow. I skipped over the time where normal women my age were drinking and hooking up with random guys. Not that hooking up with anyone was on my immediate agenda, but having fun could be. I didn't want to worry about what I wanted to do with my life or the fact that I had a difficult tenant who I hated, yet felt weirdly attracted to.

I closed my eyes and an arm slid around my shoulder, snapping me out of my reverie. I yelped and spun around to find a bemused Josh. He handed me a beer. "My shift's over. Addison sent me over to dance with you."

I glanced around the bar, searching for Addison. Instead, my eyes collided with Caleb's. Speak of the devil. He was leaning against the wall, his arms folded across his chest, studying me with casual boredom. I must have missed his arrival. Addison mentioned he's stopped by here before, but I was surprised to see him. She made it sound like he didn't come around much.

He examined me in one fast, thorough sweep of his eyes. His perusal felt like a shot of adrenaline in my veins. I told myself to look away, but my body refused to obey. Even though we didn't exactly get along, I lifted my hand to wave. Rather than return the gesture, he pushed away from the wall, closing the distance between us with his smooth, loose-hipped gait. My stomach knotted uncomfortably. His presence made me edgy.

Caleb grabbed the beer out of Josh's hand and set it on a nearby table. "I think she's had enough."

My cheeks flooded with heat, and I couldn't guarantee I was even breathing. It was pretty much a miracle I didn't punch him in the face. "Since when do you get to make decisions on my behalf?"

Caleb's eyes narrowed; something punitive and fiery zipped between us. "Since you decided to get lost in the woods, and I had to spend half my night looking for you instead of working."

Josh's eyes ping-ponged back and forth between the two of us, and I groaned inwardly. Now, the whole town was going to be gossiping about Caleb coming to my rescue because I was a colossal dumbass.

"I didn't ask for your help. Nothing was going to happen to me in the cabin."

Caleb inched closer, encroaching on my personal

space. I could smell him and only him despite all the competing scents in the room. "You sure as hell didn't look fine that night or tonight for that matter."

"Stay out of by business," I snarled, before turning to face Josh. "Thanks for your offer, but I think I'm gonna call it a night. Someone here has ruined my mood and I'm tuckered out. Maybe next time."

I turned to go, and Caleb called after me. "You shouldn't drive."

"Again, not your problem," I answered without looking back at him.

Chapter Thirteen

I pushed through the crowd, heading to the door while texting Addison so she would know I'd left. Even though she'd promised to drive me home, she was totally smashed the last time I checked. I'd be better off sitting in my car for an hour or so before driving home, or maybe I'd call a cab if this town had one. Either way, I needed to get away from Caleb. For some reason, he made me feel more than a little unhinged, almost like there was an unsettled, restless energy buzzing between us.

The second I made it outside I sighed with relief. I hadn't realized how hot and muggy it was in the bar until the cool evening air hit my skin. I started walking in the direction of my truck when something solid and firm circled my forearm. I tumbled backward and collided with a warm, unyielding chest.

"Stop doing that," Caleb growled, his breath tickling the shell of my ear.

Stunned, my thoughts scattered, and instead of focusing on his actions, I fixated on his warmth and how insanely close he was. How he smelled like the crisp outdoors mixed with paint. How his fingers dug into my forearm like claws. How his heart pounded inside of his chest against my back.

One of his hands slid around my waist, snapping me back to reality. Who did he think he was, touching me like I was his to touch? He had no business following me out of the bar. And now, he felt entitled to manhandle me.

Twisting out of his hold, I glared. "Doing what?"

He scrutinized me with a guarded gaze that missed nothing. "Being rude and walking away while we're still talking."

Okay. He had a point about our first meeting, but the second time he didn't utter a single syllable to me. "Me? You ran away last time. You didn't even bother to look in my direction."

His irritation sizzled, evolving into a tangible electric vitality spinning around us. Chaotic energy. Ruthless energy. Inexplicable energy that I couldn't begin to dissect.

"That's because that lap dog friend of yours warned me the entire time we were looking for you to keep my distance. I didn't want him to get his panties in a bunch by fraternizing with you."

"Brian?"

"Who else would I be talking about?"

While hundreds of questions about what Brian had said popped into my head, I pushed them away. I'd confront Brian later. I told him not to interfere and that I'd handle Caleb by myself.

I rested my hands on my hips and lifted my chin. "And here you are, despite his warnings."

His eyes were a rich gold like honey, mesmerizing and hypnotic, and yet they felt like…home. God, that was a messed-up thought.

"Look," he said, "I don't want to fight. You've been drinking. Let me give you a ride home. You don't even have to talk to me."

My shoulders drooped. He was right, and I really didn't like the idea of hanging out in my truck until I felt it was safe to drive home. It could be hours and I was really fucking tired.

"Where's your car?"

His eyes flared as though he couldn't believe I'd agreed. Maybe I was being stupid. He could kill me and dump me in a ditch and there wouldn't be any witnesses.

"This way. Let's go," he said, striding down Main Street, his black boots pounding hard and fast against the pavement.

Just like he promised, he didn't say a word on the way home. He even turned off the music in the car. The polite side of me demanded I ask him questions to fill the dead air and the real me wanted to study the passing landscape out the window. My head was fuzzy from drinking and I felt slightly queasy. More disconcerting, though, was the fact that the closer we got to my new home, the more intense the pulsating in my body became. I tapped my foot on the floormat, willing the building sensation away.

The minute his car stopped in front of Caleb's converted barn, I flung myself out of the car. I needed to get away from him and the unnerving feeling coursing through me. I feared if I dwelled on

83

the sensation gathering steam inside of me, I'd soon lose my hold on reality and I refused to let that happen in front of Caleb again.

I didn't get more than ten feet away from the car before buzzing erupted inside of my ears and a dark mist invaded my vision. Caleb's hands landed on my shoulders, his eyes full of something I couldn't name. "Everything is okay, Emma. Don't panic. Let me help you to bed and you can think about it tomorrow."

"No," I slurred more to myself than him, feeling everything slipping…

My muted protest failed to stop the tide pulling me under and everything in front me receded as if I were at the beginning of a long tunnel where I no longer existed.

Chapter Fourteen

Dressed in a pair of my brother's old trousers, I opened the door to the barn. The smell of oil and leather greeted me. Twelve stalls ran the length of the building, but I only cared about the horse in the last one. Serendipity was mine and mine alone, and I wanted to ride her before my parents came home. They were visiting the Cadwells, which meant I had at least a couple of hours.

As I reached for a saddle sitting on a rack, a man stepped out of the shadows, and I screamed.

"Shh." He pressed a hand to my mouth. "Elizabeth, it's just me."

Tense and jumpy, my hands thrashed around my body to regain my balance. "Darn it, Henry, you scared me half to death."

He took a step closer. "Your parents are at my house, and I had a hunch I'd find you here."

"I was taking a stroll to get some fresh air and I decided to check in on Serendipity."

"Are you planning to go for a ride?"

I shook my head, fearing my voice would betray

me. He was well aware I wasn't allowed to ride alone, not that I didn't break that rule every chance I got.

"That's too bad. I was planning to take a ride along the creek. I guess I'll have to go by myself. That is, unless you want to join me," he proposed unexpectedly, an amused gleam on his face.

"I'm not sure I should." It wasn't entirely proper to be alone with him without getting my parents' permission, and yet I wanted to go more than anything. "You don't have your horse," I remarked, retreating another step.

Henry grinned. "I tied him to a tree outside. Didn't you see it?"

"No."

"So, do you want to accompany me?"

I shifted back and forth on my feet. "You won't tell my parents?"

"No."

"Then I'll go."

He readied my horse and helped me up. I rode around the side of the barn and his black stallion came into view. I couldn't believe I had missed it earlier. He swung himself into the saddle effortlessly.

"Ready?" he asked.

Leaning forward in my saddle, I patted my mare's silky gray neck. Instead of answering Henry, I touched my mare's reins to her neck and she took off. I galloped diagonally across the open field, urging my horse to go faster when I heard the clomping of Henry's horse closing in on me.

The wind whipped around me, tugging the

ribbon from my hair. I didn't stop to retrieve it. Beneath me, I could feel Serendipity's muscles gathering and stretching as she picked up speed. When the creek came into view, I eased her back into a steady canter.

"Let's stop here," I said when Henry joined me.

We dismounted and Henry wrapped the horses' reins around an oak tree. After swinging his satchel over his shoulder, he held out his arm and I looped mine through his. We strolled along the bank of the creek, neither of us saying much. A squirrel scampered up a tree. Cicadas serenaded us, and the sun warmed my face. Everything was perfect, but then again, I always felt that way around Henry. I didn't feel the need to fill the time with mindless chatter and neither did he.

He pointed to a large rock up ahead, overlooking the creek. "Do you want to rest here for a while?"

"Just for a little bit. I have to be back soon."

We settled onto the rock and I scooped up a handful of pebbles and tossed them one by one into the water. If Henry weren't here, I'd take off my boots, roll up my trousers, and splash around in the water until my feet were numb and wrinkled. When I ran out of pebbles, I sighed and tipped my head to the sky.

He bumped his shoulder into mine. "Go ahead. You know you want to do it."

I turned to face him. A breeze ruffled his thick, coffee-brown hair. Beneath his dark brows, his tawny eyes observed me. "Do what?"

"Put your feet in the creek."

My eyes flared, surprised he had guessed my thoughts. "I don't think that's a good idea."

He laughed at me, a throaty, infectious laugh, before sliding off his brown leather boots and socks. He jumped off the rock and strode into water.

"Henry, what are you doing?"

He bent down and ran the tips of his fingers through the water, spraying it in my direction. "You have two minutes to take off your boots and join me or else."

"Or else, what?"

"I'm going to do it for you."

"You're awful ornery today," I said, reaching down to pull off my shoes and stockings.

The instant I tucked my last stocking inside my boot, Henry lifted me up and tossed me over his shoulder.

"Henry, put me down." I wiggled and pounded my fists on his back to no avail. He waded into the creek, and only then did he plop me down in the cold water. It swirled around my calves and I gasped. "You jerk."

I glared at him and kicked some water in his direction. It dotted his tan trousers.

"A water fight? Is that what you're after?"

"No." I held up my hands in surrender as I shook my head back and forth. The speculative look on his face had me hedging backward. When he took a step toward me I took off running. I slipped more than once on the slick rocks, but I kept going. The water splashed up in my face and soaked my clothes, and I didn't mind one bit. I felt free. Mama's reproving voice crept into my head and I

pushed it away. What she didn't see wouldn't hurt her.

I hadn't made it more than a couple hundred yards when Henry's arms snaked around my waist and twirled me around. "Caught you."

I gazed up at him, almost in a daze, my heart thumping like a drum against my ribcage. Gently cupping my face between both his hands, he stepped closer to me until less than an inch separated us.

"Even when you're a pain in my ass, I can't resist you." He lowered his head and kissed the tip of my nose. Instead of pulling away like he always did in moments like these, his lips lowered again and brushed along mine. His touch was so soft I wasn't sure I imagined it, and yet, I tensed all the same.

He must have realized that no other man's lips had ever touched mine, and I didn't have a clue how to respond. Propriety urged me to reprimand him for being so presumptuous, so forward, but this was Henry, the man I'd adored, nay loved, for as long as I could remember.

My heart missed a beat when he lowered his head once again. He kissed me slowly and tenderly until my head began to swim. He whispered something against my mouth I couldn't make out, and then everything faded to black.

I felt my body being carried, and I pried opened my eyes. "Henry," I mumbled.

"Caleb," he corrected.

"What happened?"

"Close your eyes, Emma. You need to sleep."

Too tired and confused to argue, I did exactly that.

Chapter Fifteen

I woke to the sound of thunder shaking the windows. My shoulders tensed and I squeezed my eyes shut, combatting a wave of emotions. Curled in a ball, I didn't dare move a centimeter. I couldn't bear the thought of opening my eyes and finding myself living another life again. My heart beat faster and faster the longer I lay unmoving. Anticipation flooded my ears with the sound of rushing blood, and I couldn't stand the mystery any longer. I had to know.

Casually, I reached out my hand, searching for clues to my location. My fingers skittered along the soft cotton until it reached what could only be the edge of a bed. That didn't tell me much. I stretched my arm farther, seeking out a nightstand and any clues on it.

"You're up."

Startled, my eyes blinked open. "Caleb?" What the fucking fuck? I propped myself up on my forearms and craned my neck to get a better idea of where I was. Sinking against the headboard with a relieved sigh, I blurted out, "What are you doing in my room?"

He ground his jaw back and forth. The penetrating edginess I recognized as being part of Caleb's inherent nature cranked up several decimals if that were even possible. Was he mad at me? Did something happen between us? My stomach dipped at the thought. Oh God, that would be more than I could process on top of the dreams or whatever kept happening.

"You fainted again last night," he finally answered, shifting in the chair next to my bed.

"Oh, weird. I must've had too much to drink."

Such a silly response given I'd fainted in his company twice now and he'd found me sleeping in a dilapidated cabin on my property. No words could explain the simultaneous surge of relief and trepidation rolling through me. I didn't want to learn I had done something regrettable with Caleb. However, the fact that I had fainted once again and lived momentarily in another century where people called me Elizabeth didn't exactly thrill me either. I desperately wanted to confide in someone, yet I knew I couldn't do that without sounding completely delusional.

"That's all you have to say?"

I gathered up my sheets and yanked them up to my neck, feeling self-conscious and exposed. Obviously, that wasn't all I had to say. It was all I had to say to him. I didn't know him all that well, and he qualified as more of an enemy than a friend or confidant. I tried to kick him out of his home, so he had every reason in the world to discredit and humiliate me. Telling him I was time traveling or having flashbacks would give him the ammunition to do exactly that.

"To you, yes."

He pushed out of the chair. All six feet of him towered over me. "All right, then I don't feel bad about what I did."

Dread crept through me, and I jumped to my feet. "What did you do?"

"I asked the local doctor to make a house call." He glanced at the alarm clock on my nightstand. "He should be here in an hour or so. In the meantime, I made coffee. I'll grab you a cup while you get dressed."

"No." I glanced down at my clothes and sagged with relief noting I still had on my jeans and black silky top. "Please. You need to cancel it."

"Then tell me what's going on."

"Why do you even care? I'm not your responsibility."

His fists clenched. "Because I'm not entirely heartless. If something is happening with you, you can't be at this house all by yourself."

I ground down on my molars and my temper flared to life like it always did in his company. I'd never considered myself someone with a short fuse. Apparently, he brought out my irrational side. "You'd like that, wouldn't you? Then you could go on with your life and you wouldn't have to move out."

A doctor couldn't treat me without my permission. I knew it and he knew it. Yet, this was a small town and having him summon a doctor to my house would cause gossip, something I didn't need or want.

"No." He rubbed his stubbled chin as he regarded me. "I don't care about that. I mean, sure I'd appreciate you giving me time to make arrangements that work for me, but I get it. You don't want me around, so I'll leave if you really want me to leave. But that doesn't mean I'm going to look the other way when something is obviously wrong with you."

"I'm overworked and exhausted. I don't need a doctor to tell me I need to slow down." My gaze went distant, recalling all of the things and people that had been stolen from me. It started with my dad disappearing, and then alcohol stole the last of my mom's sanity. Finally, Andrew, the person I had made the center of my existence, slipped away too. Maybe my mind was creating these *dreams* as a way to escape my grief.

Then again, that wouldn't be such a good thing, given my mom's history of mental illness. Maybe I took after her more than I'd thought. She hadn't always been so unstable. There was a time when she was young and beautiful, the toast of our town. She even won the local beauty pageant as a teenager and sat on a float during the Rhododendron Festival.

"Emma?" Caleb's voice interrupted my rambling thoughts.

"Yeah," I mumbled, the earlier rush of anger swallowed by my exhaustion and genuine fear something was wrong with me.

"What are you hiding?"

I watched him for a second. Concern was etched

into his face…not pity, but rather care. I sat on the edge of my bed, resting my head in my hands.

"I think I'm losing my mind," I whispered, not sure what I was doing.

Even in my hungover, shell-shocked state, I knew this wasn't a good idea. Caleb was so insanely attractive, and so infuriatingly captivating that even when he was being a colossal asshole I felt compelled to confide in him and befriend him. I found myself doing exactly that despite knowing my brother or Nora would be the more logical choice.

Chapter Sixteen

"What do you mean?"

I glanced at him from beneath my lashes. "I keep having these dreams, except they feel more real than that. Almost like…" I hesitated, not wanting to elaborate. Now that the story hovered on the tip of my tongue, I started thinking that letting the doctor look me over was the better choice. He'd take my vitals, listen to my heart, and whatever else he could do during a house call, and with any luck he'd pronounce me healthy and tell me to come into the office soon.

The town may or may not find out he made a house call. They'd probably start a rumor that I was pregnant or possessed by the ghost they liked to weave into every conversation. In retrospect, it might be the lesser of two evils here. I could endure the gossip because the truth scared me more.

"Like what?" he coaxed.

I looked to the side, chewing on my thumbnail, the uncertainty of what I should do made my hand shake. I paused, hoping he'd drop the whole thing or move on. Unfortunately, he remained stubbornly silent, waiting for me to continue. My shoulders dropped when I made my decision. I might as well run it by him to the test the waters and see how crazy it all sounded when I said it out loud to the therapist I needed to hire in the near future.

"They feel more like flashbacks of another life than dreams," I admitted, already cringing on the inside, expecting the worst.

He ran his fingers through his hair, his lips pressed into a firm line. "All right." He looked as if he wanted to say more, but he stopped himself.

"So, you see, it's nothing to call the doctor about. It's happened around you a few times, but it's not a big deal. I feel a little funky, and then boom, I'm someone named Elizabeth, living a long time ago. It's probably the stress of everything and my mind running wild with the history of this place. Before Andrew got sick, I was working toward my Masters in Civil War studies and living out here is like going back in time. So, you see I have an overactive imagination. It's nothing to worry about."

"Are you actually this Elizabeth person or are you a bystander watching her life?" He prodded, ignoring my attempt to downplay the whole thing.

"I'm her. I meet people as her. I interact with her family as her. I don't even think about what to say, I just know her life." I frowned. "That sounds crazy, doesn't it?"

"No, I'm an artist. People call me eccentric all the time. I'm not one to judge." One side of his mouth curled up like he was reminded of something else. "While this is going on, do you remember you're still Emma Clayton?"

"No. As far as I can tell, I don't exist, but I don't think these dreams or flashbacks go on for hours. They're like little glimpses into some points of her life. I don't even think they're in chronological order. It's like something that I see or hear triggers a memory." I swallowed, hesitating, not sure I wanted to know. "How long am I out?"

"The first time at the barn, not more than a couple of minutes. I'm not sure about the time we found you in the cabin. Did it happen then?" I nodded. "And last night, you kind of froze in place for a while and didn't respond. After a few minutes, I carried you into the house and you mumbled a few words. You were breathing fine, so I figured you had too much to drink. You woke up an hour later asking for water. I got you a glass and you were already asleep by the time I got back. I slept in the chair to make sure you were okay, but I didn't hear you wake up again until this morning."

I stared beyond Caleb, picturing Henry under the strawberry moon and sitting next to the creek. The desperation I felt as Elizabeth when she had found out Henry was missing and her desire to help Charles. The expression of pain and relief on Charles' face when Elizabeth agreed to shelter him until he got better. And for a second I almost wanted to slip back into their story to see what happened next. I knew Henry had died, but I didn't know how or when. My heart squeezed just thinking about him.

I shook off my musings. I couldn't let these

dreams or flashbacks take over my life, no matter how compelling or real the story seemed at times. I needed to figure out why and how this was happening so I could control it rather than having it control me.

"Addison mentioned something about this house being haunted. Do you know anything about that? Maybe that's somehow contributing to my dreams."

His lips compressed whether from amusement or annoyance, I couldn't tell. "People in town have said the same thing to me a few times."

"And?" I prompted.

"I haven't spent much time in this house other than to walk the property here and there and to let the cleaning crew in once a month. Once they left without finishing and refused to come back."

I frowned. "Why?"

"They claimed they saw a woman brushing her hair sitting on the bed. According to them, she was a ghost. I had to find someone else after that, and the new company hasn't mentioned anything to me."

"Do you think that ghost could be Elizabeth and somehow her spirit attached to me? Maybe I'm picking up pieces of her story? Or who knows, maybe I was Elizabeth in a past life."

Suddenly feeling embarrassed by the direction of my thoughts, a brittle laugh escaped my lips and I ducked my head. I'd never been one to believe in ghosts, hauntings, reincarnation, or spiritual attachments. Except here I was contemplating exactly that with a person I barely knew in the privacy of my bedroom of all places.

"Forget I said anything. I'm being silly."

"Hey." He lifted my chin with two fingers and I had no choice but to look at him. His expression was penetrating and heated. Goosebumps skittered down my neck and my cheeks flushed with heat. I picked at the hem of my shirt. I didn't want to feel drawn to him or feel anything for him except maybe friendship. Strange how I went from hating him to confiding in him.

"Don't feel like you need to make light of your feelings. Some religions believe in reincarnation like Hinduism and Buddhism. Even some ancient cultures—"

"And what about you? What do you believe?" I interrupted, not satisfied with his response.

"Well…" He shrugged. "Anything's possible."

The second the words left his mouth, a memory of the first time I saw a picture of this house came to mind. I was immediately fascinated and drawn to it. I asked Andrew so many questions about the house, I think he wished I'd never seen it. In a roundabout way, it sparked my interest in getting a masters in Civil War studies. Perhaps, my subconscious knew something my conscious mind didn't.

"Yeah, maybe you're right," I said on an exhale, feeling the weight of all this weirdness lift off my chest slightly.

He nodded, looking thoughtful, his attention fixed on his black boots. After a few moments, he lifted his head and my heart skipped a beat. When we were fighting, it was easy to forget how handsome he was. Our eyes met and held. I blinked, warmth expanding from my chest through my body. In this light, I could see the tiny flecks of olive green in his otherwise golden eyes. "Do you still want some coffee?"

"Um, yeah, sure. Thanks for making it, by the way."

Tossing the blanket from my shoulder onto the bed, I made my way out of my room, and down the stairs to the kitchen at the rear of the house. As I snagged two mugs from the cabinet and poured the coffee he made earlier, Caleb leaned his hips against the island with his ankles crossed. Uncomfortable with the weight of his stare and the thick silence, I concentrated on my task. His maleness filled the space, making it hard to focus, and I dripped some coffee on the counter. I wasn't sure if my uneasiness stemmed from the fact that I used to do this same ritual with Andrew, or maybe it was because I was hyperaware of him. And that thought discombobulated me. I didn't want to feel anything for anyone new. I wasn't ready for it, and I didn't know if I'd ever be.

I passed one of the mugs to Caleb, and our fingertips brushed. A spark of electricity zipped between us and my eyes shot upward.

"Sorry," I mumbled.

"For what?"

"I don't know." I took a sip of the coffee, letting its nutty heat warm me from the inside out. "For last night. For picking a fight with you the first time we met." I shrugged. "The list is pretty long. Do you want me to continue? Because there's probably three or four more things I could apologize for."

He threw back his head and laughed, causing a flutter in my belly. "Let's call a truce? I don't think either of us have been on our best behavior."

"I'd like that."

His eyes softened. "We can be friends, then?"

"Yeah." I shuffled my feet. "And you don't have to find someplace else to stay. I don't need the barn for any reason. It'll just be one more place I have to worry about, and I have plenty to take care of in here."

Caleb searched my face, then his lips curled up at the corners. I froze, standing there, studying him, not caring if he noticed. Something about him, being here with me, so relaxed and open made me curious about him. What would it be like to have this man in my life? What do his lips feel like? Besides painting, what did he like to do?

"Are you sure? I don't want to take advantage of the situation or make you uncomfortable."

"Oh." I waved my hand, feeling sheepish about the direction of my thoughts. "I'm not worried. We'll work something out. Actually, follow me. I have an idea." When I reached the entrance to the dining room, I paused. "I could use some help fixing this room."

"What do you want to do?"

"For starters, I hate the wallpaper. I want to take it down and replace it with something more consistent with the antebellum period."

I stared at him for a second, filled with gratitude for his desire to help me now and his willingness to do so last night despite our less than auspicious beginning. Then I was hit with the oddest feeling that we were preordained to become close friends long before our initial meeting.

"I'll help you with whatever you need, but I'm going to pay rent too." He smiled sincerely…no, not sincerely, more like intimately. A thrill of apprehension shot though me, but I didn't get the chance to analyze it because the doorbell rang.

Chapter Seventeen

I folded my arms across my chest. "Don't tell me that's the doctor."

His stuffed his hands in the pockets of his jeans and rocked back on his heels. "Nope. I made up the doctor story."

It took a lot of effort to keep my face impassive and not tumble headfirst into another fight. "What?"

The doorbell rang again, and he smirked. "You should probably answer that."

"This conversation isn't over."

When I opened the door, Addison and Josh rushed into my house, not bothering to wait for an invitation. In any other moment, I would have laughed at their antics. Right now, though, I didn't want to explain Caleb's presence this early in the morning. Despite the rather innocuous reason for him staying over, I couldn't exactly explain my repeated fainting spells and lapses in memory without opening a whole other can of worms.

"What the hell happened to you? You disappeared last night, your car is still at the bar, and you're not answering your phone. I've been going crazy. I had to recruit Josh to come out here with me in case I found your dead body or something worse."

Today, Addison's t-shirt read 'I'm allergic to stupidity.' I bit my lip, trying not to smile. I was starting to suspect these types of shirts were her signature fashion statement.

"Hey, y'all. Good to see you both." I raised my arms above my head. "And as you can clearly see for yourself, I'm alive and well."

Josh offered up a sheepish wave, his eyes darting anywhere except at my face. Clearly, he wasn't fully on board with this excursion. I sympathized with him. I'd already experienced firsthand how hard it was to say no to Addison when she got something in her head. She wasn't above using emotional blackmail or coercion.

"Don't throw this back at me like I'm the crazy person here." Addison planted her hands on her hips and narrowed her eyes, ready to battle. "You left the bar with nothing more than a cryptic text, and then I came out a little while later and saw that your car was still out front. I thought you'd been abducted or somethin'."

"Sorry about that. I should have been more specific."

"How'd you get—" The floorboard creaked and she paused midsentence, her eyes darting to the left.

I cringed, knowing exactly what or who she saw. Caleb, still dressed in his clothes from last night. This looked bad. I'd badmouthed him to Addison, then we'd had a mini blowup on the dance floor in front of Josh. Nope, I didn't like this at all. Unless I could defuse this situation, everybody in town would think we were going at it like rabbits.

Caleb tipped up his chin, a small smirk dancing teasing the corners of his mouth. "Good morning, Addison, Josh."

"Hey man," Josh responded with a similar chin lift.

Addison stood frozen in place, looking more than a little shell-shocked with her mouth hanging open and her eyes owlish.

Dammit, I could already tell she wasn't going to let this slide. She was like a dog with a bone when she wanted something.

"Emma, I'll stop by later. I need to head out. I have some work to catch up on." Without another word of explanation, Caleb slipped out the front door, leaving me with the task of cleaning up a whole lot of presumptions. Ugh, that man drove me crazy.

"So, you and Caleb, huh?" Addison said the minute the door shut behind Caleb. "Now, I see why you were in such a hurry to leave last night. I can't wait to tell—"

"Stop." I held up my hand. "You've got it all wrong. Nothing happened with Caleb."

Addison lifted her eyebrows and an incredulous laugh exploded from her mouth. "Oh, come on. You're full of crud. You don't have to lie to me. You're a widow, not a nun, and you're entitled to some fun after the last few years you've had. Even if Caleb's a giant asshole with a dangerously inflated ego, I'm not goin' to fault you for living life."

Josh backed up a few steps, his eyes wide. "Where's the kitchen? I'm thirsty and you two obviously have things to discuss that don't involve me."

I rolled my eyes and pointed to the back of the house. "The kitchen is back there to your left, and nothing happened, so you don't need to hide out like I'm going to spill a bunch of dirty secrets."

Josh shrugged. "Whatever you say, Miss Emma. I reckon it's not my business either way."

"Ugh." I stomped my foot like a four-year-old. "Honestly, Addie, nothing happened. He gave me a ride because we were going to the same place."

"That doesn't explain why he's here this morning, and if my slightly drunken memory serves me right, I think he's still wearing the same shirt, but what do I know?"

"You know nothing."

"Only because you won't share."

I blew out an exaggerated breath. It'd been a long time since I'd had to explain my actions to anybody. Andrew wasn't much of a companion for the last year and Nora deferred to me because I was the wife and she was too distraught to make decisions anyway.

"I drank too much. He gave me a ride so I didn't have to sit around in the parking lot until I sobered up or figured out how to get a taxi. I passed out at some point on the way home and he stuck around to make sure I was okay."

While the minor lie felt dirty coming out of my mouth, I didn't want to get into the whole flashback thing with her. It was bad enough I let that cat out of the bag with Caleb. I couldn't stomach telling the story again. I'd played the role of crazy girl enough today.

"Oh, well, that was nice of him. I guess I haven't really given him enough credit. Maybe he isn't as self-centered as he seems."

"Yeah." I stuffed my hands into my pockets. "I think I owe him an apology for trying to kick him out of his place. He even offered to help me strip the wallpaper from the dining room."

"Huh." She shook her head. "I'm at a loss for words."

"No way. Let me get a piece of paper to write this down. This has to be memorialized. I can't imagine this happens more than once or twice a decade."

"Hush your mouth, sassy pants." She shoved me good-naturedly. "Don't get used to it, because now that I've had a moment to reflect on this whole Caleb situation—"

"There is no Caleb situation," I interrupted. I couldn't get into it with her today when I felt vulnerable from both his kindness and the uncertainty of what was going on with me.

"Come on, Emma. You can't really expect me to believe it was totally innocent."

I rolled my eyes, becoming impatient with her. "I don't really care. You can believe whatever you want. It's the truth, though. Caleb helped me last night and we called a truce. He can stay where he is for the time being, doing whatever he does. In the meantime, I'm gonna fix up this place." I shrugged.

"Maybe I'll turn it into an inn or a bed and breakfast. God knows, I need to find something to do with my time besides stare at the walls."

The minute I said it, I knew I was going to do it. Sure, I'd toyed with the idea before, but I'd always thought of it as something I might do someday in the future. I didn't have any concrete plans. That had to change. I needed something to fill my days so I didn't lose my mind. I'd spent more than enough time stewing over the hand fate had dealt me. I needed to be proactive and do something real to give me direction. I had enough money from Andrew's mom to make something out of the place. It'd be tight and I'd have to put together a budget, but it could work. The only unknown was whether tourists would want to stay here with enough frequency to keep me afloat.

"Really?" She smiled. "I mean, you mentioned it but I didn't think you'd actually do it."

"Why are you so happy?"

"This means you'll be staying around indefinitely. So many of my friends have left for Atlanta and Savannah since graduating, and I was starting to feel like I was going to be the only person under thirty left in this town."

"You're doing a really good job of selling this place," I replied sarcastically.

"No point in lyin'. You'd only become disillusioned down the road."

"Hey." Josh wondered back into the room, a glass of water in hand. "Did you two get everything sorted out?"

We glanced and each other and burst into

laughter. "Yes," we responded at the same time.

"Well, I need to get goin'. My shift starts in an hour and I haven't eaten lunch. Addie, are you coming with me or are you goin' to stick around here?"

"No. We're both going with you. I need to get my car. That is, if you don't mind," I said, suddenly feeling unsure. I hadn't exactly put my best foot forward last night. To put it politely, I was three sheets to the wind within an hour of showing up. Then I got in a fight with Caleb on the dance floor, disappeared, and when he came to check on me the next day, he found Caleb in my house. I probably seemed like a train wreck. "I mean, if it's okay with you."

He smiled, his blue eyes warming considerably. "Don't be ridiculous. Of course, it's fine. I'm heading there anyway, and I'll be the envy of all the men in town when I show up with you two in tow at the diner."

"Ugh." Addison shoved him playfully. "You're so predictable. Let's go before all the tables fill up. It's Saturday and my dad won't make any exceptions for me. Most likely, he'll put me to work even though this is my only Saturday off this month."

Chapter Eighteen

I ran my hand along the beige textured wallpaper. A silver thread that I hadn't noticed before was woven into it. It probably glimmered in the candlelight. Objectively, it didn't look terrible with the white wood paneling. It kept the room light, and that was a good thing given that it sat on the north side of the house with heavy trees shading the long narrow windows. And yet, something about this room unsettled me. The heaviness or seriousness of the room pressed against my chest, making it hard to breathe.

The longer I lived here the more I avoided this room. I couldn't pinpoint my unease. I just knew I needed to change it, make it radically different. It didn't make sense to start my renovations here when so many things needed to happen if I wanted to welcome guests into my home. Researching the zoning was the most logical starting point. Everything would be moot if local zoning ordinances prohibited me from converting my home into a business of sorts. I shrugged away my thoughts and concentrated on the task in front of me. This room didn't feel right regardless of what happened in the future.

Taking a seat at the dining room table, I curled my bare feet into the thick rug, opened my laptop, and scrolled through a paint website looking for direction. Brian would be here later this afternoon, and with any luck, I could rope him into going with me to the hardware store. That way we wouldn't be stuck in this house all night again, staring at each other.

Feeling cold and jittery, I rolled my cup of tea between my hands. Something about sitting here made me want to run, or maybe this room wasn't the problem. The whole house was freaking me out lately.

I selected a random playlist from my phone and turned it up, wanting to drown out the strange feelings. The steady bass of the song echoed in my ears, increasing in volume until it felt as if it were coming from inside of my head instead of my phone. A spark of pain shot between my temples and spread like lightning through my body.

I suppose I could've turned off the music or left, but I felt paralyzed. Clutching the wooden armrests of the chair, I sat there in the fading light of the room, staring at my computer screen, desperately praying I'd stay rooted in the moment for as long as possible. Bit by bit, the present faded away like sand through my open fingers. A bright light flashed, my vision receded to a pinprick, and I was gone.

I hovered near the entrance to the dining room. The gas mantles shimmered on the fine silver and flocked wallpaper.

"Sit down, Elizabeth. Can we talk for a few minutes?" Henry asked.

I'd been dodging him all night, knowing this was coming, all the while hoping I could avoid it. The meal had dragged to its finish. I kept my eyes lowered, not inviting or engaging in conversation. After Pa excused himself along with Henry's dad, Thomas, I'd fled to the relative safety of the kitchen.

Mama hated it when I chatted with Axie and the other house servants. I didn't let that stop me, though. I treasured the time I spent watching them murmuring and laughing occasionally as they finished their work. It didn't take long for Mama to find me. Apparently, Henry requested a private audience before he left. My stomach flipped at the thought of him leaving. I loved him more than my next breath, but lately I'd been nervous about marrying him and all of the responsibilities of taking care of his household. I had accepted my parents' edict to put off the wedding as a gift of more time to understand and prepare for my future responsibilities. For the hundredth time, I wished I could take Axie with me when the time came. She'd make the transition so much easier, and I'd miss her.

"Sure." I picked up my crinoline-stiffened skirt and inched toward the table, settling into the seat next to Henry. I glanced toward the butler's pantry to make sure no one was lurking in the shadows. I didn't want anyone to overhear us, particularly his

113

brother, Brett. I couldn't believe they shared the same parents. Brett was Henry's foil in looks and character. Henry had nearly black hair like his father, thick and silky, with just a hint of curl and equally dark eyes. Brett, on the other hand, had dull brown hair and equally dull eyes or maybe it was just my hatred for him talking. Most women thought him attractive, though not nearly as handsome as Henry. And where Henry was admired for his honor, Brett was a bad-egg fellow who had demonstrated time and time again he wasn't a man of his word.

"You were quiet tonight," he commented, leaning over to light his cigar. The sickening sweet smell filled the room, burning my eyes. I never understood why Mama allowed the men to smoke in the dining room after dinner.

"I'm just worried and a little scared for my family and you."

He grinned. "I can take care of myself."

"I know." I sighed. "Would you like a glass of claret?"

"No." His kind, warm chocolate eyes searched my face looking for something. I glanced away, unable to hold his stare. "I want you to reconsider your decision," he finally said.

My insides trembled and fluttered. He'd always been a perfect gentleman and so decent where I was concerned, and that just made me feel even worse that I couldn't give him what he wanted. Mama didn't want to rush to put something together when we were short on time. She wanted to turn our marriage into a spectacle and for some reason Pa was letting her have her way on this; undoubtedly because he wanted to avoid another argument from her.

"I love you, Henry. You know I do. My decision has nothing to do with that."

He frowned. "And yet you won't marry me."

"Don't be purposely obtuse. I already agreed to marry you."

He puffed on his cigar and spoke with it clenched between his teeth. "Not until I return."

"We didn't plan to get married for another six months, and everyone says the war won't last ninety days. I think we should stay the course and keep the original date."

"We live in an imperfect world, Elizabeth, and I don't like leaving you here unprotected. You might also consider this: it's conceivable that something could happen to your father, or God forbid, me. It'd be better if you took my name now so you'd have access to my resources regardless of what happens. You wouldn't be left at the mercy of your mother's whims or dictates. You would have the means and freedom to decide your future. And regardless of the outcome of this war, mark my words, things will never be the same."

Fear closed in on me, making it hard to breathe, but I shook it away. I couldn't think about that. Inevitably, I'd marry Henry, I just couldn't bring myself to defy my parents on something so big.

Initially, we set a wedding date for next spring when the weather wouldn't be so stifling. I knew exactly what my life would look like after we married. I'd move into the house he'd built on the property his father gave him when he turned eighteen. If we were lucky, I'd be pregnant soon after, and I'd live the same life my mama had. Not that she'd suffered. Pa doted on her. She had everything she could ever want.

The thought of finally having Henry only to give him up a few weeks later was too much to swallow. I'd be all alone in a new house with no one for company, and since my brother was already gone and Pa was leaving too, Mama would be lonely. I couldn't do that to her. In actuality, that was probably the primary reason she refused to move up the wedding.

I reached across the table, and tapped his forearm. "Henry, everything is going to be fine. Don't fret over me. Ninety days isn't so long. Let's keep the date we planned. This war will be a distant memory, and nothing will be hanging over our heads. It'll be perfect."

"Is this your parents' decision or yours?"

"Theirs." I paused. "But it will be okay."

Henry sighed, knowing I couldn't give in when my parents were so adamant on this point. They wanted to give me a wedding that everyone would be talking about years from now, and rushing to put something together within the week wouldn't work.

"I reckon you're right, Elizabeth." He squeezed my glove-covered hand and brought it to his lips. "I guess I want to seal the deal as soon as possible. I feel like I've waited a lifetime for you already. I hate leaving, knowing everything is still unsettled between us."

"That's balderdash. It's not unsettled. I'm

marrying you, Henry, and nothing can change that. Not this war. Not the Yanks. Not anything. We will be together."

He stubbed out his cigar. "I want to believe you're right."

I smirked, feeling lighter. "You should, Henry Cadwell, because we were meant to be...so says our mamas, and who would spite those two? Dash it all. Could you imagine if we slighted their chance to reign over the perfect wedding?"

He mock shivered and came to his feet. "Walk me out, Lizzy."

I glanced over my shoulder. Since we'd gotten engaged under our favorite tree, Henry had become a little more forward with his advances, always stealing a kiss whenever possible. I suspected my parents wouldn't mind, but I didn't want to be caught acting inappropriately. I'd never live it down if anyone found out. They'd think I was acting all-possessed.

We made our way out of the house, not stopping to say goodnight to his parents or mine. When we reached the veranda, Henry threaded his fingers through mine and led me down the stairs to the side of the house where we'd be hidden in the shadows of the giant live oaks, in particular, our tree.

A sultry breeze swirled around us and the steel gray beards of Spanish moss danced on the trees. Henry circled his arms around my waist, pulling my body against him. His mouth pressed to mine, our lips opening just enough to taste each other; the kiss was long, full of passion, and a little bit of farewell. He lifted his hand up and threaded it

117

through my hair. When he pulled away, he rested his chin on top of my head, and whispered, "I'm going to miss you, Elizabeth."

I shivered. "Ninety days will be over before you know it, and you'll come back to me with hundreds of stories of your brave adventures. I think you were gone longer than that for your last trip to London."

He shook his head. When he lifted it, his eyes were suspiciously bright and he kissed the tip of my nose like he had a hundred times before. "We can only pray the war will be short-lived, but I suspect it won't be that simple. Heck, if I didn't care about hurting our families, I'd take you and get as far away from here as possible. There isn't any honor in killing our fellow countrymen to keep people enslaved."

I looked away, swallowing back my sorrow. Henry had confessed he longed to accompany a friend who'd joined the union army. "It's not too late. We could—"

He pressed a finger to my mouth. "Sometimes in life we go along with the tide because it's too hard to swim against it or because we can't figure out a way swim against it. I suspect history will judge us poorly, but this is bigger than me. Than us. We are pawns in a game that was set in motion long ago. Now we are at fate's mercy. Maybe spilling blood is the only way to cleanse our sins. I don't know the answer, Lizzy. Let's just pray those more powerful than us see the light."

When I nodded, he dropped his hand and lowered his lips to mine again. A blast of sensations ran through me, and when he angled his head as if he wanted to taste even more of me, I parted my lips wider. It was all so slow and lingering, it seemed like days had passed before he released me. My breath was ragged and my heart pounded wildly in my chest. My mouth tingled.

As I studied the bone structure of his face and each honeyed fleck in his irises, committing every detail to memory, I wondered if Henry was right about the war not being as straightforward as everyone claimed. The hatred and resentment between the North and South had passed the point of no return. The letters from my dearest cousin, Anna, who moved to New Hampshire with her husband five years ago, had become more and more alarming. In her last letter, she described being harassed by some men in town because her speech marked her as a Southerner. That men felt they could attack a woman for the slight of being from another state said a lot about the animosity brewing in the country.

I clutched the wide lapels of his long frock coat, resting my ear against the buttons of his double-breasted vest, listening to the steady drum of his heart. He held me close, his arms crushed around my waist, and I found solace in his steadfast presence. I loved him too much to ever be parted from him. God wouldn't take him away when I'd never really had him.

"Promise me you'll be safe. Promise me you'll come back to me no matter what," I whispered urgently, but what I really wanted to ask was if he'd reconsider and run away with me somewhere far away where this war couldn't touch us. Where we

119

could live happily ever after. Family obligations and politics be damned. I only wanted him. Forever. Without him, nothing mattered.

The pounding of his heart increased in volume until it felt like it had wormed its way deep inside of my bones. A bolt of lightning split the sky, trailed by a deep rumbling that shook the ground, and then there was only silence.

When I looked around, I found myself standing alone on the side of the house beneath the trees, barefoot in the yoga pants and the sweatshirt I had pulled on earlier that morning. I was Emma again. The wind howled, whipping my hair around my face and I lifted my gaze to the sky. I needed to get inside before I got caught in the rain.

Chapter Nineteen

I glanced back at the house. Too deep in the flashback or whatever these episodes were, I hadn't bothered to shut the front door. The thought of going back in that house right now unsettled me. The feelings of sitting in the dining room with Henry clung to me like a shroud. Love mixed with a deep reluctance to disobey her parents was the only way I could describe it. On top of that, I suspected Elizabeth never saw Henry again.

A jarring pain ripped through my center. "Oh my God," I mumbled, collapsing to the ground.

It all made sense now. Elizabeth allowed Henry, the man I somehow inadvertently spent an hour or so with, to walk out of her life and he'd died. Instead of being relieved that I was putting the puzzle pieces of Elizabeth's life together, I felt empty and strangely guilty, as though I had deprived Henry of something. He clearly loved Elizabeth, and I felt her love for him, but if that was the point of the story, what role did Charles play?

Tears slid down my cheeks, and I hadn't even

realized until that moment I was crying. This was insane. The thought of slipping into Elizabeth's world again scared me. The future awaiting her scared me. It was silly for me to sit here crying for people who had long since departed this world. Their story was written over a century ago. Mine, on the other hand, wasn't. I needed to focus on moving forward with a definite plan and maybe Elizabeth's life would stop haunting me. Maybe this was happening because I felt so aimless and lost and somehow my energy was tapping into hers.

Instead of going back to the house, I ventured toward the barn. I didn't want to be alone. I needed someone or something to take my mind off Elizabeth and Henry. Caleb hadn't shared his schedule with me, so there was a strong possibility that he wouldn't be around. Addison hinted that he left town often. Either way, the exercise would do me good.

I ran along the path, ignoring the pebbles digging into the bottoms of my feet. When I reached the door to the barn, I paused to knock instead of letting myself in unannounced.

The door opened almost immediately. "Emma, what are you doing here?" Before I could answer, he frowned, his eyes scanning my face, then moving on to my body. "What's wrong? Did something happen? Are you hurt?"

I lifted my hands to my tear-stained face, horrified that I hadn't bothered to remove the evidence of my breakdown before I stormed over here.

"I don't know." Then I covered my face, not

wanting to see his reaction. "No, that's not true. It happened again."

He grabbed my fingers, tugging them away from my face, and steered me inside to his kitchen. "It's nothing to cry about." His deep, strong voice calmed me in a way I couldn't explain except that in his presence I felt safe, protected, and most importantly, not judged. "You're just a little shocked, that's all. You'll feel better in a couple of minutes."

He kept talking as he pulled out a chair for me and warmed a mug of water in the microwave. I didn't listen to his words, but the assured tone of his voice and his efficient movements around the kitchen were enough to pull me out of the overwhelming despair and guilt that was suffocating me.

He dropped a teabag into the mug and plopped it down on the table in front of me. "Tell me what happened."

Attempting to pull myself together, I wiped my cheeks with the sleeve of my shirt. "I'm afraid she sent him away thinking she didn't love him," I mumbled, staring unseeing at the paintings lining above his bed on the opposite side of the barn. "And he left for the war and he never came home. Or at least that's the way it seemed. Maybe I'm wrong, though. I'm getting confused because of the other man I've seen."

"Who are we talking about?"

"Elizabeth, the woman in my flashbacks, and Henry. She was engaged to him, and I remembered from one of the other times this happened that

Elizabeth's mama was discussing Henry's death. I finally put together some of the pieces, and I feel so empty. Remorseful too. I feel like I did something wrong, or rather I did something wrong as Elizabeth." I fiddled with the teabag, avoiding his gaze for a moment. "Is that weird?"

I had no clue why I was asking him this. Clearly, my feelings were bizarre to put it mildly. The fact that Elizabeth's life was partially eclipsing mine to some degree disturbed me and from the look on Caleb's face, it bothered him too.

"Were you alone in the house when it happened this time?"

"Yes, but when I came out of it, I was standing barefoot in the grass on the side of the house."

"I don't like this. It's not safe for you to be wandering around in a trance."

"Well, it's not like I can control it." Frustration bubbled inside of my chest, and the tears started flowing again. I never asked for this. Who the hell would want to slip in and out of consciousness and wake up somewhere new? Not me. That's for damn sure. "It just happens. There is nothing I can do about it. I tried this time, I did."

"What do you mean, you tried to stop it?"

I rested my head on the table. "There's a pattern. I can feel it coming. This time, I tried to hold onto reality as long as possible and it didn't work."

I jumped up from my chair, suddenly wondering why I went running to Caleb. He wasn't my friend. Yeah, I shared a couple things with him about this. That didn't mean he'd help or even that he wanted to hear about it. The chair tumbled backward, and I nearly stumbled in my rush to get the fuck out of there before I made a bigger ass of myself.

Sadly, I couldn't make my feet move closer to the door because I didn't want to step foot in my house right now either. God, the thought of rambling around in that big old place made my stomach churn.

"I've gotta go," I squeaked out, after staring at the door like a lunatic for a few minutes. "Sorry I bothered you. I'm sure you have better things to do than indulge someone losing their grip on reality."

Somehow my life had come down to me confiding in a virtual stranger, though he didn't feel like a stranger. There was a depth and understanding in him that made me feel like he was an old soul, or an old friend. He was honorable and unbendable. I was sure these characteristics were what had caused Addison to label him aloof.

"Hey, hey." Caleb wrapped me up in a hug I didn't even know I needed until that second. It'd been so long since anyone cared enough to comfort me. Following his diagnosis, Andrew retreated into his head and I became an afterthought. Affection was a one-way street in the last years of our marriage, not that I could blame him. "It's okay. There's no need to get all emotional."

I scoffed, rubbing my face against the soft cotton weave of his shirt, soaking up the warmth and strength of his body beneath the fabric. "Of course you'd say that. You're not the one slowly sliding into madness, one hallucination at a time."

"There's nothing wrong with a hallucination here or there. You're in good company." He was smiling. I could hear it in his voice, and rather than feeling upset, I felt the muscles in my shoulders release bit by bit.

"Oh, yeah, like who?"

"Catherine of Siena, Saint Francis of Assisi, and Joan of Arc…to name a few."

"Saints? You're giving me a list of saints as a frame of reference."

"I went to Catholic school as a kid. It was the first thing that came to mind."

I lifted my head, and was frozen by the look on his face. I studied him, my gaze fastened on his striking mouth, scarcely absorbing his words. "I don't know what I'm doing."

I wasn't sure what the comment meant.

"I think you're handling everything well, considering," he said softly.

I gave him a half smile. "Oh, yeah?"

"Yeah, I really do."

I looked around his place and realized that except for the landscapes hanging near his bed, his paintings were gone. "What happened to your artwork?"

He pointed his finger toward the stairs. "I moved them to the loft."

"Oh, okay."

He stared at me carefully without offering an explanation. After a few beats, he nodded and slipped one hand beneath my hair, around my nape, and a prickle of uneasiness went through my body. I felt so tiny in comparison to him, so dominated, so…desirable. His palms were heated and rough, awakening my entire body until I was buzzing with illicit anticipation.

Slowly, like he was testing the waters, he lowered his mouth to mine, and then he paused for a millisecond. While I was still trying to sort out what the fuck was happening, his lips brushed over mine again.

Holy shit. Caleb was kissing me.

Kissing me.

And I didn't want to step back or push him away or tell him no.

His lips were firm and fiery, prompting me to think of all sorts of things a newly widowed woman shouldn't want. I missed this. The closeness. The intimacy. But mostly the promise. There was so much damn promise in his kiss that my mind whirled, trying to understand what it meant.

Startled by the direction of my thoughts I lurched back, and his hands dropped to my waist and tightened as if he didn't want to let me go. My heart froze with a ludicrous combination of hope and dismay.

"No," I sobbed, petrified I had made everything in my life infinitely more complicated. This wasn't right. It shouldn't be so simple to move on after Andrew. And yet, falling into Caleb's arms seemed almost natural, a foregone conclusion.

"Shh," he coaxed, rubbing his hands up and down my arms. My arms tingled where he touched me. Standing this close to him, I could smell his pine scent mixed with the fresh paint on his skin. "It's all right, Emma. It's just a kiss. You don't have to deprive yourself to prove you loved him. You can have a life. No one would fault you for doing this."

My lips parted as I sucked in a shocked breath. A thousand damning retorts sat on the tip of my tongue, and yet I couldn't bring myself to say a single one. He was right. It was one kiss…could it really be wrong? To steal something from myself when life had already robbed me of everything I held dear. This wasn't about replacing Andrew. It was about living, and after everything I'd gone through, I damn well deserved to live.

Most importantly, though, I didn't have anything to prove. I had nursed my husband for two years. I never once strayed or even considered straying. It wasn't bad to want to feel something again. I didn't need to make this a big deal. It was just me adjusting to my new reality. The reasons I had resisted my attraction to him flapped away on noiseless wings, leaving me without an objection.

I hedged closer, seeking the low hanging fruit he dangled in front of me. I nodded my consent, and his eyes widened, the black pupils dilating until only a thin rim of amber remained. When he lowered his head once again, I wasn't fully convinced of my logic, but I knew I wouldn't stop him. I lifted my hands and splayed them on his chest, and a shiver cascaded through him.

His lips were soft and velvety as they met mine. I made a feeble sound of trepidation, and he quickly smothered it with his mouth. He angled his head and amplified the pressure of the kiss, forcing me to open. Blood thundered inside my eardrums. The instant his tongue swept along mine, he groaned, his entire body tensing like a stretched spring.

My neck arched under the pressure, and my thoughts scattered. His taste was flavored with coffee mixed with a hint of sweetness. My tongue coiled around his, holding him within my mouth for a second. He walked me backward, forcing me against the kitchen table. Wind rattled the windows, but the barn felt hot and charged with the energy crackling between us.

Caleb's hands circled my thighs and he lifted me onto the counter. Sparks fired along my skin unlike anything I'd ever experienced before. The more I kissed him, the more I felt as if I were drowning, but at least I wasn't alone. He was right there with me, and I clung to him like he was my lifeline, and for more reasons than I could describe, he was exactly that.

He wedged his body between my legs, and I mewed softly. Distantly, I realized this was going too fast, but I was too caught up in the sensation to stop him. He nibbled at my neck, wrapping my hair around his hand. His other hand explored my body—my chest, waist, thighs—acquainting himself with every curve, swell, and dip.

"What the hell is going on here?"

Chapter Twenty

The roar battered my senses. I shoved Caleb and slid off the counter, severing all contact with him. My face drained of blood when I pivoted toward the door and saw Brian.

His facial features were contorted into a sneer as he stood just inside the door, glaring at Caleb. He glanced at me quickly, clenching his hands into white-knuckled fists. As Caleb closed the distance between him and Brian, mortification clawed at my stomach.

Caleb's jaw flexed once, twice, before he visibly forced his muscles to slacken. "Calm down," he said in an even tone.

Brian pointed at me. "Let's go."

"She doesn't answer to you," Caleb snapped.

"She's vulnerable. She isn't making good decisions right now, and you're taking advantage of her." He tugged at his hair. "I knew I shouldn't have left her alone with you."

"Get out of my house before I do something we'll both regret," Caleb growled, his voice so low and icy that chills danced down the length of my spine. Flags of red stained his cheeks, but his gaze was steady.

Brian shoved him. "Fuck you. This is Emma's house. You're just some jackass she's too nice to kick out. And you're trying to turn her into a fuck buddy because you know she's too vulnerable to tell you no."

Caleb lunged for him, and I snagged the back of his shirt, trying to hold him back. I didn't need a keeper and I certainly didn't need someone telling me what I wanted or needed. I'd been taking care of myself for as long as I could remember. I wasn't fragile. I wasn't a wilting flower. Crappy neglectful mom, MIA dad, growing up in poverty, terminally ill husband. I had experienced it all, and I was still standing.

"That's enough," I yelled. "Brian, you may be my guest, but you have no right to barge into Caleb's home. Let's go."

I stormed out the door, not bothering to see if Brian followed me. I needed some distance from Caleb, from his golden eyes, from the way my body lit up around him.

Now dark outside, I couldn't see the ground beneath my bare feet and the pebbled dirt path stabbed at my flesh. I didn't care about that, though. My mind was hung up on the shit show I'd just witnessed. I couldn't believe the trash that just came out of Brian's mouth. Well, maybe I could. He'd been hinting at being attracted to me, and to the best of my knowledge I hadn't intentionally encouraged him. But who knew what went through his head.

Maybe he thought my consent to stop by on his way back to Atlanta was all the reassurance he needed or maybe he was simply looking after me like he promised Andrew. Either way, he needed to back off.

When I reached the foyer of my house, I continued up the stairs, not ready for a confrontation with Brian. I needed a few minutes to myself so I didn't rip his head off. I heard the front door click shut behind me.

"Where the hell do you think you're going?" Brian shouted.

"To bed," I answered without turning around.

"Are you mad at me?"

"What do you think?"

"Jesus, Emma, I was protecting you."

I whirled around when I reached the second story landing. "I don't need to be coddled or protected."

His jaw ticked. "You're confused and grieving. You don't know what you need."

"Don't demean me. I'm free to live my life how I see fit, and if that includes kissing Caleb, so be it. I don't need your permission, and I sure as fuck don't need to explain my actions to you."

He grabbed my upper arm. "When I pulled up, your front door was wide open and you were nowhere to be found. You know what that tells me?"

"I don't remember asking your opinion, and I don't really care." And truthfully, I didn't want to talk about it. It was like opening Pandora's box. If I explained the whole flashback thing, he'd undoubtedly lose his shit and be on the phone with

Nora within minutes. She'd show up within twenty-four hours with a team of psychologists in tow. Hell, they'd probably put me on an involuntary seventy-two hour psych hold.

His hand tightened, digging into my pale skin. "You're walking around with your head in the clouds, not giving any thought to your safety. Then I find you throwing yourself at that scumbag artist. I know Andrew found you in some dirty town in West Virginia, but I'd thought six years of being around him had gotten rid of that part of you."

My vision misted red. I ripped my wrist out of his hold and slapped him across his face. "How dare you?"

He rubbed his cheek, his eyes narrowed. "I dare because I care about you and that's more than I can say for Caleb. I know his type. He's a user, and you're his next victim."

"I don't believe that for one second."

He chuckled. "Then you're a fool," he whispered derisively, the burn of rage creeping out of the collar of his white and blue pin-striped shirt and climbing fast.

I absorbed the pain of his words, and buried it in my innermost self where the damage wouldn't hurt. I schooled my expression into a mask, smooth and vacant as a doll's. "I think you should leave." I paused a beat, and added, "Please, Brian. I can't deal with this right now. We'll talk in a couple of weeks when we've both had time to calm down."

"No." His focus zeroed in on me like a sharpshooter finding its target. He inched so close to me I could see the gold striations in his blue eyes.

When I backed up, my heel teetered on the top step, and I snagged onto the railing to prevent a fall.

Abruptly, my body started trembling from the top of my head to the tips of my toes as if the floor were shaking. I couldn't tell which. A dull roar filled my ears. *No. It was happening again.*

Struck with the realization that I might be able to run away from this flashback, I lurched forward. Darkness encircled my vision, preventing my escape. Instead, I collapsed against a closed door, trying to hold onto the present. "No," I mumbled. "Not now. Please don't let this happen."

I could hear Brian calling out to me, but he sounded garbled, as if he were talking underwater. The flames of fear licked at me and I knew without a doubt that if I succumbed to this memory and slipped into the past, my life would never be the same. I clawed at the door behind me, desperate to stay in the present.

The walls appeared wavy and somewhat transparent, sparkling and swaying. Brian raised his arm, but I couldn't determine his purpose because his face rippled, his facial features morphing into someone altogether different. Someone unknown, yet familiar too.

"First Corinthians 15:33, 'Be not deceived: evil communications corrupt good manners,'" the man going in and out of focus warned.

"Stop this. I'm not ready," I chanted, my lips moving except no sound surfaced, or at least nothing I could hear. My hands balled, curling into my sides as I fought against the invisible hand pulling me into the past. I squeezed my eyelids shut, refusing to see anything, whether as Emma or Elizabeth.

Next to me, I heard Brian call my name again, more forcefully, the translucent quality of his voice long gone. My eyes fluttered open, baffled for a moment, then suddenly alert, realizing I was still in the present. I was Emma. Thank God. I released a long, drawn out breath.

When I lifted my head, Brian loomed over me, his brow furrowed, and his face pale. "Are you okay? I'm sorry if I lost my temper. I didn't mean to scare you. I wasn't going to hit you."

For a prolonged beat there was silence, broken only by the scrape of a tree branch rubbing against the window. I didn't know what to say to explain my reaction, and I certainly didn't want to continue our conversation when I felt so drained.

When Brian spoke again his voice was soft. "I really am sorry. I'll drive to the motel outside of town."

"No." I shook my head. "It's fine. You can stay. I'm going to bed anyway. I'm feeling out of sorts."

"Okay." He scanned me from head to toe, searching for something. "Is there something else going on with you?"

My heart felt as if it had stopped beating momentarily. While he'd witnessed some sort of out of body experience, the truth was so far-fetched, it was impossible he could guess with any accuracy. Still, I didn't feel comfortable confiding in him.

I started to shake my head and he held up his hand.

"You don't have to divulge anything to me, but

maybe you could call your brother or Nora."

I veiled my thoughts with my lashes, careful not to look directly at him. "I'll think about it, and I appreciate your concern even if I don't like the way you show it sometimes."

He nodded as if satisfied. "Okay, then. I'll see you in the morning before I leave. And, Emma, I am sorry for meddling in your life. I just want what's best for you. Whatever that means."

"I get that. Thanks."

Chapter Twenty-One

My eyes burned as I stared sightlessly at the ceiling, the cloying darkness weighing me down, asphyxiating me. I struggled to drag oxygen into my lungs, counting my breaths so I didn't spiral into a panic attack. I had experienced several of them after Andrew's diagnosis, and I didn't want to go back to that place again.

Between kissing Caleb and whatever happened in the hallway with Brian, my brain was on a continuous loop. I couldn't stop reliving that kiss over and over again. I definitely felt something, and I had no clue what that meant.

Worse, though, I sensed whatever was about to happen in the hallway to Elizabeth would be unsettling. Even though I had ended it before it'd gone too far, I didn't know how to replicate it. The only thing I'd done differently was quickly identifying the signs that a flashback was about to happen. Then I'd concentrated on pushing it away. But the most important thing was that I had some control over it, whatever it was.

After a while, my racing thoughts retreated, and I no longer felt as if I were about to come out of my skin. I closed my eyes, finally feeling like I might be able to fall asleep.

Not too long later, footsteps echoed in the hallway, pulling me out of my light slumber. I scanned my surroundings. The full moon was the only thing illuminating the room. Whoever it was halted just outside my door. My breath became ragged as I laid immobile from momentary shock.

Logically, the odds of a stranger wandering into my home were small given its remote location. More than likely it was Brian, and I definitely wasn't up for a heart to heart with him right now.

The door crept open, and I shot up in my bed, prepared to run or confront whoever was there.

"Emma?" Caleb whispered, and my shoulders dropped. I'd said all I had to say to Brian earlier, so finding Caleb here was a reprieve from the uncomfortable conversation I needed to have with Brian before he left tomorrow.

"Yeah," I responded, leaning my head against the headboard.

"Did I wake you?"

"Not really." I'd barely slept more than a few minutes here or there. "What's going on?"

"I wanted to make sure you were all right. I didn't like how things went down today. Brian was pretty pissed. I shouldn't have let you leave with him."

I chuckled. "That was pretty awkward."

His nostrils flared. "I can't believe he came into my place without knocking. What's he doing here anyway?"

"He stopped by on the way back from Savannah. He's just here for the night."

He didn't speak for a while, and I thought he'd leave any second. "I'm sorry if I pushed you today," he finally said.

"You didn't push me."

I'd been drawn to him since the moment I'd first seen him. If he hadn't instigated the kiss, I wouldn't have pursued anything out of respect of my relationship with Andrew. Or maybe I was afraid of losing the last piece of my life with Andrew. Now, though, it didn't seem so black and white. I could love and miss Andrew without giving up on my future.

"Are you sure?"

I held my torso very straight and immobile. "It was as much my choice as it was yours. Besides, like you said, it was just a kiss." Saying the words created a small ache beneath my breastbone. Truthfully, the kiss felt like more than a kiss. It was like an inferno burning me from the inside out.

He tugged on the pull chain of the pink lamp on my nightstand and I flinched, preferring the secrecy the darkness provided. His impenetrable, golden gaze left me feeling emotionally naked. My lower lip wobbled with insecurity, and I quickly schooled it.

He searched my face, trying to read my thoughts. "You never finished telling me what happened with Elizabeth and…"

"Henry," I finished. "Can we talk about it later? Another episode started when I was arguing with

Brian. It only lasted for a few minutes, but I still feel a little unsettled." I glanced at the clock. "It's already one in the morning and I've barely slept. My mind has been racing and something about being in this house is freaking me out. Certain rooms feel strange. I know that sounds crazy, but..." Overwhelmed with everything, I didn't finish my thought.

"I don't like this. It seems like these visions are coming closer together. I should stay."

"Brian is right down the—"

His brows scrunched together. "I don't give a fuck about Brian. What if you wander out of your room and fall down the stairs or go outside to the road? I don't think it's a good idea for you to be alone so much."

"It's okay. Really. I don't think anything bad will happen to me."

He exhaled. "Just let me stay here so I don't lose my mind. I'll sleep on the chair again."

I knew I should fight him on this, but I was too overwhelmed and scared to push him away. Honestly, I didn't want to be alone either. I sucked in a deep breath and scooted over.

"I can't let you sleep on the chair again. We can share the bed." The invitation hung in the air, swirling around us like static electricity. "Just to sleep," I added, not wanting him to think the invitation included more than a bed to sleep in rather than a chair. I still hadn't fully come to terms with what happened between us earlier.

He swallowed hard. "Are you sure? If you have some spare blankets, I can stretch out on the floor. I don't want to make you uncomfortable."

"I'm okay with it if you are."

He yanked his shirt over his head, and I had to tear my eyes away from his sculpted abs before my gaze dipped any lower. He pulled on the chain of the lamp again and slid in next to me. My heart began sprinting a mile a minute, threatening to explode out of my chest. It didn't last long, though, because after fifteen minutes, his breathing evened out.

"Caleb," I whispered, suddenly feeling like I had a million things I wanted to tell him.

He didn't stir, and I sighed, knowing the opportunity to talk had passed. I studied his face. He looked handsome, yet boyish and innocent with his eyes closed. For the first time, I understood why some people enjoyed watching another person sleep. His slightly parted lips looked too tempting for my own good. His forehead was free of everyday lines and worry, and the sharp angles of his face didn't look so intimidating any more.

I had to resist the urge to run my fingertips along the stubble covering his cheeks. Andrew had shaved every single day without fail, and I wondered what it'd feel like to the touch. I lifted my hand to find out and decided against it. Instead, I curled onto my side, facing away from him. I thought of Elizabeth, Henry, and again wondered what role Charles and Brett played in her life. After a while my eyes became heavy and I drifted to sleep. I dreamed of Elizabeth and Charles, the Union soldier she found in the woods.

Chapter Twenty-Two

I watched Mama leave for a meeting at the church in Henry's parents' buggy. Everybody was up in arms because the Yankees had crossed the Chattahoochee River outside of Atlanta weeks ago and were shelling the city nonstop. I told her I wasn't feeling well. In truth, I couldn't spend another day hearing the complaints and sad reflections of our friends about this war. Every conversation made me feel so desolate and fearful for the safety of all of the soldiers and what little remained of my family.

Besides, I needed to check in on that Yankee. He didn't look so good when I left him in the abandoned cabin. I'd be surprised if he weren't half-dead this morning. I ran down the path leading to the cabin and pushed open the door.

I found him lying on the cot, unmoving. I closed the door securely behind me and pulled a short candle out of my apron, placing it on a nearby barrel.

His eyes were fever-glazed and he was shivering.

I pressed my hand to his neck. Alarm raced through me. "You're burning up. I need to get help."

He snagged my hand, but his grip was weak. "No," he implored in a hoarse voice, as if his throat had been scraped raw.

"You'll die if I don't do anything."

"I have no intention of dying."

"Hm." With a trembling hand, I rolled up the leg of his trouser to take a look at his wound. The makeshift bandage was stained with blood. Guilt flooded me for not making time to stitch it up like I promised yesterday.

"I have to take care of this. I need supplies."

Instead of arguing with me, he sighed and closed his eyes, succumbing to the peace of sleep and fatigue, however fleeting. I ran all the way back to the house.

"Axie," I yelled when I flung open the kitchen door. "I need your help."

A deep frown of concern marred her face. "Now, Miz Elizabeth. Whad you gone and done this time? Tell me right now!"

Her response didn't surprise me. I was always getting into trouble, and Axie had known me my entire life. She was Mama's midwife and she helped Mama tend my brother and me when we were babies. She'd been in my life ever since. In fact, I'd likely spent more time with her than most of my family members.

"I need Mother's salves, a stack of linen towels, and a large pan of hot water. Oh, and grab my book off my dresser."

I didn't know how long I'd be sitting around. I

might as well have something to entertain me.

Axie rested her hands on her broad hips. "No. Not 'til you explain what's gotten into you."

"Hurry, Axie. I found a Yankee, but I think he might die if I don't help him."

"Honey chile, yer mammy will be right mad. Let 'em die, I say. T'wan't right to do this."

I pinched the bridge of my nose, frustrated with her and myself for getting caught up in this. "I can't."

"Why is dis Yankee so impo'tant to ya?"

"I can't explain. Please, just help me. You're good with things like this. I can't do it without you." I could help Charles to some extent, but Axie always had good ideas, even if they sounded crazy. She gave women whiskey and cloves during labor, watermelon seeds to help with the kidneys, and mustard plasters for congestion. She had herbal teas for everything. My mother didn't like it when I drank the stuff, but it was better than nothing, especially with the shortages of doctors due to the War.

"Yer puttin' me in a bad fix askin' fer dis. You sho' you can trust dis Yankee?"

I thought about Charles for a second and even though he had threatened me by the creek, I didn't think he was bad. "I do, and don't you dare say a word to my mother. You know how she is since my father died. I don't want her to worry when nothing bad is gonna happen. Charity and helping is a good thing. A godly thing."

"Yas'm, Miz Elizabeth, I believe yer right." Axie stared at me long and hard for a second, then

nodded. "No disputin' yer gentle heart, chile. I'll help."

Within minutes, we were running back to the cabin, supplies in hand. After setting up everything on the floor next to the cot, I removed the makeshift bandage and dipped a linen towel in the warm water and washed away the dried blood. His leg jerked in pain at my first swipe, temporarily reviving him, but he quickly slipped back into unconsciousness.

Axie leaned over my shoulder. "Maybe yo' better put a poultice on dis here wound."

"Good idea. It's likely infected," I muttered distractedly as I studied Charles' face.

God, please don't let him die. I couldn't explain why I cared so much. Maybe it was because this was my chance to stop some of the death around me. Or maybe somehow I'd tied the fate of this man to Henry's.

For an hour or more, I wiped his fevered head and held his hand. At some point, Axie slipped out the door with nothing more than a murmured goodbye. Occasionally, a groan would slip through Charles' lips and his eyes would flutter open for a few seconds, but for the most part he remained still and unresponsive. Dark circles marred the thin skin beneath his eyes and his cheeks look gaunt.

Knowing I needed to get back soon, I stood and dusted off the drab gray hoop skirt and matching jacket I wore when I was around the house. I made quick work of picking up all the supplies and stuffing them in the now empty pot.

"Elizabeth?" Charles croaked.

I whirled around and hurried to his side. "Yes. Are you in pain?"

Charles shook his head lethargically on the cot. "I think I'd rather be dead, but ask me again on the morrow."

"Seems to me, Yankee, you're mighty lucky. Not every man can say that."

He snorted caustically. "My name isn't Yankee! Just like your name isn't Rebel," he growled.

"I know, it's Charles, and I'm Elizabeth."

He rubbed his temples. "I guess I shouldn't be lying here feeling sorry for myself when more than half of my friends are resting in a graveyard or that awful prison, Andersonville."

His voice sounded so despondent my heart softened a little bit more. The indescribable urge to show him kindness swelled inside of me. Maybe he could be my friend, and one day when this whole damnable war ended, we could exchange letters. My family would be friends with his. We'd be a shining example of how to mend the divide between the North and South.

"Are you leaving?" His voice intruded on my consciousness, wresting my thoughts from the unorthodox path they had taken.

"Not if you want some company. I brought a book with me. Would you like me to read to you for a little while?"

"What book did you bring?"

I flipped the cover of the book toward him. "Paradise Lost."

He closed his eyes. "Hm. All right."

I removed everything from the top of the upside-

down barrel, scooted it close to the cot, and perched on top of it. The more I read, the heavier my eyes became.

"Miz Elizabeth, git up. Git up. Yer mammy's hollering down the big house lookin' fer ya."

Chapter Twenty-Three

My head snapped up. My body buzzed with electricity, every nerve ending on edge and tingling. In a blind panic, I searched out every corner of my room. My eyes told me I was Emma again, but I still felt tethered to Elizabeth's world. I inhaled shallowly as I turned my head to the side, looking for any evidence of Charles or the woman called Axie. I came face to face with a very awake Caleb.

"Hey," I said, my voice a little shaky. "You sleep all right?"

"I don't think I moved an inch all night. What about you?"

"Same," I answered, not wanting to get into my dream.

He stretched his arms. "I need to go to Savannah today. Do you want to tag along? We won't be back until late, but it might be a good change of pace for you to get away from here for a few hours."

"Do you have work?"

"I have to deliver a couple of commissioned pieces to an art gallery, but that will only take a few minutes. Afterwards, we can eat lunch and walk around town."

I hesitated, not sure whether I was comfortable with this. We had kissed, but this sounded suspiciously like a date. As soon as the thought came, I tamped it down. There were no rules for being widowed at twenty-six, and I could use some time away from here to get my mind off the strangeness of the past few days. Besides, I hadn't been to Savannah for years.

"That sounds nice. When do you want to leave?"

He rolled off the bed and snagged his shirt from the floor, exposing all of the enticing dips and ridges of his bare chest and back. Long buried emotions swelled in me, unfolding and unfurling. I shook my head hard, and forced myself to look away before I said or did something stupid.

"Maybe an hour or so. Is that enough time to shake Brian?"

When I glanced up, he grinned at me, looking so self-satisfied I smiled in response. The air was thick with something other than the heady promise of a day away from this place. It both delighted and horrified me. Whether I wanted it or not, there was definitely something between us, and I wasn't going to fight it any longer.

Caleb may not be my forever, but he could be my right now and I was fine with that. If life had taught me anything, it was that I couldn't predict what direction it would go. I just had to learn to enjoy the ride.

"I think so." Standing up, I grabbed a sweatshirt draped over my chair and pulled it over my head.

He placed an arm on my lower back and led to me to the door. I paused, thinking about the ramifications of strolling downstairs with Caleb in tow. While I truly didn't care what Brian thought, I also wasn't in the mood for another confrontation.

I paused, my hand on the doorknob. "Would you mind waiting here for a few minutes until I can distract Brain?"

His jaw ticked, his eyes dark and narrowed. "I don't know where things are going with us, but I won't let you hide me away like I'm some goddamn dirty secret. If you're worried about what other people think, then we should end whatever this is right now." Then he lowered his voice. "I won't let people dictate what we do again."

"What do you mean, again? And I'm not worried what other people think. I just don't want to deal with Brian right now and have him ruin my day again."

He made a sound of muffled anger and irritation and shoved his hand into his hair. "I hate that asshole."

"I'm beginning to see that."

He wrapped his fingers around my waist and drew me flush against him. His body was refreshingly hard and his breath a warm seduction against my ear.

"I get wanting to be cautious and not rock the boat." I opened my mouth to interrupt him, but he kept going. "We don't have to talk about what's happening between us right now. We'll wait to talk when you're ready, but there's no fucking way I'm tiptoeing around him like we're doing something wrong. We're adults. We don't answer to him."

"I know. I told him as much yesterday." I paused, trying to come up with another way to persuade him to wait here, but he didn't give me the chance. He feathered his lips across mine, and I trembled from the simple yet affectionate gesture. If I had questioned whether yesterday's kiss was a one-time thing, I had my answer.

He opened the door and held his hand out, signaling me to go first. "Come on. We'll face him together," he ordered, and I didn't mind his forcefulness.

I eyed him incredulously, making a half-chuckle and half-groan sound. "I don't think that worked so well yesterday."

Instead of starting a fruitless argument, I headed out my door and down the stairs, wondering how I got myself into this situation. I was tumbling headfirst into a web of intimacy with Caleb, a place where he would want and deserve more than the empty shell of grief I'd been for so long. But as his hand pressed against my lower back again, reassuring me, I found it hard to care about all of the reasons I might be making a mistake.

All of the worry about reigniting Brian's ire proved to be a waste of time. He was long gone by the time we made it downstairs. He left a note apologizing for upsetting me last night, and promised to check in with me in a couple of weeks. While I appreciated his attempt to smooth over our fight, I did notice he hadn't apologized for his behavior only my reaction to it.

I was pretty sure Caleb realized the shortcomings

of the apology too because he mumbled, "Typical," before balling it up and tossing it in the trash.

Chapter Twenty-Four

Caleb and I strolled side by side through an archway of trees. Spanish moss dangled from the limbs above us. The afternoon sun forced its way through the long branches, throwing jagged lines of light onto the pavement. Empty park benches and magenta flowers lined the pathway. Savannah was picture perfect and a big part of me relished escaping from my life for a couple of hours and basking in the vibrant beauty of this place.

Caleb adjusted the two crated paintings he was holding into one hand.

"Are you sure you don't want me to carry one?"

"Nah, I'm good."

A line of quaint shops came into view. Colorful awnings adorned the stacked brick buildings with tall, slim windows. As we crossed the street, I spotted the name of the gallery where we were headed.

I ran ahead, spinning in a circle, my raised fingertips grazing the feathery moss dangling above me. "Holy shit," I breathed out. "I'd forgotten how magical this place is."

Caleb leaned his paintings against a bench and dug his phone out of the front pocket of his black jeans. He held it up. "I hope you don't mind if I take some pictures."

I froze in place. Normally, I would wave away the camera or turn my back. I hated looking at myself in pictures. But something about being here in this place with this man where all my worries were far away made me feel fearless.

"Keep doing what you were doing," he prompted.

"Sure," I said, then immediately burst out laughing as I raised my hands above my head, the breeze teasing my hair.

He glanced at his screen. "These are great. The light is fucking fantastic right now."

My heart danced inside of my ribcage. I couldn't recall the last time I felt so free and so damn alive. Every one of my senses was heightened. The sun bathed the area in a golden light. The air was fresh and full of life and warmth. Standing below the wavering trees, the heat of the sidewalk radiating through the thin soles of my boots, I felt the new beginning I'd been searching for since Andrew had died.

"Are you going to paint me? Like this?" I scooped up one of the pink flowers on the ground and tucked it behind my ear.

"Now, you look perfect," he muttered.

Everything around me blurred, taking on a slightly muddled quality, yet not fading entirely. On the periphery of my consciousness, I knew I wasn't quite in my world or Elizabeth's, but that awareness wasn't enough to pull me out of the moment.

I could see Henry standing in front of me, leaning against a tree, one leg propped in front of the other, twirling a flower in his hand.

"Come here, Elizabeth, let me put this in your hair."

"You and your flowers, Henry," I replied, sauntering toward him while I twirled my parasol.

"I can't help myself. You love them." He held out his hand. "Take a stroll with me."

"As you wish, Mr. Cadwell."

He led us through the formal garden to the creek behind my house. The sounds of revelry from my parents' party became quieter and quieter until it disappeared entirely. I looked up at the streaks of orange and red in the late afternoon sky.

"Do you think anyone will notice our absence?"

"No, and I don't care if they do. I've barely had a chance to see you lately. I want to know everything that happened over the past couple of weeks."

Henry had taken another one of his trips to Atlanta with his father for business.

"You first. Tell me all about Atlanta."

He paused by a tree and pulled something from the pocket of his coat. "There's not much to tell you, but I brought you back a present."

A huge smile split my face. "You did?"

He opened his hand. Resting on his palm was a hinged gold bracelet with a Bohemian garnet set in the center surrounded by tiny diamonds.

"Oh, Henry, this is too much."

"Put it on," he directed, ignoring my protest.

I fastened it around my wrist and twisted it in a circle. "It's beautiful. I'll never take it off."

As fast as the vision came, it faded back into the present and Henry and Elizabeth were gone. I blinked, staring up at the clouds in confusion, my chest squeezing at the loss of them and their world. I wanted to see more of them together like that.

Caleb wrapped his arms around me and held me close, his hold so caring and protective I didn't even consider resisting it. I rested my head against his chest. Beneath his white button up shirt, I could feel his heart drum in an unhurried, even rhythm, calming me.

"Emma, you're okay. You're here with me. There's nothing to be afraid of."

"I saw them again."

"I figured as much." He exhaled sharply out of his mouth and pulled away from me. He stared at the ground for a second before rolling back his shoulders. "Come on. I told the owner of the gallery I'd be there by now."

We wove our way through the people lingering on the sidewalk.

"This is it," Caleb said, pausing midblock, next to a gallery. The lettering on the black awning was discreet and tasteful, announcing "Gallery 1525." I assumed the name had something to do with the address. Caleb opened the door and a bell chimed, broadcasting our arrival. Inside was a narrow, rectangular room painted stark white with artfully displayed paintings.

"Do you sell all of your work through this place?"

"Some people contact me directly through my website, and I have a handful of repeat customers, but yeah, I have a contract with this gallery. For the most part, Olivia does a good job of moving my work." He hesitated for second, like he had more to say about that. "It's all going to change in a few months when my contract's up. I think I'll test out the waters elsewhere when the time comes."

A woman with shoulder length, glossy black hair, and upturned dark eyes above well-defined cheekbones approached from the rear of the building. I thought she possibly had Polynesian heritage. Whatever it was, she was absolutely beautiful, and I immediately regretted my choice of ripped jeans, a gray cropped sweater, and my favorite boots. I looked cute in a girl next door way. She, on the hand, looked elegant and impossibly sophisticated. Something about her made me dislike her on sight.

Old instincts had me curling my shoulders forward to sink into myself. The second I caught myself doing it, I straightened my spine and lifted my chin. Sure, she was cultured and beautiful, but during my marriage to Andrew, I encountered hundreds of women like her. I wasn't that poor white trash girl from West Virginia anymore. I had an education. I was financially independent. Most importantly, though, I was a fighter. Life had taught me a lot of hard lessons, and one of them was not to sell myself short.

"I think I heard my name. It's good to see you. It's been too long," she said as she air kissed him on both cheeks. She had a faint sing-song quality to her voice that made my southern accent seem crass in comparison.

"Olivia." He stepped away from her and motioned to me. "This is Emma. She made the trip with me to Savannah today."

I held out my hand and Olivia's eyes narrowed for a beat before lifting hers, offering only her cold fingertips like I was somehow contaminated. I doubted her reception was normal. She wouldn't sell many paintings treating her customers that way, but what did I know about art? Not a whole hell of a lot. I glanced at Caleb to see if he noticed, but he kept his attention firmly on Olivia, his gaze cool and unreadable.

"I don't have time to catch up. Emma and I have plans, but I brought the paintings for the Conners and the Devons."

Olivia smiled but it didn't meet her eyes. "Would you mind putting them in the back for me? Oh, and uncrate them and lean them against the wall. I'll put them on display for a few days until they come in to get them. Your work always generates so much interest."

Caleb squeezed my upper arm. "I'll be back in a few minutes."

I frowned and nodded. "Don't worry about me. Take as much time as you need. I'll just look around."

Chapter Twenty-Five

Instead of suffering under Olivia's expectant stare, I wandered to the opposite side of the gallery. Unfortunately, she didn't take the hint that I didn't want to chat. I heard her heels clicking over the hardwood floors.

"Are you in the market for some artwork?"

"Not now. I just moved and I'm still deciding what to do with the place," I answered evasively, before moving to the next picture. Too bad the gallery didn't have more than one large room. There wasn't anywhere for me to hide from her.

"Have you known Caleb for long?" she probed, tracking me with her gaze.

"Not long. A few weeks."

"Ah. Do you live here or in that backward little town Caleb calls home?"

"I live in that backward little town," I answered, hoping she'd go back to doing whatever art gallery things she normally did.

No such luck. "Caleb's so charming and good looking. He has that elite prep school charm, which

159

helps to sell his work. He went to boarding school in London. Anyway, some artists are so eccentric, they can be off-putting for the more pedestrian clients. Not Caleb, though."

I cringed at her choice of words. "I didn't know he went to school in London."

"His mom is from there. Sometimes when he drinks, you can pick up a little bit of an accent, but I'm sure you've noticed that."

I hadn't noticed. He certainly didn't have a Southern accent, but I hadn't really thought about it too much either way. "Hmm," I answered, detecting more than a little possessiveness in her questions and tone. Increasingly eager for Caleb to return, I glanced toward the back of the gallery. We hadn't discussed what our kiss meant or where this was going, if anywhere, so the direction of this conversation was making me increasingly uncomfortable.

"Caleb and I used to date. Did he mention that to you?"

Ah, so there it was. "No. He didn't." I actually managed to sound uninterested, and I gave myself a mental pat on the back.

She waved her hand. "I guess he wouldn't want you to know he works closely with his ex." Her voice sounded bitter instead of nonchalant and the urge to wait outside for Caleb intensified. I'd just lost my husband and I had no desire to be embroiled in some love triangle. If I was going to date someone, I wanted it to be simple. I hadn't dated much before Andrew, so in the scope of the average twenty-six-year-old, I definitely still had on my training wheels when it came to all of the intricacies of relationships. I needed to end this conversation before it spiraled into something even more uncomfortable than it already was.

I swiveled to face her. "Caleb rents the barn from me. You know, where he lives and paints. I moved into the house on the property a month or so ago after my husband died. I needed to get away from Atlanta for a while and start over. Did I give you the answers you were looking for or was there more you wanted to know?" I wanted to tell her to back the fuck off. That Caleb and I were dating, but caution held my tongue. For all I knew, Caleb and I were friends and that's all we'd ever be. Besides, I didn't want to invite Olivia's scrutiny more than I already had. Obviously, she was still hung up on whatever happened between the two of them.

"Oh." Olivia laughed, a faint blush tinging her cheekbones. "You own the Clayton farm. I didn't realize anyone lived there. Caleb gave me the impression it was pretty much vacant."

I shrugged. "It's not a farm anymore, but yes, I own it, and I live there."

Caleb's shoes clipped over the floor. He paused in front of us, his eyes searching my face. I kept it purposely blank. I didn't want to give anything away in front of Olivia. She was like a shark scenting blood in the water. He stepped closer to me and settled his arm around my waist, tightening his fingers briefly as if he could sense the tension or maybe he heard part of the conversation. Olivia's eyes zeroed in on the point of contact and her whole body tensed.

161

"We're together," I heard Caleb say, his voice unobtrusive but firm. "I don't appreciate you trying to pry information out of my girlfriend. My private life isn't your business."

"Girlfriend?" Her face blanched, then she turned to me. "You conveniently left that out."

A wave of apprehension traveled through me. Caleb shot me an unfathomable look and turned his attention to the woman in front of us.

"She didn't need to tell you anything. Like I said, my life doesn't concern you."

With wide eyes, I turned toward him, my pulse in full blown mutiny. Caleb lowered his head, skimming his lips along my cheek. Nothing inappropriate, just a simple gesture. It didn't stop there, though. His mouth inched lower and he planted a short, hot kiss where my collarbone and neck met, making an unequivocal declaration that we were together.

My face heated, and I tried to pull away from him. I didn't want to be used as a tool to get back at this woman regardless of how bitchy she'd been to me.

"How dare you come in here and flaunt her in my face. You wouldn't be anything without me. I made you and I can ruin you."

"You don't want to do this, Olivia," Caleb warned softly.

Uneasy, I peeked at his hard profile. His expression was unreadable.

She shook her head and clenched her hands into fists. "Don't you dare tell me what to do."

"Stop it. This isn't the time or the place."

"Tell me, Caleb, when is the right time? You won't take my calls and the only time you return a text or an email is when it has to do with work."

He sighed, running a hand through his hair, but the set of his face stayed harsh, unyielding, as if it had been sculpted from granite. "I can't keep doing this with you. I'm going to call Morris and ask him to release me from my contract. I've kept this to myself because I know how much you love this job, but I'm done. You said you could keep things professional, but it's clearly not possible. You have a knack for making everything personal."

Caleb guided me toward the door, his fingers digging into my side, as if he could tell I was getting ready to run out of there with or without him. While Olivia seemed a little unhinged, I was irritated he put me in this position. He knew she'd be there today, and from the sounds of things, he suspected she'd react like this.

She trailed after us. "Damn you, Caleb, you can't go to Morris. You promised—"

"I can and I will." He opened the door. "We were over almost a year ago. I'm going to tell Morris it's you or me, and I don't give a fuck which he chooses as long as this bullshit stops."

Caleb guided me out the door, leaving Olivia inside the gallery, the heat of her stare boring into the back of my head. We were both quiet as we strolled down the sidewalk. I'd learned more about Caleb's personal life than I'd wanted and I didn't know what to say.

"I'm sorry," he said abruptly after a few minutes. "She wasn't supposed to be there today. I set up the meeting with Morris, the owner, and she normally isn't there on the weekends. I guess she got wind of it and decided to change that. As you could tell, we dated briefly, if you can call it that. We never lived in the same place so it didn't really go anywhere and it was never exclusive. She's been a pain in the ass ever since."

His explanation soothed my irritation. I had a past too. One that came with a lot of complications, and if he didn't get mad about Brian's freak out, I couldn't exactly claim the moral high ground now.

"I don't want her to ruin your career. I should've waited for you in the park."

"I'm not worried about her. She knows a lot of artists, but she doesn't own the gallery. She's more of an artist groupie."

I laughed. "Um, yeah, so I could have gone without knowing that."

Caleb's facial features softened, and he pushed back a strand of my light hair that had dipped in front of my eyes. "She tried to give you the impression that we were a whole lot more than a few nights. We weren't. She's only interested in me because I've made a name for myself in the art world. If my paintings weren't selling, she wouldn't have looked at me twice."

"You don't have to tell me this."

"I don't want you to get the wrong idea."

"Thanks for clarifying." I bumped my shoulder into his, trying to lighten the mood. "You know, I'm not a big fan of confrontations with old flings. It was a little awkward."

He glanced at me. "A little?"

A wobbly laugh escaped me. "Okay, a lot awkward. She was really intense. I thought she was going to rip a painting off the wall and hit me over the head."

He chuckled. "Yeah. I was worried for your safety for a minute there."

"You should have stuck with the friend angle. I think I had her pacified until you came back and claimed me as your girlfriend."

Caleb halted on the street, lacing his fingers between mine, and pulled me against the side of the building. Caleb looked up, his eyes bright with something I couldn't name. "I'm not—" He paused and forced out an exhalation. His voice was gruff like a scrape of gravel along my nerve endings. "I already told you I wasn't interested in subterfuge. We are what we are."

I couldn't look away from him. "But we haven't discussed anything. We kissed once and you pulled out the "g" word like it was no big deal."

"Are you saying it was all wishful thinking on my part and you're not interested?" He frowned. "Or maybe you're not ready?"

While my first instinct was to slow this down, I pushed away the inclination as fast as it came. Life was short and I needed to start living, exploring, and finding myself.

"No to all three, but I am nervous." I moistened my lips. "I've only been with my husband, and this feels different."

"Different how? Do I scare you?" His free hand glided down my neck.

I nodded, frustration balling up my insides.

165

"With Andrew I felt like I went along for a ride and then I was hit so hard I didn't think I'd ever get up again. It makes me a little gun-shy, like I'm waiting for the next bad thing to hit me instead of expecting the best." I rolled my eyes. "That's dumb, huh?"

Rather than answering, he covered my mouth with his. Powerless, I returned his kiss, my fingers grasping the soft cotton of his shirt. His hands speared through my hair, curving along my scalp. The people around us faded into nothing. I concentrated on his mouth as he explored me, searching for hidden angles, until my whole body thrummed with urgency. A feeling of rightness rippled through me, and I sensed in the deepest reaches of my soul that I was exactly where I was supposed to be. Slowly, he pulled away and I felt more of a loss than I'd ever admit out loud.

He rested his forehead against mine. "You want to grab something to eat or are you ready to head back?"

I glanced around us, getting my bearings, kind of like I was just waking up from a long sleep.

"An early dinner, then let's get out of here."

"Emma. Emma. Emma Clayton, is that you?" I whirled around and came face to face with some old friends from Atlanta. Apparently, it was the day to face present rather than past ghosts.

Chapter Twenty-Six

I didn't recall ever feeling as conspicuous in my life. I wrung my hands as I watched Noah and Lainey close the distance between us. I pasted a big fat smile on my face, attempting to appear relaxed, attempting to act like I wasn't making out with some man on a street corner in the middle of Savannah a few minutes earlier.

Yeah right, my heart was pounding so fast I kind of wished I could have one of those flashbacks before they reached me. I swiped my hand across my lips to erase the evidence of the last minutes. God, I couldn't remember the last time I'd made a spectacle of myself. As a rule, I avoided them because growing up my mom did it often enough for our entire family. I resisted a grimace as Lainey wrapped one arm around me, stealing a glance at Caleb from the corner of my eyes.

"Lainey, Noah, this is Caleb." I probably should have offered more of an explanation, but unlike Caleb, I had a hard time blurting out the details of our relationship to every Tom, Dick and Harry.

Caleb shook Noah and Lainey's hands. We all stood facing each other. Despite the fact that I'd been out to dinner with them too many times to count, we might as well have been strangers with all of the awkwardness of our greeting.

"What are you guys doing in Savannah?" I asked to break the awkwardness growing by the second.

"We're taking a quick weekend trip to celebrate our anniversary," Noah answered, stuffing his hands in the front pockets of his pressed gray pants. It was startling how different he was from Caleb in his ancient black jeans that molded the long muscles of his legs like they'd been custom tailored for him. Noah was cleanly shaven whereas Caleb was rocking the two-day stubble.

"That's great. How many years?"

"Seven years," Lainey answered, a bright smile on her face. That was right. They had married right before I met Andrew. A little twinge worked its way through my chest. Our seven-year anniversary was right around the corner, not that it counted in the true sense of the word. Our story had ended, theirs would continue.

"Congratulations."

I'd always liked the two of them. Unlike a lot of the other couples in Andrew's network of friends, they adored each other. Lainey and her family were in the restaurant business and Noah was a professor like Andrew.

"Yeah, we're looking for some artwork for Noah's office."

"Really," I said, latching onto the opportunity. "Caleb is an artist. I'm sure he could give you a few pointers."

Noah laughed. "That'd be great. I don't have a clue what I'm looking for."

I glanced at Caleb and he smiled, but there was a glint in his eyes that heated my skin.

"Sure," Caleb said, "I can tell you some galleries to stop by, and if you give me a price range, I can suggest a few artists."

"That'd be great. Come have a glass of wine with us. We were just going to take a break." Lainey looked back and forth between Caleb and me, and held up a bag. "Noah hates shopping and I've dragged him all over looking for a new dress. Now it's his turn to have a little fun. The concierge in our hotel recommended a wine bar around the corner."

I wanted to refuse. I really did. Noah and Lainey were some of Andrew's best friends, and it felt strange hanging out with them with a new man on my arm, almost like more of a betrayal than dating someone new. I hesitated, not wanting to outright reject them, and I did miss Lainey. In the end, Caleb made the call for us.

"Sure. We don't have much time, though, because we're leaving tonight."

Lainey slipped her arm through mine, guiding me inside the wine bar, rattling off every detail of my old circle of friends' lives. Caleb and Noah headed to the bar to order our drinks while we found a table near the window.

Lainey folded her arms across her chest. "You've been ignoring me. I didn't even realize you'd left town until I stopped by the house and saw

169

the 'for sale' sign."

"Yeah." I winced internally. "I couldn't imagine staying there without Andrew." I didn't want to get into the gory details of Andrew leaving the house to his sister. I understood why it happened and there wasn't any reason to cast Andrew in an unfavorable light after he was gone. Before we married, Nora pressured him into making a will that essentially excluded me and he caved to her demands. In the end, everything worked out and Nora made amends for both of them. I would have hated living there without him, and I wouldn't have been able to sell it, feeling like I was throwing away his memory.

"Did I do something wrong? I know we didn't come around often toward the end, but Noah had a hard time dealing with Andrew's death. I wasn't even sure you wanted us around. I'm sorry if I let you down."

"No." I reached across the table and squeezed her hand. "I'm not mad. I've been busy with the move and I feel a little detached from my old life, like it was all a dream. And honestly, it's hard being around people who remind me of the past. It's not fair to you guys, and for that I'm sorry. I've been a shitty friend."

"Hey, don't apologize. I get it. I watched my mom lose my dad. As much as she loved seeing her old couple friends, she hated it too. So, maybe we could start over with a clean slate. I miss you."

"I'd love that."

Lainey glanced over her shoulder. Noah and Caleb were still engrossed in conversation at the bar. "So, tell me about this new guy. Is it serious?"

"It's new, but things are going well so far."

"I'm so glad. Andrew told us he was worried you wouldn't move forward with your life after he was gone. He felt so damn guilty about marrying you when you were so young and getting sick not too long afterward. He thought he had ruined your life. He'd be so proud of you. I told him you were strong and you'd make it, but you know Andrew. He hated not being able to plan every last detail."

Tears welled up in my eyes, and I didn't know what to say. I didn't realize Andrew had talked to anyone about me. After his diagnosis, our life was a whirlwind. We barely had time to make plans, and every time he brought up my future, I refused to talk about it and he never pushed. At the time, I didn't want to face a reality without him. Now, I regretted being such a coward. I'd give anything to have that conversation with him, or any conversation for that matter.

"Thanks for sharing that with me, Lainey. I mean it. It's been hard trying to pick up the pieces of my life. Andrew had everything mapped out for us and when I lost him, I lost my compass. Now, I'm just concentrating on enjoying life and not stressing about where it takes me."

As the words left my mouth, I thought of Elizabeth, Henry, and Charles. In a roundabout way, they were part of my life, and I knew I needed to stop stressing about the visions or whatever they were. Maybe if I stopped fighting them, I'd understand why I was having them, and they'd stop. Acceptance could be the key to everything. My emotions veered abruptly from grief to happiness.

Lainey kept talking and I nodded where appropriate, but the bulk of my attention was focused on Caleb and the sincere way he interacted with Noah. He didn't mind that he'd been roped into having a drink with Andrew's friends. He looked content to be there. A warmth settled inside of my chest and I felt grateful for this time with old friends and the opportunity to experience something new with Caleb. I didn't care what others thought of my decisions. If we were alone I would have shared all of this with him, but instead I smiled when I caught his gaze, hoping he could read my thoughts.

As a kid, I used to think there was one perfect person for everyone—a soul mate. When Andrew died, I was convinced I'd lost mine. Now I was coming to appreciate the idea that if you were fortunate, you might meet a few important people who were right for you at that moment. Not because the timing was perfect or the other person was perfect, but because together everything made sense. While it may or may not last forever, the ephemeral nature of life just made it imperative that you cherish every second you had with that person.

Chapter Twenty-Seven

By the time we returned home, my mind wasn't on Caleb, Lainey, Noah, or even crazy Olivia. I knew what I needed to do to push forward Elizabeth's story. Rather than waiting for it to unfold at its own pace, I had to seek it out. I wouldn't be a passive spectator. I'd force them to come one way or another.

Caleb parked in the roundabout in front of my house. Not waiting for me to invite him in, he grabbed a duffle bag from behind his seat and rounded the front of the car to open my door.

I grinned. "I take it you're planning on coming inside with me regardless of what I want."

"You're right, but I have to leave early in the morning. I'm behind on a few commissions, so I won't be able to help you out with the dining room this week," he said ruefully.

My shoulders sagged, both with relief and defeat. Although I hadn't been comfortable in the house by myself lately, I wanted to spend some time planning how to fast forward the piecemeal revelations of Elizabeth's life. It sounded like his days would be filled for a while, so I'd have all of the time I needed to implement whatever I came up with.

Caleb shadowed me upstairs to my bedroom. I immediately excused myself to the bathroom to get ready for bed. By the time I returned to my room, I felt as if I were coming out of my skin.

Caleb was stretched out on my bed on top of the covers, wearing his gray boxer briefs and reading something on his phone. Plucking nervously at the hem of my sleep shorts, I trained my eyes on the floor as I passed by him and perched on the opposite side of the bed, my back to the headboard. He placed his phone on the nightstand, and the soft thud was enough for me to jump.

"You're nervous again." It wasn't a question, yet the soft, almost raw sound of his voice combined with the mocking smile on his lips made me relax a notch.

"No, well, maybe a little."

"You think I'm going to pressure you into something you're not comfortable with."

Staring at him unblinking, I shook my head almost imperceptibly, not wanting to admit it. He pulled me next to him until my head was on his shoulder and my chest pressed against him, highlighting the contrast of his hard muscle with my softness. I squeezed my eyes shut, mortified by the way my heart sped up and my breathing became noticeably choppy.

"Then I should kiss you, so you'll stop worrying. Anticipation is deadly, you know." His dark head bent. He lowered his mouth to mine, lingering for a moment as if he wanted to savor me. His mouth tasted like wine. Being linked with him like this brought an overwhelming sense of connection to Caleb in some hidden part of my soul. I couldn't fully explain it if I tried. All I knew was that if I could wrap him around me like a blanket, I'd do it and still feel the need to be closer to him— physically and emotionally.

His hand slipped under my camisole, cupping my breast on the underside. His lips lowered and he drew the tight peak of my covered nipple into his mouth. All uncertainty forgotten, I wriggled beneath him, incapable of remaining still. He drew me further and further into him with every swirl of his tongue and brush of his fingers.

Impulsively, I coaxed his lips back to mine, needing to taste him again. The bulk of his hand rested heavy on my lower belly just beneath the elastic of my sleep shorts. My stomach muscles quivered. I arched into his caress, imploring him without words to continue.

His hand skated lower, his fingertips grazing my entrance. My insides pulsed on the emptiness. Until then I had never considered the idea that it was possible to die of unfulfilled need, but that was exactly how it felt. I balled up my hands, trying not to beg, but it had been way too long since I'd felt anyone's touch. I fumbled with the waistband of his boxers and his hand stopped moving.

"Do it," I gasped, my toes curling into velvet soft duvet. "Caleb, please—"

"Do what?" he rasped, sliding his fingers back

and forth but not quite where I wanted him.

I parted my thighs wider, groaning with need and a little frustration. "Stop teasing me."

A sigh resembling a purr escaped his mouth, making my lips tingle. Slowly, he pulled his hand out of my shorts and he gently dragged his lips from mine. He dipped his head, kissing my still exposed belly. Then he sat up and brushed my hair back from my face, his amber gaze studying me. I assumed I was quite the sight with my fidgety limbs and uneven breaths.

"Why are you stopping?" I asked, my voice husky. I caught his hand in mine and tried to pull him back to me. "I want to be with you. I want this."

"No. Not tonight." Caleb broke my hold on him and faced away from me on the bed, his legs hanging over the side. He rested his elbows on his knees. "Not like this, Emma."

Briefly, I didn't comprehend his words. Trying to think straight was like trying to see the bottom of a murky pond. Then it hit me, and a toxic concoction of anger and embarrassment rolled through my gut.

"What's wrong with tonight?"

Caleb took what seemed like an hour to answer me. He swiveled to face me, and quickly reached out to pull down my camisole to cover my stomach.

"You're not ready," he said. "Like Brian said, you're vulnerable, and he doesn't even know the half of it. These flashbacks are disorienting. I just wouldn't feel right about moving things forward until you understood everything."

My lips parted, so many rebuttals on my tongue, yet none of them came. I couldn't believe he was actually rejecting me. Everything had been going so well. My nerves had faded to nothing, and I thought we were on the same page. If I'd taken a second to think about it, it seemed too good to be true, and apparently it was.

"You're making a big deal out of nothing," I complained. "I want this."

"Trust me. I want this too, but the timing isn't right."

"What are you talking about? The timing for you?"

"No. For you. For us."

"Does my opinion count? Or are you saying only Brian's and your opinions matter? If so, that seems a little high handed of you."

He shot me a disbelieving glance, then tipped up his head and started chuckling.

My lower lip quivered and I covered my face with my hands, not wanting him to witness my fragile ego shatter in front of him. "You're a jerk."

"Jesus, Emma, look at me," he said between bouts of laughter.

"No. You should go. I think I need to be alone tonight." I refused to let him stay here another minute. If he did, I'd probably jump on top of him and beg him to continue, and I'd lose what little dignity I still had. This probably wasn't an example of successful adulting, but I didn't care. He teased me until I was aching and then he pulled back, claiming the timing wasn't right. What a load of shit.

"Not happening," he said firmly, peeling my hands from my face, tilting my head so I had no choice except to look at him.

I jumped up. "If you're not leaving, I am."

He rubbed his temples, his brow furrowed. "I'm trying to be the nice guy here."

"I'm not looking for a nice guy."

He snagged my shoulder and turned me around. "What's this really about?"

I stared down at my bare feet, my eyes tearing up. God damnit, I was such a nutcase. First, I was coming out of my skin at the thought of us doing something more than kissing. Then five seconds later, I was begging him not to stop and acting like a lunatic because he pulled the handbrake.

"I don't like being rejected," I mumbled, feeling totally ridiculous. I only needed to flip my hair and stomp my foot and I'd be mistaken for a teenager. The silence that followed was deafening. And so extremely fucking awkward.

"I'm not rejecting you," he finally responded.

"Well, it sure as hell feels like it." He scooped me up like I didn't weigh more than a feather. "Put me down right now, Caleb." I pounded on his chest, and he dropped me on the bed. The bed whined in protest.

"I'm not kicking you out of your bedroom. Just go to sleep and I'll sleep on the couch downstairs."

"No, God, Caleb, this is stupid. I don't know how this escalated. I'm just confused. You tell me you don't want to hide our relationship, but you don't want anything to do with me sexually. I don't get it."

"Of course, I want you. That's not what this is about," he murmured. The sound of his voice freed the tight clamp around my heart. I released a long breath as I absorbed his words. The tone of his voice conveyed a sincerity that convinced me he was telling the truth.

I groaned. "Don't leave. I really don't want to be alone, and this whole fight is dumb."

He crawled in bed with me. "I'm not going anywhere," he said. "And Emma, I'm not rushing things between us because I don't want you to question my motives."

Before I could second guess what I was doing, I curled my body around his. His arms went around me, and I nuzzled into the crook of his neck, inhaling his unique scent. Tonight, this was enough.

Chapter Twenty-Eight

When Caleb left the house the following morning, I spent some time texting my family and friends. Seeing Lainey made me realize I'd been so caught up in my life I'd neglected the people who cared about me. Nora, Brock, Lainey, and Addison deserved more. I didn't want to wake up in a year and find myself alienated from everyone not just in miles but also emotionally. As the responses poured in, I smiled. Just because I planned to spend the day chasing Elizabeth didn't mean I had to ignore my real life.

Once the texts stopped, I powered down my phone and went in search of supplies. I'd gathered a couple of candles, snacks, a blanket, and some water, and stuffed them in an oversized canvas bag. I didn't know if I'd be gone for an hour for five. Then I left the house.

I roamed the property for a half an hour without triggering anything before I saw the cabin off in the distance. From the little information I had, it appeared a lot of Elizabeth's relationship with

Charles happened there. If I wanted to learn more about him and how he fit into her life, it seemed like the best place to start.

My mind made up, I picked up speed until I was nearly sprinting. I flung open the door, looking around me. It was exactly as I remembered it. Old, run down, and musty. No one had bothered with this place for years.

I spread out the blanket on the worn floorboards beside an old barrel. I placed the candle on top of the fragile wood, and lit it. I didn't know much about inviting supernatural visions, but I'd read an article about candle meditation, or trataka, for some psychology class a few years ago. I'd even experimented with it as part of a class research project years ago. It was effective for meditating, so it seemed like a good starting point for what I had in mind.

Sitting cross-legged, I took five long, deep breaths, then I brought my attention to the flame dancing above the candle. I softened my gaze, and within a few minutes my muscles relaxed. I visualized love and healing spreading outward from the candle and slowly my mind began to wander.

"Darn it, Charles. What are you doing? You were burning up all day yesterday and there's a damp bite in the air. You'll catch your death, and I will have gone through all of the trouble of saving you for nothing."

Charles focused on my face and swayed slightly. "I'm fine." His speech was slurred.

He was as drunk as an owl. "Sakes alive! Did

you get into the whiskey I left here?"

"What else did you expect me to do?"

I picked up the book from the makeshift bedside table. "Read. I left the book for you." I lifted the linen sheet from the cot. "You're gonna hurt yourself. Rest up and you'll be as good as new in a couple days. Then you can catch up with your regiment."

"Stay, madam. I don't feel like lying in bed. Read to me. Tell me a story or something. I'm losing my mind."

"I really don't have time for this today." I slammed the book down and headed for the door. "Mama's carrying on about getting ready for some dinner party with our neighbors."

Charles snagged my arm before I could unlatch the door. I whirled around in surprise, afraid to protest. He loomed over me and my heart battered inside my chest. He hadn't touched me since the day I'd found him by the creek.

"How about a kiss," he mumbled, "lest I die while I wait for your return." He drew me against his chest and the pungent sweetness of brandy filled my senses. "Just a small sampling so I'll have something to think about in your absence."

"You're awful irritable today. My fiancé would skin you alive if he knew you were talking to me like this." I looked down my nose at him exactly like my mama, but the demanding pressure of his body against mine quickly doused my confidence.

"So, you have a greyback fiancé. How do you know he hasn't been mustered out?"

"You're too familiar with me by far. He's not

your concern."

He picked up a piece of my hair and twirled it around his finger, his blue eyes luminous in the candlelight. "In times like these, you have to take pleasure where you find it and not worry about the consequences. God knows, most of us won't be around long enough to face 'em."

"Do you have someone you fancy back home?"

"I thought so, but she sent one letter and I haven't heard from her since. She probably wrote me off as a hopeless cause or married someone else. I can't say I blame her. We've all been through the mill and hoping she'll still want me or I'll live long enough to see her again are luxuries I can ill afford of late."

A strange feeling wormed though me, and I didn't like it one bit. I hadn't heard much from Henry before he was injured. He sent letters to his parents and occasionally he'd include a short note or sketch for me. Now his behavior had me questioning if he had the same attitude as Charles. I was so sure of his love, but maybe I'd misread him. I know my refusal to marry him before he left wounded his pride. Maybe he decided I wasn't worth the wait. With willpower I didn't know existed, I forced down my traitorous thoughts. Henry was true, loyal, and honest. I didn't know the story of Charles' lady friend, but I did know mine.

When I opened my mouth to reprimand him, I found my lips ensnared by his, and while his touch was gentle and cautious, a scratchy feeling clawed at my chest. The sound of my heart pounded inside of my head and I squeezed my eyes closed, wanting to disappear.

Unfortunately, the hard pressure of his body against mine made me all too cognizant of the fact that a strong, handsome man that wasn't Henry was kissing me. Futilely, I wondered whether I'd ever see Henry again or if our last kiss under the oak tree was a goodbye forever instead of a goodbye for now. I whimpered at the emptiness building inside of my chest.

He pulled back, his eyes boring into mine. My head spun with melancholy and betrayal, and I feared I might swoon if I took even a second to reflect on what I had done. I attempted to quiet the vicious tremor that overtook my body and a tear slipped down my cheek. Angrily, I turned my head and swiped at my cheeks. I refused to cry over that stupid kiss.

"Please don't do that again."

He frowned down at me. "Haven't you ever been kissed before?"

Confused, I stared at him, until the hasty realization dawned. He saw my tears. I blushed furiously, but I managed to duck my head.

"That is none of your business."

He wrapped his arms around me again. Not knowing where to put my arms, I balled them into fists and wedged them between our bodies. He kissed the top of my head. "My apologies, madam. Brandy and a beautiful woman don't always make a good combination. My mind is fuzzy from the pain and drink. Come read me a couple of chapters and we can forget that happened. I don't want you to be vexed with me and leave me out here to die, or worse, send someone out here to kill me."

"No," I said, my voice wispy and lacking substance. "I have things to do today that don't include nursing a presumptuous Yankee with poor manners."

"I'm not trying to offend you. It's just that from the moment I saw you near the forest with your blonde hair tumbling around your shoulders and your vibrant blue eyes, I could think of little else. Do you know how beautiful you are?"

His words made me pause. There was no way he actually thought I was beautiful in a sticky ivory muslin dress that clung to me like a second skin. Sensing another motive, I asked guardedly, "Is this an attempt to soften me to you so I'll—" I couldn't finish the sentence. No doubt, Charles was a fine-looking man, but not so much that he tempted me to make poor decisions. My heart belonged to Henry.

"Is it a crime to desire you? You're beautiful. You have to know that. I'm sure your greyback has told you that many times."

"What do you want me to say?" I shook my head. "I don't mind helping you as long as you don't have designs on my heart. Any cordiality on my part shouldn't be misinterpreted because I'm spoken for, and I don't appreciate you pawing at me after everything I've done for you."

Charles closed the space, and seeing the heat in his gaze I almost retreated, but I straightened my spine and held my ground.

"I'm very grateful it was you who found me in the woods. Your care and attention were more than I expected, and that begs the question? Why did you *help me?"*

My shoulders sagged, and I found myself wanting to reveal everything to him, which made me realize how lonely I'd been these past months. Henry was my only confidant, and he'd been gone so long I was starting to forget the things that made him special. And Mama, well, she might as well have been buried right next to my father. She went through the motions of life, but she didn't really care about anything. The fact that she had no idea I was harboring a Yankee on our property for nearly two weeks showed just how little interest she had in anything other than her misery and her bottle of sherry.

Calmly I met his glower. "I got word Henry was wounded some time ago. Since then, we haven't heard a thing. For all intents and purposes, he's missing. When I saw you, I thought if I helped you, perhaps someone out there would extend the same kindness to him."

"Ah. I see." He stumbled toward the cot and sat on the edge. "You love him?"

"I have known Henry my entire life," I answered evasively. This man didn't need to know the details. I didn't owe him anything.

"So, love has nothing to do with it?"

I leaned against the door, pondering his question. "I love him. What about you? Do you love that woman back home?"

"I thought I did. Now, though, when I think of going home, it isn't to see her. It's to be with my parents, my sister, and my friends. If I loved her, she'd be on that list, so I'm fine with it if she's

pledged herself to another. I think the more people I meet and the more of this country I see, the less I credit the idea that I loved her. She lived in our town, and I'd known her for quite some time. I believe I was fond of her. That is all, and even that has faded these last three years."

"Hm," I answered, even though his story made my stomach turn. I hated that Henry could be out there saying something similar to whoever would listen to him. I'd die if he gave up on us so easily and sought another. "Bully for you. I think I can spare twenty minutes to read some poetry."

He grabbed the book and held it out to me. "I think you stopped reading on page fifty-four."

"I reckon so."

Chapter Twenty-Nine

By the time I left the cabin, Charles had fallen asleep. I picked up my skirt and ran toward the house. Though I'd been gone for nearly two hours, I doubted Mama had noticed my absence. She was in a mood today. Lunch came and went and she still hadn't come downstairs. I shoved open the kitchen door and slammed it behind me, not heeding the way the windowpanes shook menacingly.

"Miz Elizabeth, I sho' hope yo' ain' visiting that Yankee again," Axie said, her attention on whatever she was preparing for dinner.

"Somebody has to do it. I can't just let him rot in the cabin. Besides, the sooner he gets better, the sooner he can get out of our hair."

Axie draped a towel over her arm. "If you say so. If yer mammy finds out, she'll be in a fine pucker. I think you gone done 'nuff for dat man."

"No one will find out, and he's still hurt. I can't exactly let him fend for himself."

"When is you gonna stop traipsin' 'round in da woods and start actin' like a lady? Mistah Henry

would not like this."

"*What, and lay around in bed all day like Mama? If that's what a proper lady does, then no thanks."*

Axie shook her head and leaned over the pot.

"*What's for dinner?" I inquired, wanting to change the subject. I should've kicked Charles out the moment he pressed his lips to mine. That I didn't was a sin to Moses.*

"*Terrapin soup."*

Hopefully, Mama planned to make it out of bed by then or I'd be eating alone again. Lately, Axie was my only company unless we made it to church or Henry's family joined us for dinner.

At the thought of Henry and my betrayal of him with Charles, my stomach flipped. Charles had painted such a bleak outlook on life and love, and in the process, he brought out all of my fears. That Henry was truly dead. That Henry wouldn't forgive me for not marrying him before he left. That Henry didn't want me any longer. That what Henry felt for me was a manifestation of our proximity and his lack of choice in the matter.

"*I'm going to rest before dinner. I don't want to be disturbed," I said, needing to be alone. Needing to think.*

"*I ain't got around to cleanin' yer room yet wid all dis mess down heah."*

"*I'll take care of it myself. You have enough to do between cleaning, cooking, and looking after Mama."*

I brushed past Axie. Lifting my skirts to my ankles, I fled up the stairs to my bedroom, not caring if my heavy footsteps disturbed my mother or amplified whatever malady she claimed to have today.

I opened the door to my room only to find Mama perched on the floral chair near the fireplace.

"Where have you been?" she demanded sharply.

Oh, so now she cared. I marched past her, tossing my bonnet on the rumpled, unmade bed. "I went for a stroll."

"You what!" Mama shrieked, coming to her feet. Her eyes darkened to indigo. "I've told you not to wander around by yourself. You endanger not just yourself but all of us. How dare you!"

"My! My! What do you expect me to do? Stare out the window all day or maybe lie in bed until dinner like you?"

"Don't be sarcastic. It's unbecoming," Mama retorted. "This is for your own good. What would Henry think of his future wife roaming around by herself? He might decide you're not worth the trouble. And he's probably right. You're too headstrong to make a good wife."

I threw up my hands in resignation. Axie and Mama were ganging up of me, making me feel unworthy of Henry. I'd had enough. "Pshaw. You're right, as always, Mama! In fact, he possibly isn't injured at all. More likely, he found the perfect woman. One so much better than a ragamuffin like me, and he'll never be back. After all, there's nothing here for him."

"Elizabeth, I didn't mean—"

"No, Mama. Not now. I don't want to hear it. Just let me be. I'm tired. I've heard this all before.

190

I'm not good enough. I'm lucky a man like Henry wanted me at all. I let the sun ruin my skin. I stained the hem of my skirt. Is there anything else you'd like to add to the list of my faults?"

Mama lifted her chin indignantly, narrowed her eyes, swiveled on her heels, and stalked out of the room. The door slammed behind her, and my shoulders sagged as I listened to her heels clicking against the hardwood floors. Without Papa or my brother as a buffer, we were likely to kill each other before the war ended. I should've defied my parents and married Henry before he left. Then I wouldn't have to answer to her or worry Henry might abandon me for another.

The soft patter of raindrops tapped the roof, filling the sudden silence of her departure. Given the dark clouds outside, it was likely a prelude to a big storm. Lightning lit up my room and thunder rumbled, shaking the windows, making me flinch. The daylight wouldn't hold much longer.

I lit a kerosene lamp perched on the bureau and made my way to the armoire in the corner of the room. Crouching on the floor, I lifted a few floorboards. Inside I stored all of the stuff I wanted to keep out of Mama's reach. Blindly searching the opening, I grabbed the stack of sketches and letters Henry had given me over the years. I nearly sobbed in relief as my fingers touched the bundle. They were encased in a scrap of oiled cloth and tied with a faded blue ribbon. I unfolded each one, careful not to tear them.

The newer sketches were stacked on the top. The first was of a large, sloping meadow with log

191

structure surrounded by tents with the soldiers standing nearby in various poses. He had included several drawings depicting the landscape of various places he'd been along with some dried flowers. He knew how much I loved flowers. Even in harm's way, he hadn't forgotten that.

The rest were the ones I wanted to see so I could remember how things were before all of the hardship and suffering. Henry had given me dozens of sketches of myself in various poses. Sitting at the dining room table. Drinking a glass of tea on the front porch. Lounging on the swing he hung from a tree on the side of my house with a book in my lap. The last was a drawing of Henry and I laying on a blanket by the creek weeks before he left. Mama would have a fit if she saw it. As much as she desired the match between Henry and I, she never permitted us much time alone. That day, I'd snuck out and met him. I studied the final picture, looking for clues that he cared, that he'd wait for me, but most importantly I wanted to feel a connection to him. I needed to know he was still out there somewhere.

Finally, I came to one of the few letters from Henry:

"*Dear Lizzie,*

Sitting by the dying firelight on the ground, I'm writing you a few lines. I am worn-out tonight, but I suspect I will be much more so on the morrow. The thought is gaining ground that we will have a fight in a short time, and this sad excuse for a letter may be the last one that you or my family will receive from me for a while. From the little information I have heard, we will be attacking the Yanks.

By the grace of God, I have survived seven engagements without so much as a scrape, but conceivably I may not be so lucky in the future. I would be glad if we could settle this affair without further bloodshed for there surely has been more bloodshed in this wicked war than anyone could imagine.

I can't thank you enough for your letters. I would be ashamed to admit how often I have read them. I can't express in words how much I look forward to the day when circumstances will let us meet again.

All of my love,
Henry"

I stared at the letter so long tears slid down my cheeks, splashing on the papers clutched in my hand. I curled onto my side, letting the pain pass through me in seemingly relentless waves. Not knowing if the person you loved most in the world was alive was the worst kind of torture. It almost

193

felt physical. When I finally pulled myself together, I folded and retied the bundle and put them back where no one could find them. Henry had gifted them to me, and I didn't want to share them. They were our private story, one that I prayed with all my heart hadn't already ended.

I rubbed my trembling fingers against my temples. Between the emotional rollercoaster of not knowing whether Henry was alive and harboring an enemy, I was bone tired and longed for sleep, but I'd subject myself to another confrontation with Mama if I didn't show up for dinner neat and presentable.

The clock on the bureau daintily chimed the late hour. I blinked a few times, wondering where the time had flown. The nap would have to wait.

Chapter Thirty

My body vibrated and the purr of the radiator echoed in my ears. I looked around and I was in my room, but as Emma, not Elizabeth. I blinked a few times, my heart racing like a jackrabbit. Oh my God, I had made the trek from the cabin back to my room, wholly unaware of my actual surroundings. I breathed in and out, trying to calm myself.

Then it hit me. "Shit! The candle." With my luck, I knocked it over and set the cabin on fire. I didn't have a clue how long it'd been since I left. It could've been ten minutes or an hour.

I took off, running out of my room and down the stairs, adrenaline surging through me. I jumped off the top step of the porch and kept going. By the time the cabin came in view, I was winded, but I didn't smell or see smoke, which was a positive sign I hadn't inadvertently burned down a piece of history. Not yet anyway.

Fires spread fast, at least from my experience. When I was seven my mom fell asleep with a cigarette in her hand. My brother and I were both sleeping. I'll never forget how I woke up and gawked in puzzlement at the curious red luminosity that saturated the front of our trailer. The intense heat coupled with acrid air burned my eyes and nose. My brother wasted no time dropping me out the window. I didn't know how he managed to drag our mother out of there and douse the flames, but he did. We had to stay with some friends for a couple of weeks while everything was cleaned.

When I stepped over the threshold of the cabin, I examined it in a new light, speculating about all the untold stories that transpired here, not just Elizabeth's. The now burned out candle sat abandoned on the stool exactly where I had left it. I scooped it up along with the blanket and bag I had brought with me and left.

The adrenaline now long gone from my system, I moseyed back to the house, taking in my surroundings. The sun was setting over the trees, and the sky was a vibrant hue of coral mixed with shades of pink. When my house came into view, I paused, searching out the tree from the sketch Henry had made for Elizabeth. Over a century had passed and that tree could be long gone, but something told me it would still be there. After all, live oaks could live several hundred years.

Excitement exploded inside of my chest when it dawned on me. This was my chance to prove Elizabeth existed, and I wasn't going crazy. I picked up my pace until I was jogging. I reached the field on the side of the house, and I found myself beneath the branches of what looked like Elizabeth's tree. Sure, the branches shaded more of the field, but something told me this was the place.

I circled the wide trunk, dragging my fingers along the rough, uneven bark, pausing at a hollowed knot. My insides tingled with familiarity, and I lifted my gaze, searching for ruts in the limbs caused by the ropes of a swing. The instant I spotted them, my heart beat quicker, harsher, stormier, and I slouched against the trunk of the tree, straining to catch my breath. My vision blurred and I blinked repeatedly, trying to bring it back into focus.

When it cleared, I saw a man crouched down in front of me.

"I thought I'd find you here," Henry said, his brown eyes glinting with mischief.

"I suppose I've become quite predictable these days."

"Not at all. Quite the opposite, in fact. You're always disappearing."

"Not always," I answered evasively, even though it was true.

I'd been right huffy ever since Pa refused my request to go with Henry and him to Great Britain. While I loved Henry, I resented that he traveled endlessly with my father to bring our cotton and tobacco to the European market. I wanted to travel with them. I wanted to see the world. If my father had his way, I'd never go anywhere. He thought my place was at home with Mama.

"What's wrong?" He frowned. "Don't tell me you're still upset about my trip."

I inhaled a deep breath. The air smelled of violets and sun-warmed grass. "I wish I could've gone with you."

"If it were up to me, you would have."

"Really?" My voice cracked on the word.

He hadn't pushed the issue when Pa refused my request. I was spitting mad at the time, but deep down I knew it wouldn't have mattered. Everyone knew a proper Southern gentleman must not only be honest and independent, but also exercise complete control over his wife, children, and slaves. We were nothing more than property. As such, as an unmarried woman, Pa had the final say on what I did and where I went. With Mama always whispering in his ear that he gave me too much freedom, I didn't get to do much of anything.

"Of course." He cleared his throat. "That's part of the reason why I was looking for you."

His eyes searched my face with so much optimism, I could hardly draw in a breath. He lifted one hand and unfurled his fist. I swallowed hard, scarcely able to glance at the ring balancing on his palm. The cushion diamond surrounded by a halo of rose cut diamonds caught the light and sparkled like a cluster of stars.

I couldn't even examine it because all I saw was Henry. Henry, the boy I had known forever was proposing to me. I'd suspected he would propose soon, especially after he kissed me, but I couldn't believe it was actually happening. I waited for what seemed to be a never-ending minute, terrified to speak, my entire body strung tight with anticipation.

"Elizabeth, for as long as I can remember, you've been part of my life. I can't pinpoint the exact moment I knew I'd marry you, but it seems *like I've been waiting for you to turn twenty for a lifetime already. I don't want to wait any longer. Please say you'll marry me. And before you answer, yes, I know you're frustrated with the restraints your parents put on you, but as my wife, you may do as you wish. Ride your horse through the countryside with abandon. Accompany me on every trip. Wear those trousers your mama hates. I don't care as long as you're mine."*

My throat was dry, yet I already knew what I would say. "Yes."

He wrapped his arms around me and leaned his forehead against mine. I shivered at his touch. "We're gonna be so happy, Elizabeth."

He stared at me for a beat and then his gaze dipped to my lips. My pulse rate jumped as his face inched closer. I squeezed my eyes closed. When his lips brushed across mine, heat rushed down my spine like flint clashing against steel. He traced the outline of my lips with his, his hot, sherry-scented breath fanning my face. His tongue slipped inside my mouth and I felt his touch all the way down to the tips of my toes. Goosebumps dotted my skin.

"Henry, what are you doing?" I whispered. Distress mixed with something like longing whirled inside of me. He tightened his hold on me to stop me from stepping back. His expression reminded me of the single-minded look of a hunter, as if he had no intention of releasing me. The thought made me dizzy with happiness.

His calloused palms cupped my face. "Making sure you know you're mine and mine alone."

"Yours?" I laughed. "There has never been a

doubt. You, on the other hand, have paraded all those awful girls in front me every chance you've got. You don't know how many times I suffered while people laughed behind their hands saying you would eventually tire of me and I'd wind up an old maid."

"Madam, it amazes me how little you see your appeal. What about Thomas? He's always trailing after you like a puppy after church. Then there's my younger brother. If I turned my back for a minute, he'd find a way to slink into your good graces and usurp my position. If I took all your admirers seriously, I'd be fighting a duel every month."

Unclear whether he teased or spoke the truth, I glanced at him and his wide grin said it all. "You tease me."

"Certainly not. You're a portrait of beauty. Never have I seen such fairness. No one compares. Not here nor in any of my travels." He tucked a strand of hair behind my ear. "But that's not the most important thing about you. You embody unquestionable loyalty, kindness, and best of all, grit, and I absolutely adore you. And if you don't marry me, I'll follow you around in this life and the next."

I chuckled because I couldn't imagine him doing anything of the sort, but he'd always had a way with words. "Promise?"

"Of course, Madam. You shall not get rid of me easily. I'll beat down the gates of heaven or hell to find you."

My belly fluttered, and I grinned so hard my cheeks hurt. "I shan't forget this, Henry."

"So, you forgive me?"

"Forgive you?"

"For not intervening when your father forbade you from joining the trip. I know how much you wanted to see London. I couldn't pull you away from those Charles Dickens' books in the months leading up to the journey."

"Pa wouldn't have changed his mind no matter what you said. If you wanted me there, you would have had to hide me in your traveling trunk."

"No doubt." He offered his arm and I threaded mine through his. *"Come on. We should go inside and tell our parents. I'm sure our mamas are waiting on pins and needles."*

"Like there was ever any doubt I'd say yes."

"I wasn't entirely confident I still held your affection. I heard Matt stopped by a couple times requesting to court you."

"Is that what this is about? You were worried about Matt?"

He stopped walking and faced me. *"Matt and the rest of them. You better believe I am most anxious to guard you from the lingering gazes of every swain you meet, but that doesn't diminish what I confessed earlier. I love you, and I can't imagine a time when that will ever change."*

I shook my head. I felt like I was floating. The joy blooming inside of me, the amazement, it was beyond anything I'd ever experienced. Henry loved me. I knew he cared about me, but this was almost too good to be true. Was this real? Was I dreaming?

"And I love you too, but you know that. Surely

you noticed how pathetic I am when it comes to you. I've followed you around since I could walk. You probably wanted to send me on my way more than once, but you were too kind to break my spirit."

"Your nearly white hair was like a cloud of angel fluff, darting behind trees and crouching next to fences. It always gave you away."

"A cloud of angel fluff?" I laughed. "I think Mama has checked my head for devil horns no less than forty times."

"You're perfect the way you are. I wouldn't change a thing."

I smiled so hard I was surprised my cheeks didn't crack. "Do it again."

"What?"

Flames licked my face. "Kiss me."

"You liked it?"

Dazed, I nodded and tipped my head upward, struggling to get air into my chest.

His gaze lingered on me with dark, hooded eyes for a moment of suspended time. Then unhurriedly, Henry lowered his mouth to mine for the second time that day. Every time I moved to pull away, he pressed harder, coaxing me without words to let him take the lead.

I squeaked into his mouth, but he didn't let me go, and I didn't want him to do anything of the sort. I wanted to feel his lips against mine forever, his tongue caressing me. It was so different from what I thought of as a kiss, or at least the ones I'd witnessed.

When Henry finally straightened somewhat, and his eyes held mine. "Lizzy, you were made for me."

Chapter Thirty-One

I opened my eyes and the sky had darkened, twilight only a few moments away. The house in the distance loomed menacingly between the shadows. Funny how I'd wanted this place from the second I saw the picture in Andrew's office and now that it was slowly doling out its secrets, being here unnerved me.

Pushing away from the tree trunk, I shook off my maudlin feelings and made my way back to the house. As I rounded the corner, I saw Caleb sitting on the front porch steps, his elbows braced on his knees. He had a pair of aviators hanging from the collar of his black shirt. His hair either looked windblown or as if he had spent the entirety of the day running his hands through it. When I got closer, I saw paint threaded into his hair, and I realized it was the latter.

"Rough day?" he asked, his expression unreadable.

"What makes you think that?"

"You looked so defeated walking over here."

My head dipped. "Not defeated, just confused."

"How so?"

"Elizabeth loved Henry so much. I can still feel her happiness and her love." I tried to rub away the weird sensation growing under my chest. "Maybe she always did. I don't understand what Charles has to do with this. The way Elizabeth and Henry were together was..." I shook my head, unable to find the words to describe what was going on in my head. "If they are the point of the flashbacks, why do they keep coming? Am I missing something?"

A full grin spread across his face. It was so goddamn dazzling—his blindingly white teeth, and holy shit, the way his full lips tilted up at the corners—that I froze, unable to do anything except stare.

"You think I'm crazy talking about these people like they're real, but I think they are. I saw the ruts in the oak tree from the swing Elizabeth loved. They're still there. Come on. I'll show you."

He ran his hand along the underside of his jaw, and his golden eyes were practically smoldering. "I believe you."

"You do?"

"Yeah."

"Oh, okay. Anyway, how was your day?"

"My day was productive. I got a lot done, but I don't want to talk about that."

I tilted my head to the side. "Really? Are you sure? You seem a little off or something."

"Not off. Happy. Come here." He grabbed my hand and guided me onto the step next to him.

A second later, his fingers rounded the back of

my neck. A shudder of anticipation rolled through me, goading my heart into a reckless, frenzied beat. His hands kept moving until they cradled my face with a gentleness that caused a lump to well up in my windpipe.

Then his mouth dipped down to mine, all velvety and scorching with an intensity that seemed unwarranted given the simple moment and our awkward position on the front porch. That didn't stop him, though. He kissed me over and over, lingering, borderline lewd kisses that made me dizzy. The longer we kissed, the more I was convinced I would go up in flames. I moaned at the merciless exploration of his tongue. Instinctively I reached for his wrists, both still cupping my face, and I clung to him, thinking of no one but him, aware of no one but him.

I strained closer. I couldn't remember anything that had tasted this appealing or felt this exhilarating. He shook off my hold on one of his wrists and moved his hand down the side of my body. Then, as if he realized where this was going, his kisses slowed until he finally pulled away.

"What was that for?" I asked, a little stunned.

"You being you."

I rubbed a smudge of paint from his forehead. "So, do I get to see any of these paintings you're working on?"

He stood up and stretched his arms above his head, and I caught a little sliver of his golden skin. "When they're done. I hate sharing my work before I think it's ready."

"I guess that explains why you freaked out on

me the day you found me in your place looking at your art."

He made a sound in the back of his throat. "Yeah that, and I didn't know who the hell you were at first."

"Did you eat?" I asked, standing up and brushing the dirt from my jeans.

"Not really. What about you?"

"Nothing since this morning." At that exact moment, my stomach growled and I shrugged sheepishly.

He appeared to consider my statement for a second before frown lines appeared between his brows. "You need to take it easy. You don't have to force anything. You'll eventually learn what you need to know."

I winced. "Yeah, you're probably right. I guess that means I shouldn't tell you that I did some trick to induce the flashbacks after you left this morning."

His eyes widened. "Shit, Emma, I don't know if that's a good idea."

"I don't care. Right now, I'm just so damn lost, both emotionally and physically. I need clarity, and this thing I did today, well, it worked. I can't keep living in limbo, and not only with Elizabeth's story, but I've been in this limbo-like hell ever since Andrew got sick. The faster I can get to the point of this whole story, the faster it will be over and I can reclaim my life."

"It's not mutually exclusive. You can do what you want with your life. Elizabeth's life doesn't have to interfere with that. You can work on getting the bed and breakfast up and running. You can find a job. Whatever you want. You said money wasn't a motivating factor, so I take it you're covered for a while. But...I feel like you're on a path where you're refusing to let yourself be happy. I see glimpses of it here and there. So, all I'm saying is you need to try to treat yourself with more kindness. Enjoy the ride wherever it takes you."

I dipped my head, my throat closing in on itself. I didn't know if I remembered what it felt like to be carefree. Sometimes in the last few weeks, I felt a glimmer of that around Caleb, but then I defaulted to the same overarching sadness that had ruled my life for the last few years.

He put his arm around me. "Come on, I'm going to feed you."

I nodded feebly, and he led me inside my house. I wasn't sure I could move forward with the bed and breakfast plan anymore, much less live here. Instead of being this magical place, the house felt sad now, and I couldn't imagine planning my entire life around it. I would commit to figuring out the point of Elizabeth's story and how it related to me, but beyond that, I wouldn't make any plans.

Honestly, I wanted to ask Caleb if I could move into his place for the indefinite future until I could get over these feelings or decided to give up on this place entirely. That seemed a little presumptuous, especially since he didn't like to share his artwork.

"Sit here," Caleb said, pointing to a backless stool at the counter in the kitchen.

"I don't have much in the way of food."

"You have eggs?"

Yes."

"Cheese and maybe a vegetable or two?"

"More than likely."

"Then we're having breakfast for dinner."

Caleb was rummaging around in the refrigerator when the doorbell rang.

"You expecting someone?" he asked, his head popping out from behind the stainless steel door.

Chapter Thirty-Two

"Nope." I pushed back from the counter. "I'll be back in a minute."

I opened the door to Addison's big smile. "Hey stranger, I haven't seen you in a month of Sundays. Are ya gonna let me in or what?"

"Yeah. Yeah. Come in." I opened the door wider and she stepped inside, wearing another one of her crazy shirts. This time it said, 'world's okayest friend.' "What are you doing all the way out here?"

"Oh." She glanced at her scuffed up black Vans and rocked back on her heels. "I tried to call you all day and you didn't answer your phone, so I thought I'd stop by."

"Sorry about that. I was out exploring the property and I had my phone on silent."

"Not a big deal. Um, did you want to go somewhere and grab a bite to eat? We can go to my dad's diner or somewhere new. Anywhere but the bar."

My eyebrows pulled together. "Did something happen at the bar?" She let out a sob, and I pulled her into a hug. "Oh, shit, Addison, what happened?"

"I'm being stupid."

"Of course you're not. Does this have something to do with Josh?"

Her eyes flared. "How did you know that?"

"I was pretty drunk at the bar the other weekend, but I saw the way you were looking at him when we went to lunch the next day."

She rubbed the back of her hand across her cheek. "I just can't figure him out. I thought he was interested in me and now he's blown me off since that day at your house. I don't get it."

"Caleb is making dinner. Do you want to join us? You don't have to spill the whole story, but it might take your mind off things for a couple of hours. And I miss you."

"He's here? Right now?" Her lips barely moved, and I was kind of afraid she was going to run out the front door. For some reason, she froze up when Caleb was in the vicinity.

"Yes."

Her eyes turned to slits. "I think you have some stuff to tell me too. So, you know what that means?"

"A girls' night out in the not too distant future?"

A giant smile spread across her face, and I knew whatever came out of her mouth was something I didn't want anything to do with. "You're coming to church with me next Sunday."

"No way. That's not gonna happen. I'm not a big fan of that sort of thing these days."

With all the cursing I'd done at God over the past few years, I'd probably spontaneously combust the second I crossed the threshold. Between giving me a father who died, a mother who was a drunk, and killing off my husband way too soon, I still had a bone to pick with Him. He'd certainly given me the shaft more than once in this life. Then again, like Caleb suggested, I should probably relax and enjoy the ride. I'd carried my grief and resentment long enough, and I was tired.

She rolled her eyes. "Well, I'm not taking no for an answer. You owe me, and besides, it's the only way I can see Josh. He escorts his mom every Sunday and since he's ghosted me, I have no choice except to show up there."

"There's always the bar. That seems like the most logical place to talk to him."

"Nah. He'll be working, which won't make it easy to confront him, and knowing him, he'll ask to be switched to inventory the second he sees me."

"It's that bad, huh?"

"I didn't think so, but yeah, I'm not kidding about the ghosting thing. I don't understand why he does this."

"He's done this before?"

She nodded. "I don't want to get into it right now with Caleb right down the hall."

"Fine, but I vote you give him the middle finger and move on. Now come eat with us."

When we reached the kitchen, Caleb was standing in front of the sink cleaning the vegetables.

"I have an interesting theory about cooking for other people," he announced in the even tone of a person about to discuss something infinitely important.

211

"Oh, yeah." I grinned at Addison as I pointed to a stool at the island. "Go ahead. I'm all ears."

"It's really simple. If you don't help, you don't eat," he answered handing me a green pepper and a package of bacon.

"What about Addison? She needs somethin' to do too."

"Nah, she's our guest. She can entertain us while we cook. Isn't that how Southern hospitality works?"

"Ugh, I thought you were gonna do all the cooking, and I could relax. You know what? I'm regretting letting you step foot in my house. In fact, I changed my mind. You can fiddle with your paints for a couple more hours while Addison and I have some girl time."

His brows scrunched together like he was trying to remember something. "What do you Southerners say? Don't get your knickers in a knot. Come over and help me. It'll be fun."

I snagged a dish towel from the handle on the dishwasher and snapped it, landing a teasing smack on his shoulder.

"You two are cute, kind of like an old married couple," Addison said, propping her elbows on the counter, her eyes sparkling with mischief.

I swallowed hard, the ever-present guilt over Andrew settling around me like a cloud. It wasn't only Andrew that was bothering me, though. It was Elizabeth too. God, I was a wreck. Self-conscious, and trying desperately to act like everything was normal, I busied myself searching the drawer for the perfect knife to cut the pepper and the bacon.

Sensing the sudden tension, Addison slid back her stool and stood. "I gotta go to the bathroom. I'll be right back."

In a noncommittal voice, Caleb said, "Don't get stuck in your head. We're having a good time."

"People probably think I'm heartless for moving on."

"Noah and Lainey didn't have a problem with it," he pointed out. "Do you always worry about what other people are saying about you?"

"It's one of my countless faults. I think it stems from having a mother who was always the talk of the town and not in a good way."

"What's wrong with your mother?"

I raised an eyebrow at him. "What isn't wrong with her would be a better question."

He cracked the eggs one after another into a glass bowl. "Are you going to elaborate?"

"It's complicated, but I'll give you the quick rundown. It seems pretty clear she's bipolar, but instead of getting the help she needs, she drinks. Well, that's not entirely true. Sometimes she dabbles in other stuff too, but alcohol is her preferred poison. When my brother and I were growing up, she'd go through these phases where she was the perfect mom. And then, boom, she'd morph into something else altogether. She'd start drinking again. She'd lose her job. We wouldn't have any supervision or food for months on ends.

"The cycle still hasn't ended. My brother takes care of her now. I've been begging him to move closer to me for years, but he won't leave her to fend for herself. When Andrew showed up, it was

213

like God finally remembered I existed. I couldn't get out of there fast enough. I don't regret leaving even though I miss my brother every day."

He brushed a strand of hair away from my face. "I'm sorry."

"Sorry for what?" I whispered, mesmerized by the golden hue in his eyes.

"Sorry you had a shitty childhood. Sorry for not leaving you alone when I know you're still grieving. Sorry I can't stop thinking about you. Sorry for being pushy about sleeping at your house. Fuck, I don't know." He raked a hand through his hair. "Sorry for being so damn selfish that I won't walk away from you even if you ask me to."

I trailed a finger along his cheekbone down to his square jaw, and over his full lips. "Well. I'm sorry to render your ethical conundrum null and void because I'm not interested in letting you go either, Caleb. So, you better get over yourself."

He grinned. "Is that so?"

"Yep."

Addison's footsteps echoed down the hallway, suspiciously loud, almost like she wanted to announce her presence, and I was pretty sure she had been eavesdropping.

"What'd I miss?" she said as she entered the kitchen, her hands on her hips.

Caleb glanced at me, cocked an eyebrow, and we both burst out laughing.

Chapter Thirty-Three

That night I dreamed of Elizabeth again.

I set my fountain pen on my desk. Why did I continue writing Henry? I didn't have any idea where to send the letters. We hadn't heard anything about him for a while, and I was starting to lose hope he was still alive.

A hesitant knock sounded at the door. "Elizabeth, honey, are you in here?" Mama asked.

"Yes."

When I opened the door, my stomach pitched. Her eyes were red and her cheeks were flushed and Mr. Caldwell stood behind her.

"We would like to have a word with you."

I covered my mouth with a hand. There was only one reason he'd be here. Henry was gone.

"Miss Elizabeth." Mr. Caldwell removed his black hat. "I came here to inform you we received word last night that Henry has passed."

Everything he said after that was a blur. I shook my head back and forth, unable to believe I'd never

215

see Henry's face again. This couldn't be how our story ended. We were supposed to get married and grow old together. Finally, the bedroom door closed, leaving me alone with Mama.

"Lizzy, I know how close you were with Henry, but I'm here for you," Mama whispered.

"No," I screamed, crumpling the letter I was writing him into a ball and throwing it across the room.

Even though Henry was injured, I'd never wanted to believe he could actually die. He was the center of my life for as long as I could remember. My escape from Mama's nonstop criticism. He understood me in a way my family never had. Around him, I could be myself.

Desolation settled inside my chest as countless tears rolled down my face. It wasn't fair. I needed him to be alive. How could he be gone? I wasn't ready for him to die. We had plans. We had a life to live.

Mama pulled me into her arms. All my life I'd wanted her to show me affection, but now I felt lifeless, alone, and miserable. I didn't want to live without him.

"He's dead. He's really dead," I whispered when she released me.

She wrapped an ivory woolen blanket around my shoulders, and pressed a kiss to my forehead. "Don't cry. We all suspected he was gone for a while now."

"I know. It's just hard. Deep down, I feared he was gone, yet I wanted to be wrong. He deserved more than that. He was a good person. The best.

216

Even if he found someone else or changed his mind about being with me, I had hoped..."

"Shh. Why don't you take a nap and we'll talk later?"

"No. I need to take a walk."

"I don't think—"

I didn't wait to hear what she said. I ran out of my bedroom, down the stairs, and out the front door. I didn't realize where I was going until I flung open the door to the cabin.

"Elizabeth, what happened?" Charles questioned, surely noticing my state of disarray.

"Henry's dead," I blurted out.

Through the glow of candlelight, his serious eyes met mine and a tormented understanding crackled between us. Words weren't needed. While we were on different sides of war, we both had experienced more hardship and grief than someone our age should. Over the last three years, we'd lost people we loved. Loss and grief had become the rule, not the exception.

"I'd hate to leave you now that we know for sure he's gone. I suspect your mama isn't up to the task of looking after you, but I can't stick around for long. I need to pull foot and join back up with the Union."

"I know." I chewed on the inside of my lower lip. "I'm scared. I don't want something to happen to you too. My family would think I'm crazy as a loon, but you've become my friend."

"That's why people call this the war of brothers. This war happened because the South rejected the inescapable changes happening in the country, but

217

we aren't really enemies. We're just caught on opposite sides of a country."

"Perhaps. I remember when this all started and everyone was saying it'd be over in ninety days. Well, it's been over three years now. I just want it to end. I can't stand it anymore. I want to be far away from here where the pain and loss can no longer find me."

"You can come with me. I know I asked you before and you refused, but now that Henry's gone, there's no reason for you to stay. I'd make the move as easy as possible on you. It might help to be somewhere new. I could even help you find your cousin in New Hampshire. You could stay with her."

Heat flooded my cheeks and warmed my ears. "I can't."

A wave of sadness struck me hard, nearly taking me to my knees. I needed to get away from him. Everyone really. I took off running, not bothering to shut the door of the ramshackle cabin behind me. I could hear Charles' heavy footsteps behind me. My eyes burning with tears and clasping my side against the pain both physical and emotional, I fell to my knees.

Charles crouched next to me and I sprawled out on my back. "I didn't mean to upset you. I know I can't replace Henry, but I am fond of you and maybe in time you'll feel the same way."

When I opened my mouth to reject him, he pressed two fingers to my lips. "You don't have to make a decision now. Think about it. It won't hurt to stay a few more weeks."

I wiped my face with the back of my hand. "I won't change my mind. I can't leave everything I've ever known. What would Mama do?"

"Let's talk about it later." He scooped me up, carried me back into the cabin, and placed me on his narrow cot. "Rest."

"I can't. Mama will—" I tried to sit up, but he gently pushed me back down.

"I'll wake you up in an hour."

I stared at him, my common-sense warring with the need to escape for a while. Mama, she loved me. I didn't doubt that. Not for one second, but she couldn't be there for me. She was caught up in her own grief.

My mind made up, I nodded, rolled over, and closed my eyes. He ran his fingers repeatedly through my hair. I could sense sleep coming, roaring toward me like a shadowy tide of nothingness. I embraced it, badly needing the peace that came with unconsciousness. My eyelids were too heavy to remain open a second longer, and within minutes, I succumbed.

Chapter Thirty-Four

When I woke up the next morning, tears still stained my cheeks, and my heart was heavy with grief for Elizabeth. I rolled over, searching for Caleb. He was pulling on his clothes.

"Rough night?" he asked, likely noticing my red, puffy face.

"Yes." The second the words left my mouth my silent tears morphed into loud sobs. He immediately pulled me into his arms. He didn't ask what happened and I knew he wouldn't. He never pushed.

When my weeping eased into weak whimpers, I raised my head. He stared down at me with so much care and understanding, the tightness in my chest lessened.

"I dreamed about the day Elizabeth found out that Henry had died," I whispered.

He brushed the hair from my face tucked it behind her ears. "I'm sorry, Em."

"Just hold me a little longer please," I replied.

I shifted onto his lap until I was straddling him.

His hands dropped to my waist.

"Caleb?"

"Yes?"

"Thanks for being here for me. I don't know why you're so understanding, but I appreciate it. More than I could ever express. I don't know what I'd do if I had to do this alone. And not just this. Andrew's death too. You saved me."

He kissed the tip of my nose and took my face in his hands, and I realized I was trembling. For endless heartbeats we silently gazed at each other, his irises glimmering in the morning light. I didn't know what twist of fate brought him into my life, but I was grateful. So damn grateful. It was like the universe knew I was drowning and it threw me a lifeline.

"I wouldn't want to be anywhere else. We're right where we need to be."

My muscles relaxed, and so did my soul. His words brought me the peace and serenity I'd been missing since I woke up. Despite everything Elizabeth and I had lost, despite all the ways my life had unraveled, we truly had each other and that made up for all of the heartache and disappointment.

"I'm starting to believe you're right."

He set me on my feet and got up. "Maybe you should go into town today and meet up with Addison. You could use a break."

"I'll think about it," I said instead of making any promises.

The mystery of Elizabeth's life was driving me crazy. I needed to understand why this was happening to me, and I didn't like the idea of hiding from something that seemed inevitable. To truly move forward, I had to put this behind me.

After Caleb left, I roamed the house, trying to figure out what I was missing and what I needed to know or understand about Elizabeth's life. While my location seemed to trigger the flashback and what part of the story I saw, I wished they came in chronological order instead so it'd be easier to put the pieces together.

I knew Elizabeth loved Henry. I knew her parents asked her to delay their marriage. I knew Henry died before she ever had the chance to see him again. I understood why she helped Charles. I knew her mother wanted her to marry Henry's brother, but Elizabeth despised him. Her mother knew that, but she didn't care. From what I learned, her mother didn't really understand her at all.

Unlike yesterday, I decided to start in the kitchen and see what I could discover about Elizabeth's home life. Clearly, she had issues with her mother. I wanted to understand more about it.

My mind made up, I placed the candle on the kitchen counter, and stared into it until my vision blurred. Less than ten minutes later, blood started drumming loudly inside of my ears, and everything around me faded.

"Miz Elizabeth," Axie said as I entered the kitchen through the back door. "Yer mama's in de parlor. And Mistah Brett's with her. I don't know why he's here, but she wants you to join them."

I smoothed my high-necked gown of blue muslin.

"Apparently she failed to tell you, Axie. My mama plans to get me out of her hair once and for all."

"Huh?" Axie pursed her lips.

"She wants me to marry Brett."

Axie gawked, her dark eyes wide. "But Mistah Henry—"

"Is dead," I finished, my gut rolling, and I pressed a hand to my stomach. Saying those words still made me sick with regret and longing. This war and my parents' refusal to let me marry him before he left had robbed me of my future.

"Ain't dat quick."

"Too quick," I mumbled.

She grabbed my hand. "I gots somethin' to tell ya. Come find me when dat man is don gone. It's 'bout dat Yankee."

I nodded, and with reluctant feet, I strolled toward the parlor.

"Mama, Brett. I'm sorry if I kept you waiting. I was checking on my horse." I bowed my head and sat in the large, overstuffed chair, the farthest from Brett. I had successfully avoided him since he had returned by pleading sickness more than once. Apparently, Mama had tired of my antics and decided to ambush me.

"Elizabeth, you look lovely," Brett said, a pleasant enough smile on his face. It still didn't bring me any closer to trusting him. His injury may have softened him, but I suspected the old Brett was still lurking inside.

"Thank you, Brett. You look well. I take it you've adjusted to being home."

Brett heaved a long sigh. "Somewhat. It's been

hard adapting to having one hand."

My gaze darted to his left hand and then quickly back to his face. The cuff of his coat was conspicuously empty. Not wanting to be rude despite all the cruelties he subjected me to as a child, I schooled my features. *"Understandably so. I hope it doesn't pain you."*

"Not too much," he answered, angling his body so I couldn't see his injury without moving. *"Thank you for asking."*

Mama rose and adjusted her yellow taffeta dress. *"If you will excuse me, I need to check on the refreshments."*

My temper flared at her blatant attempt to leave us alone, but I managed to keep the smile on my face, refusing to give her additional reasons to lash out at me. *"How nice of you to come visit with my mother. She's had a hard time of it since Pa died."*

"I didn't come to see her. I've been wanting to talk to you."

"Oh?"

"With Henry gone, I know your mother has broached the subject of the two of us marrying. While I've heard you aren't entirely amenable to the idea, I'd like you to reconsider. It seems to me, Elizabeth, that you rejected the idea out of your loyalty to Henry."

"Henry may have had something to do with it, but I listened to all of Mama's reasons for the match, and simply do not believe we are compatible. You've made it very clear over the years that you do not like me, and while I am not naïve enough to believe I will find love again, I do

224

think some degree of affection is necessary to make a marriage work."

Axie entered the parlor carrying tea service along with some sweet breads and cold meats. Neither of us spoke while she set up the table, which suited me perfectly. While I trusted Axie, I didn't believe for one second that Mama didn't send her in here at this exact moment so she could report everything I said.

Brett leaned forward in his chair, frowning. "My behavior did not accurately reflect my feelings for you. I have always held a certain fondness for you, but I tried to discount it because Henry had claimed you as his, and I didn't want him to suspect I had feelings for you as well."

"No." I shook my head wildly. "I do not believe it."

"Why is it so hard to believe me, Elizabeth? You are by far the most beautiful woman in the county."

I stared at his face, trying to decipher if his words held any truth or maybe to find some resemblance to Henry. While his words were pretty enough, I didn't believe him, and even if he did have a certain fondness for me, I didn't feel the same. Far from it. He'd taunted and tortured me every chance he'd got right up to the day he left for the war. I'd never forget how he stopped by the house to drop something off for his mother and he'd told me if Henry had any sense he'd break off the engagement and find someone worthier.

I searched my brain for a logical way to refuse him without angering Mama, but nothing came to mind. The only thing I could offer was honesty.

"I'm sorry, Brett. I cannot accept your offer. I don't return your feelings."

The muscles in his neck corded and his cheeks flushed. This was more in line with the Brett I remembered. *"I doubt that you have taken the time to reflect on the full depth of your family's predicament. Without the benefit of a man to guide the business of your planation, you and your mother will be in dire straits."*

I lifted my chin. *"We will manage just fine. Thank you."*

I knew this wasn't true. Many of our farm animals had been lost or stolen during the war. With most of our labor gone and the embargos, we hadn't seen much return on our investment. Mama hadn't offered any details, but I could see the decay of our home since Pa left.

As he stood up preparing to leave, he tossed an envelope on the table. *"This letter came to my family yesterday addressed to you. It was in Henry's personal effects."*

My eyes beginning to water, I snatched up the envelope and clutched it to my chest. *"I thank you kindly for bringing it by. And Brett, I'm really sorry I cannot accept your proposal. If I have hurt you, please forgive me. It was not my intention. I haven't been in the right state of mind since I learned of Henry's death."*

He picked up his top hat by the brim and held it next to his side, tapping it rhythmically against his thigh. *"I understand that so I'll overlook your rash refusal for the time being. Just remember, it was your father's dearest wish that our families would unite. For that reason, I will leave my offer open for a few days should you reconsider. When you think upon all the hardship and losses our families have endured, I'm sure you will come to the correct conclusion and do the right thing. There isn't a feasible alternative. I'll see myself out."*

When the front door slammed behind him, I knew my reprieve wouldn't last long, and I was right. Mama stormed in the parlor, her shoes banging like cannons against the hardwood floor. She halted in front of my chair, her nose flaring, her eyes wild. She drew back an arm and slapped me across the face.

My face stung and throbbed, making my heart race. The metallic taste of blood coated my tongue. I clamped my teeth together and glared my disgust through the sudden hopelessness threatening to consume me. "What in Sam Hill is wrong with you? How dare you lay a finger on me after everything I've done to keep this house together while you drank yourself silly."

"Nonsense. What I do is none of your concern."

"You're revolting. I don't have to listen to you."

"You don't have a choice." She grabbed my arm, yanking it hard. "Did you honestly think it was a good idea to send away Brett like that? What will his family think of the way you have treated him since he returned? He's a hero."

"That you embarrassed us both by persisting with this madness. I don't want to marry him, Mama. He's a bad man. You might be happy to whitewash his faults, but I won't do the same. I will never marry him. I don't care what you say."

227

"Great God! This has gone on long enough. Your penchant for recklessness and irresponsibility continues to surpass your common sense. So, hear me now, you will marry Brett and you will do it with all due haste. I will not broker anymore of this nonsense. I don't care if you dislike that man because without him, we will be destitute and unprotected.

"Why, Sherman's army has already taken Atlanta and the opinion is gaining ground that they're heading our way. He cast out all of the women and children living in Atlanta without much more than the clothes on their backs. Then they burned most of it to the ground.

"You can act right huffy about this marriage all you want. I don't care. You will marry Brett in no more than a day or two hence with a smile on your face and gratitude pouring from your wicked heart."

I couldn't speak. My throat was thick with pent-up cries. If she had any more agony to pile on me, she stopped herself from continuing and moseyed out of the room as if she weren't attempting to ruin my life.

Stunned with the events of the last hour and the tales of the Union army, I stared out the window. The dying sunset poured through the glass, bathing everything in a golden hue. The house purred with silence, almost as if the last hour hadn't happened.

I could tell from the tone of her voice that she had no intention of letting this go. She was singularly focused on me marrying Henry's brother, and I'd never willingly concede. My mind scrambled for a way out of this folly, and the only solution I could come up with was to run away with Charles. It wouldn't be easy leaving everything and everyone I knew behind, but Mama had forced my hand. If my choice were between living a life chained to Brett and running away with Charles and living in a place where I might never be accepted, I'd choose the latter.

My mind made up, I tucked Henry's letter into the waistband of my skirt, tip-toed out of the parlor, and out the front door.

Chapter Thirty-Five

"*Charles? Charles?*" *I yelled, flinging open the door to the cabin, the weather-worn hinges groaning in protest.*

He sat on the edge of the cot, thumbing through another book I had loaned him from my personal stash. Today, he wore some of my brother's old clothes. They didn't fit him well. The pants were too short, the shirt too baggy around the waist, but they were better than the worn uniform he'd been wearing since I met him.

"*Madam.*" *He smiled. "To what do I owe this pleasure?*"

I carefully shut the door behind me and leaned against it, not sure how to broach the topic I had in mind. While he'd offered to take me with him on more than one occasion, I'd be a burden. I wouldn't be able to travel at the same pace as him. I had no clue about the world beyond the boundaries of my small town other than what I'd read in books. From my cousin's letters, I knew the Northerners didn't like Southerners.

"I changed my mind." I paused, chewing on my lower lip. "I want to go with you. I can't stay here any longer."

He frowned. "What's going on?"

I shrugged, not sure how to explain that I didn't want to marry Brett without making it seem like I was only choosing him because mama had forced my hand. Then again, starting a life with him, if that's what he wanted, based on lies wouldn't be helpful to either of us.

"Mama is going to force me to marry Henry's brother. I can't do it. I know this isn't the most auspicious way to start our journey, but I don't have the luxury of waiting around any longer." The second the words left my mouth, I felt as if I had hopelessly bungled my proposition. "That is, if the invitation is still open."

Charles stood and wrapped me in a tight hug. "God almighty, I was certain I'd be leaving this place without you. I know you'll never stop loving Henry, but if you give me the chance, I know I can make you happy."

I placed my hand on his lightly bearded cheek. "I think so too. And I'm ready to make a new life away from this place. I thought I needed to stay for Mama, but she'll never forgive me if I don't marry Brett, and I fear she won't allow me to refuse him anyway."

"I don't know her, yet I suspect you're right." He chuckled, his eyes filled with hope. "Elizabeth, I thought I'd died and you were an angel when I saw you by that creek. I was still alive, but you were definitely my angel with how you nursed me back to

231

health, sheltered me, and now I'm gonna return the favor by helping you."

I lifted my hands, and rested them on his chest while I peered up at him. "What are we gonna do, Charles? When will we leave?"

He pushed my hair away from my forehead. "Pack your valise. You should grab anything you have of value and we'll need some food. Will two days be long enough for you to put everything in order?"

A ripple of fear zipped through me. I didn't have two days. Hell, I wasn't sure I had more than a few hours. "I can be ready by nightfall. I don't want to stay any longer than absolutely necessary. I don't trust Mama or Brett."

He pressed a kiss to my cheek. "Tonight, then."

"Wait. We have so much to figure out. Where will we live—"

"I suspect we'll live on the farm with my family in New Hampshire in the beginning. Even with your unmistakably Southern accent, my parents will love you. We'll build our own home, though. Everything will be fine. I can tell you everything about my home on the journey. We'll have time."

"Okay. I need to get back. Someone might come looking for me," I said, finally feeling a little more optimistic about the future.

I opened the door to the cabin and folded my arms against the brisk early December breeze.

Brett appeared from around the side of the cabin. A scream ripped from my lips. Charles ran outside and placed himself between Brett and me.

A sardonic smile spread across Brett's lips.

232

"Your mama mentioned you were always roaming the property by yourself, and now I understand why. You've been throwing yourself at this damn bluebelly. What would your precious Henry think of you now, trailing after one of his murderers like a strumpet?"

He lifted a cap and ball pistol and cocked it, the clicking noise more threatening than anything I'd ever heard in all my born days. Brett scowled at us with such loathing and rage that the gun shook in his hand. Immobile and mute with disbelief, I stood stock still, my eyes wide and my heart pumping frantically.

Charles didn't hesitate. He shoved me to the ground and dove shoulder first into Brett. The air burst from Brett's lungs in a grunt. Their bodies flew backward. When they hit the ground, the crack of the gun rang in my ears. Smoke from the gunshot burned my nostrils.

Smelling the metallic scent of blood, I clambered to my knees. Charles'? Or Brett's? Charles lay sprawled out on top of Brett, unmoving. I heard a groan and Charles rolled off Brett, leaving him splayed out on the ground, except he wasn't moving much. Blood spread out from his shoulder, turning his white shirt almost black near the sleeve.

I crawled to his side, his dark eyes held mine, blinking slowly. I cupped his face, my stomach swimming with regret. If these past years taught me anything, it was life was fragile. I couldn't lose him too. "Charles, I'm so sorry. This is my fault. I should've forced you to go weeks ago."

"Not your fault," he grumbled, wincing with

pain.

I didn't even get a chance to respond before Brett yanked me by my hair and pulled me to my feet. My scalp burned.

"No," I screamed, tears dripping off my chin. "Please. Let me help him." I tried to turn my head over and over to see if Charles was dead. Brett kicked me in the leg every time.

"Wave goodbye to your Yankee because you'll never see him again."

"Please. I don't care what happens to me. Just let me help him, and I'll do whatever you want. I'll marry you tonight if you let me help him. Is that what you want?"

"Shut your mouth. Everything that comes out of it is a lie."

My heart sped up, and I swung my fists and kicked my legs, desperately attempting to land a blow on any part of his body. He used his hold on my hair to drag me toward my house. I dug my fingernails in his hand, trying to force him to release me.

His temper escalated to a full boil. Filthy words I'd rarely heard spilled from his lips like poison while he continued to yank my hair harder and harder. My mind and emotions detached from the violence swirling around me like a hurricane. Numb, I wondered if he'd kill me now. Part of me didn't care either way. With Henry gone and causing Charles to be injured or killed, it didn't matter one way or another. No, I wanted to die, especially if it meant I could escape marrying this monster.

Mama flung open the door the second we reached the porch. Her face was fiery red, an almost comical contrast from her faded blonde hair.

"Please help me," I said, my voice a strained whisper.

Brett's low, unnerving chuckle sent a spike of fear down my spine. "She's not gonna help you. Who do you think suggested I watch to see where you were going? I'm not surprised you were sneaking out to meet a Yankee all this time."

"Really, Mama? Why would you let him treat me like this? Do you hate me so much?"

"Escort her to her room," she barked without acknowledging my question.

Brett finally released my hair, and I fell to my knees. "Walk!" he shouted, his face scrunched up, his jaw grinding side to side.

When I didn't move, he kicked me in the ribs and pain exploded on my side. I could hardly suck a breath into my chest.

I pushed to my feet, swaying like a rag doll, my mind blank except for the pain throbbing in my body. Barely able to see through my tears, I stumbled up the stairs. Once I reached my bedroom, I crumpled into a ball at the foot of my bed, glaring at Mama, who stood at the door, hands on the waist of her yellow gown.

"Don't look at me like that. You have no one to blame but yourself and your obstinate refusal to obey me." She shook her head, her lips turning downward. "To think my own daughter is a traitor."

"The war is lost. You know it. I know it.

Everyone knows it. Our lands are devastated, so many homes and businesses burned, and our money is gone. You admitted as much. Soon the union soldiers will show up at our home, and if we're lucky, they will quarter here rather than burn it down. I refuse to make matters worse by marrying Brett and fantasizing the war can be won. No, this war was lost from the start, and clinging to the idea that my marriage to Brett will save us from ruination is lunacy. Brett has a hot temper and he lacks honor. He's not the right person to help us."

"You're still spoiling for a fight, I see. Even now when your treachery has been exposed, you're still trying to justify your actions."

"Please, Mama," I begged, not even knowing what I wanted her to do. I wouldn't find any sympathy or compassion from her. Any love she had for me died along with Pa, or maybe she never loved me in the first place. My brother had always been her favorite and with him in London, she didn't have anyone to talk sense to her.

"I don't want to hear it. You will stay in this room until I come and get you when the reverend arrives to marry you and Brett tomorrow morning. If you make any more trouble for me, you'll regret it. Your pa was too lenient with you, but all of that ends now."

"How could you do this? He'll destroy me and you're helping him do it," I screamed.

"You left me no choice."

When the door slammed, I heard the key turn in the lock from the outside. Short of jumping out of the window, I had no way to escape. Humiliation and defeat spread through me.

I swallowed hard and stretched out onto my side, cradling my sore ribs. I heard the front door open and slam several times. I prayed and prayed that Charles wasn't hurt too bad and he would find a way to escape this hell. Maybe Axie would get wind of what happened and help him.

Chapter Thirty-Six

After too many hours to count, I sat up and tenderly poked at my ribs. Each touch sent sparks of flames shooting through my side. Hunger gnawed at my insides, but maybe starvation would be a better fate than marrying Brett and living a lifetime with that monster.

Slowly, I slid off my clothes, needing to change into something looser. The envelope from Henry tumbled to the ground. I picked it up and stared at it for so long, the letters in my name blurred together. Instead of opening it, I sought out my hiding place in the floorboards beneath the armoire. I couldn't read it right now when my life was falling apart, and I didn't want to taint what I had with Henry by the events of today.

Just as I replaced the floorboards, a key turned in the lock. Axie stood at the threshold with a tray. Seeing her, I broke down into tears. She set the tray on my bed and gathered me into her arms.

"Shh now, chile. Yer mammy asked me to bring you some powders so you can sleep. I just don't

*know what to do. She is ravin' about you keepin'
that Yankee in the cabin."*

*"And Charles, the Yankee? What happened to
him?"*

*Axie released me and fiddled with her apron. "I
patched him up and sent him on his way. I told him
to be careful Mistah Brett don't find 'em. He
wanted to come after you, but I told him don't stop
fo' nothin'. I'd take care of you. He gave me dis."*

*She reached into her apron pocket and handed
me the last book I'd been reading him. I cracked the
cover and saw an address along with a hastily
written note to come find him after the war ended. A
crippling sadness flooded me, and I grabbed the
frame of my bed to keep myself from falling to my
knees. If Mama had her way, I'd be married to Brett
tomorrow. I hated him and Mama both. I truly did.*

*"I've gotta get out of here. Will you help me,
Axie?"*

*"Miz Elizabeth—" she started in an
apprehensive tone, but I interrupted.*

*"You have to help me. Brett will kill me. I just
know it. He's evil."*

*"I'm gonna be in a fine bit of trouble if I help
you and not jest from yer mammy. If Mistah Brett
ketches us, I ain' gonna be no better off'n that
Yankee of yers. I can't help you no more."*

*"I'm sorry for asking, Axie." I sagged with
defeat. I wanted to be angry with her, but I couldn't.
She was right. Brett would kill her if he discovered
her betrayal and I couldn't stand the thought of any
harm coming to her. Other than Henry, she'd been
my only other true friend and I loved her.*

239

She lit the lone kerosene lamp on top of my bureau. "Take the powder and sleep, Miz Elizabeth. Yer bound to feel better in the mornin'."

"You're probably right," I mumbled, not believing the words. I'd never felt more alone in my life.

As if she sensed my despair and couldn't witness it, she lowered her eyes. "I tried to tell you dat they knew 'bout dat Yankee, but you left 'fore I could warn you."

Without saying anything else, she left the room, locking the door behind her. I opened my window and leaned against the sill. The scent of pine trees was weighty in the air. Below was a thick, foreboding hedge. I'd never survive the fall unscathed, especially with my ribs aching like the devil. A branch of the tree where Henry asked me to marry him nearly reached my window, but it wasn't close enough. I drew in a long breath, trying to calm my nerves so I could come up with a plan.

When I shut my eyes, tears flowed freely down my cheeks. In the past few minutes, the air had grown thicker, hinting at yet another coming storm. I should probably shut the window or at least the shutters, but I couldn't find it in myself to care if the rain poured into my window and damaged the floor. I was out of time and options. Barring divine intervention, I'd be Brett's wife before the end of the day tomorrow.

I fell to my knees, my head resting against the windowsill. Lord, my Savior, please intercede on my behalf and stop this wedding from happening. I promise I'll—

An incessant ringing filled my ears and my body swayed. The next thing I knew I was back in the present day, on my knees next to the open window in my bedroom. Salty tears stained my cheeks. My knees ached, and I wondered how long I had kneeled on the hardwood floors. The lace curtains fluttered in the breeze and noticed that the daylight had faded to dusk.

I looked around the room, taking in the differences between now and during Elizabeth's life. A wave a nausea hit me when I realized the bureau was the same. The fireplace mantle was painted white rather than natural wood, but it had the same intricate swirls.

"Oh, God," I mumbled to myself. I stood up and slammed the window. The glass rattled in the panes. There was no way in hell I could stay in this room or this house. I didn't want to know what happened to Elizabeth. She'd already lost Henry, and I couldn't stomach it if she woke up the next morning only to marry Brett. No. I didn't want to know how her story ended.

Chapter Thirty-Seven

I grabbed a duffle bag from the top of the closet and stuffed as many clothes as I could inside. I made a quick trip to the bathroom to load up my toiletries, not even paying attention to whether I had everything I needed. It didn't matter. I could buy whatever I left behind. Getting away from here was the only thing I cared about.

Maybe the emotions rolling through me had more to do with the desperation Elizabeth felt awaiting her fate than my need to escape, almost like an emotional hangover. Either way, I refused to stick around long enough to process which feelings belonged to her or me. The house that had once bewitched me now felt eerie and unnaturally quiet.

Fearful something might trigger another flashback, I didn't let my eyes linger on anything in particular as I fled the house. I got in my truck and headed toward the gates. I had no clue if I planned to drive all the way back to Atlanta or stop at the nearest hotel. Nora would welcome me into her house for a couple of days, no questions asked, or I could reach out to Lainey. Nothing had to be decided right now. When I pressed the button to open the scrolling iron gates, a wave of guilt hit me.

"Fuck!" Squeezing my eyes, I banged my fist on the steering wheel. If I ran, I might escape Elizabeth's memories. If I ran, I might be able to stop thinking about her. But I couldn't leave without telling Caleb. He'd freak if he came to the house tonight and found me gone. I turned the truck around and headed to the barn.

I banged on the wooden door to the barn five times in quick succession. "Caleb. Caleb," I shouted, my hands shaking from the electric energy humming through my body.

He opened the door, looking tired and disheveled. His dark hair was sticking up and it was feathered with paint again. A pang of longing rippled through me so intense I rubbed the center of my chest. "I'm leaving. I can't stay here."

He frowned. "Wait. What? Slow down. Come in and talk to me."

"No." I shook my head from side to side. I didn't have time. I needed to get out of here before the flashbacks pulled me back into *her* world. "I need to get away from here tonight. I can't explain everything right now, but I don't want to have any more flashbacks. I'm done with this. I don't want to know what happens to Elizabeth."

"Wait. Slow down. Why do you want to leave?"

Warm water dropped from my chin and splashed against my shirt. I rubbed at my face but it was useless. Tears were spilling down my cheeks. Jesus, I hadn't even noticed I was crying.

243

"Because what's coming is bad, and I don't want to experience it. I can't." My entire body wilted at the truth of my words.

Our eyes locked for the slowest of seconds. Then tenderly, his thumbs brushed across my tear-stained cheeks.

"Okay, but I'm coming with you. Wait in the car. I need to clean up and grab a few things."

Since I'd left Elizabeth's life and found myself on my knees in my bedroom, I'd had an unbearably tight knot in my chest making it hard for me to breathe. Now, as I stood on Caleb's doorstep with him offering to come with me, the sensation lessened a little bit.

"Really? You want to come with me? What about your work deadlines?"

He ducked his head, studying me closely. And then, goddamn. He kissed the tip of my nose, and I trembled down to the tips of my toes with the familiarity of the action. It was almost as if he'd done the same thing hundreds of times.

"They can wait. You can't."

I went back to my truck, anxiously waiting his return. Everything around me felt overly loud and vivid. I turned off the radio, hating the way it buzzed in my ears. The interior lights glowed ominously. I tapped my fingers on the steering wheel and bounced my leg.

"Hurry up," I mumbled even though it hadn't been more than a few minutes. But damn it, I felt like I had this invisible ticking time bomb strapped to my chest. I rested my head against the seat and closed my eyes, concentrating on evening out my inhalations and exhalations.

The driver's side door opened after a few minutes.

"Let me drive," Caleb said.

Without complaint, I climbed over the center console and into the passenger seat. Caleb tossed a small backpack behind the front seats, and drove away from the barn and through the gates of my property.

After he'd been driving for ten minutes, I realized we hadn't discussed any destination. "Where are we going?"

"There's a small island off the coast where I go to think. Tybee Island." He glanced at me and turned back to the road. "Have you been there?"

"No. Do you want me to search for a hotel on my phone?"

He scratched the underside of his jawline. "No. I have a small home there not too far from the beach. It's nothing special, but it's a good place to get away for a couple days."

"Wait." I frowned. "I was under the impression you didn't have anywhere to go when I told you to leave."

He glanced at me, his smirk and his eyes full of mischief. "I might have stretched the truth. But in my defense, the house is tiny and the light sucks. I never paint there. It's my retreat from the art world and life in general. I go there to think, not work."

"I should be mad at you, but I can't. I'm glad you stayed."

He reached across the console and squeezed my thigh. "I'm glad too."

When we finally made it to his house, it was exactly as he described. Tiny, but I loved it. The seafoam green house with crisp white trim sat on cedar stilts. I could hear the slow lapping of the waves in the not too far distance. The air was salty and warm.

I sucked in a deep breath as we climbed up the outdoor stairs, and my muscles finally relaxed for the first time in hours. The flashbacks had been taking more of a toll on me than I'd realized. This home felt like the reprieve I needed. I could see why Caleb liked it here.

When he opened the front door, I fell a little bit in love with his home. It had white shiplap walls, greyish hardwood floors, and a tiny white kitchen with marble countertops. Two stools bookended the pint-sized island. The family room consisted of a navy loveseat, one wooden side chair, and a round natural rattan coffee table. The only bedroom didn't accommodate much more than a queen bed and one nightstand. A large rectangular window spanned the opposite wall. Caleb was right. He didn't have any room to set up an art studio, much less paint, without getting rid of all the furniture.

Caleb set our bags on the floor at the foot of the bed. "It's not much and we might go stir crazy in a couple days if the weather is shitty, but it's not anything like your house."

"It's perfect." I studied the tapestry hanging above the bed. "I don't see any of your artwork in here.

"No. Like I said, this is my retreat. I don't want to look at my work while I'm trying to unwind. I'd get caught up in critiquing it, and I might as well be working."

"Yeah. I get it. Speaking of retreats, I don't want to talk about..." I froze, not wanting to say Elizabeth's name, afraid I'd inadvertently trigger a flashback.

"I get it," he said, thankfully not forcing me to elaborate. "While we're here, none of that matters."

Yawning, I flopped backward on the bed. "I can't keep my eyes open."

"Go ahead and sleep. I'm going to run into town to see if I can grab some food and coffee for the morning."

I closed my eyes and nodded, sleep already calling me.

Chapter Thirty-Eight

Sunlight streamed through the window and the sound of birds chirping filled the room. I actually felt well-rested. I didn't have a single dream or one that I remembered anyway. It felt good to be normal. I grinned and settled even further into the soft sheets. Ordinarily, when I woke up, I didn't waste any time relaxing in bed.

My entire life I had things to do. As a teen, I started working at the local restaurant, first bussing tables and working my way up to waitress. Once I married Andrew, I had my studies, and then caretaker duties when he became too sick to take care of himself. Today, I decided I wouldn't move from this bed until it was absolutely necessary, and then only to walk along the beach. It'd been so long since I'd seen the ocean.

I rolled onto my side and came face to face with a sleeping Caleb. My smile spread even wider. The way he dropped everything yesterday and put my needs first...it took my breath away. I ran my hand along his face, following the sharp angle of his jaw.

248

His stubble prickled the pads of my fingers. His lips were soft yet firm to the touch and his long lashes shadowed the top of his cheekbones.

As gently as possible, I kissed him. Caleb's entry into my life was an unexpected curveball. When Andrew died, I never thought I'd find someone to love again, who made my world spin and my stomach flutter. As the thought passed through my head, I froze, acknowledging the truth of it.

Oh God, I loved Caleb.

I inched closer him until I could feel his warmth melting into me. I didn't know why fate had given me a second chance at life and love, but I had no intention of throwing it away. While Caleb and Andrew were nothing alike, I found myself drawn to Caleb in ways I couldn't explain. I loved how he took care of me even when I fought with him. I loved how he didn't blink when I shared all the crazy things happening to me. I loved his creativity, though I wished I'd paid more attention to his work the first day I met him. He'd been so secretive about it ever since, even going so far as to move it to the loft, and always meeting me at my house instead of his.

His eyes popped open, and almost like an automatic reflex, his arms circled me, molding his body to mine. My breath stalled mid-inhalation. Butterflies swirled in my stomach. With his languid gaze and his wild dark hair, he looked more stunning than normal and that said a lot, because he always looked good. He nuzzled my neck and dropped a kiss on the tip of my nose. The feeling I got when he did that was beyond anything I could explain.

I inched closer to him. "Good morning."

"Mornin'."

He rolled on top of me, wedging his hips between my thighs. His eyes were like sunbursts. All of the pent-up desire of sharing a bed for the last week or so made me feel like I would lose my mind if he kept holding back. Okay, who was I kidding? I'd lost my mind a long time ago.

"Caleb," I entreated, running my hands up the ridges of his abs and finally looping them over his bare shoulders.

He brushed my hair away from my face. "Yes, Emma."

"I want you."

He laughed softly. "We talked about this. Not until this thing with Eliz—"

I slapped a hand over his mouth. Didn't he get it? I couldn't care less about any of that, at least right then. I wanted to be impulsive and irresponsible and not worry about what would happen tomorrow or the next day. Time wasn't always on my side and I didn't want to waste any of it.

"We said we wouldn't talk about that. For all intents and purposes, she doesn't exist while we're in this house. This is about you and me. Caleb and Emma. Nobody else matters. I need to live in this moment, not a century and a half ago, not last year, not ten years ago. Now."

"Emma." He drew out my name. "I don't want to complicate an already complicated situation by taking advantage of you."

I punched him in the shoulder. "Stop trying to be so fucking noble. You're not taking advantage me. In fact, I'm pretty sure it's me who's trying to take advantage of you."

"I think I might like this feisty version of you." He started to roll off me and I held him tighter.

"Come on. You're really pissing me off right now."

He feigned confusion. "Me? Piss you off? When has that ever happened?"

"I want this. You want this. No more holding back. No more games, okay?"

After a few seconds that felt like hours, he nodded, and my breath whooshed out of my lungs. I couldn't believe he was giving in so easily. I didn't have time to gloat over my victory because he dipped his head, tasting my mouth. His kiss was gentle at first, but it quickly went wild. His hands brushed along my arms, my hips, my chest, seeming to be everywhere at once. His lips moved down my neck as his hands worked my shirt over my head, revealing my breasts.

He alternated between running his tongue over the soft swells and nipping at them, and then using his tongue to soothe it gently. I cried out and threaded my hands in his hair. A torrent of emotion sparked inside me: exhilaration, apprehension, happiness, and fear. Fear because there was no guilt or regret, only elation. Waves of pleasure rolled through me.

I felt his smirk against my skin as he slipped one hand inside my panties. I was already wet, but when he stroked me softly, his smile was supplanted with

251

a growl. Then he yanked my panties from my legs.

My body arched, resenting the second of cool air when he temporarily lifted his body from mine. He shoved my thighs apart. I paused to commit the raw need on his face to memory. His fingers slid inside of me again and he kissed me, his tongue and fingers moving in tandem. I felt dazed and half-asleep, yet on top of the world. Toe curling sensations hit me and bursts of light exploded behind my eyelids. I wanted to moan, but I dreaded doing anything that'd break the spell and have him pull away again.

"You can't imagine how long I've waited for this," he said, his voice gruff, and I raised my lids to see him. The look on this face was so penetratingly exposed, my heart faltered in my chest. This was it. There was no going back for either of us.

He stripped off his black boxer briefs. I couldn't stop myself from sneaking a peek. My eyes flared as he grabbed his cock and aligned it with my entrance. I felt the slight pressure of his head begging for admittance. Having been almost two years since I'd had sex, my body clenched with need. I didn't want to wait.

My hands smoothed over his back and ass, holding him firm against me. I opened my legs wider, urging him on even though the foreplay had scarcely begun. There'd be time for all of that later. Right now, I just wanted to feel him.

His eyes found mine as he edged inside of me slightly and pressed a kiss to my lips, stretching out the moment. Stretching out the anticipation. Feeling like I had already waited decades to feel him inside of me, I squeezed my hands on his ass, arched my hips as much as possible and rasped out a pleading "please."

With a groan of defeat, he pushed his hard length inside of me in one game-ending stroke. The initial pinch caused me to suck in a deep breath through my teeth.

"Does it feel okay?" he whispered next to my ear.

"God, yes."

We stared at each other and in that block of time every inch of my heart, body, and soul belonged to him and some part of me sensed he belonged to me too. His lips searched out and found mind again.

He was rock-hard and moving in and out of me with slow, even strokes. I wiggled beneath him with impatience, the sheet rustling beneath me, our breaths mingling. I wanted him to move faster.

His gruff chuckle, low and deep, tickled the shell of my ear, but he kept moving at his pace and after long minutes of those disciplined thrusts, I relaxed, letting him take the lead, following him wherever he wanted. When I thought I'd die from want, he picked up the pace, our bodies slapping and molding into one. An insatiable hunger for him rolled through me. I could only describe it as a need to be connected to him on every level possible.

"God, Emma," he whispered shakily, almost as if he were losing control, and the hairs on the back of my neck lifted.

My spine arched, and I dug my fingers into the smooth skin of his shoulders. The need to beg, scream, and laugh hit me all at once with the force of a tidal wave. A trickle of alarm ran through me at the strength of our connection, but I quickly pushed it away and concentrated on the feeling building inside of me.

He lifted my hips, sending me hurtling over the edge. When the last twinge of pleasure whirled though me, Caleb sped up, climaxing with violent pulses. I pressed my hands against his chest, loving the feel of his ragged breath and shuddering body. On a grunt, he rolled us both to our sides.

We stayed in each other's arms, and he breathed out my name again. I felt the hot slick of him between my legs, but my eyes were too heavy with exhaustion and satisfaction to do anything about it.

My stomach rumbled.

"Breakfast?" Caleb asked.

I didn't open my eyes. "I don't think I can move."

"Rest," Caleb crooned, drawing the blankets over our bodies.

"What about—"

He pressed a finger to my lips. "It can wait."

I burrowed into his side and dozed off before I had a chance to second guess his suggestion.

Chapter Thirty-Nine

After our initial round of lovemaking, Caleb dragged me into town for a late brunch. Then, rather than take a walk on the beach like I'd wanted earlier in the morning, we'd found ourselves in bed again, surfacing only to eat dinner. Finally, we fell into a drained slumber later that night. The next two days followed along the same pattern, and I had to admit that being carefree felt good.

With every passing day of our self-induced isolation my fascination with Caleb increased. I told him everything about me and I asked him every question I could think of. We traded information about hobbies, favorite foods, least favorite foods, families, friends, and political beliefs. Nothing was off limits. Even though I'd only known him for a short while, I felt like I knew him by heart, almost as if we'd been around each other for a lifetime instead of a month.

The sun was high in the sky when I woke up on the third day wrapped in Caleb's embrace. I felt unequivocally satiated and thoroughly peaceful lying there. A slow smile slid across my face, and I traced the lines of Caleb's body.

"What's that smile for?" Caleb's husky voice had me lifting my head. He was leaning up on one elbow, an appreciative grin on his face. He kissed tip of my nose as was becoming his custom.

"I don't know. What about you? Are you smiling because I'm smiling or because I have drool on my face?" I joked, sounding a little unsure. This thing between us was new, and before him, I'd only been with Andrew. I didn't know how this dating thing went. Andrew seemed to be all in within a handful of days. Being younger and less experienced than him, I was starstruck, so I had blindly followed his lead, which had me walking down the aisle and living a life beyond my expectations within a matter of months. I didn't expect things with Caleb to fall into line that easily.

"I'm smiling because I'm damn glad we came here."

I sighed, rolling onto my back. "Yeah, it's been a good change of pace. I haven't thought about anything in days."

"Not a thing, huh?"

I poked him in the chest. "Well, you, of course, but I should have done this dropping off the face of the Earth thing sooner. God, I can't believe I haven't even charged my phone or pulled it out of my purse since I left."

"You and me both. Although I do this sometimes so no one will notice."

A niggle of unease ran through me. Other than Nora and Brock, I didn't have many people looking for me on a regular basis, and as long as I made it back by Sunday to sit by Addison in church, she wouldn't notice my absence. Brock and I talked once a month. Nora, though, she could be a problem. She checked in on me every week, and it'd been longer than that since we'd spoken. She'd be worried, especially if Brian reached out to her and fed her a bunch of nonsense about Caleb.

"Shit." I sat up and scraped my hair away from my face. The long blonde strands were wild from showering and climbing into bed with wet hair last night. Undoubtedly, I looked a little crazy this morning, not that I could tell from the way Caleb kept his gaze glued to me.

"What's wrong?"

"Nora's probably wondering where I am. I wouldn't be surprised if she made the drive to the house. Knowing her, she's probably filing a missing person's report as of right now."

"Who's Nora?"

I swung my legs over the side of the bed. "Andrew's mom. We're still close. She's actually the one who gave me the house, not Andrew."

"Really?"

"It's a long story, but he didn't leave me much of anything in his will at Nora's request. She thought I was kind of a—"

"Gold-digger," he finished and I flinched.

"Yeah. Anyway, during his illness, Nora and I became really close. Now, she's more of a mother to me than my own. She gave me the house to 'right a wrong,' or so she claimed."

"Seriously?" He shook his head, his voice rough.

"He basically left you destitute after you nursed him for years because that's what Mommy Dearest wanted. What a prick."

My face heated. "It wasn't like that, and either way, it doesn't matter. It all worked out in the end."

"How long after his diagnosis did he die?"

Heavy with feelings I couldn't even begin to process, I pulled on a sweatshirt, snagged my purse from the floor, and made a beeline for the living room. I didn't want to talk about this. Sure, I had a lot of unkind thoughts after the reading of the will, but Nora stepped in so quickly, I hadn't dwelled on them for long. Maybe she did it because she knew the whole thing would sour my memory of Andrew.

I tried not to let his actions hurt me, but I wasn't blind to Andrew's faults. He hadn't been perfect by any stretch of my imagination. He could be authoritarian at times, and I hated how he never defended me when Nora insulted me to my face. Despite all that, he'd opened so many doors I hadn't even known existed. He supported my studies, and he loved me. Maybe not enough to challenge his mother, but he didn't expect to die so soon. I'm sure he would've changed his will if we had children or more time had passed. Besides, there had to be a rule somewhere about not speaking harshly about the dead.

"A couple of years, but I don't want to talk about this. It's irrelevant."

He scoffed. "That's plenty of time to change his will. It was a dick move and don't even get me started on his mother. She sounds like a piece of work."

I whirled around. "Drop it. I don't want to talk about it. Nora and I had our issues, but we've put it behind us and she's important to me. Anyway, it's in the past and it's not your business."

His jaw flexed and he massaged the back of his neck. "Fine. We won't talk about him. It just pisses me the fuck off that they treated you that way. I don't like to see people get taken advantage of, and that's especially true when it comes to you." He blew out a breath. "I'm going to run into town to grab some food for breakfast."

"Ugh," I grumbled and tossed my purse on the kitchen counter. I needed to use the time alone to call Nora and my brother anyway. "Maybe you'll come back in a better mood."

He scooped his keys off the counter. "Who says I'm in a bad mood?"

"Me, and now you're storming off because I don't want to talk about things that don't matter anymore."

He framed my face with the palm of one hand. "I'm not mad at you."

"Still, I don't want to fight," I whispered, barely managing to get the words out of my mouth.

For some reason, I had this feeling that our relationship was ephemeral, almost as if I didn't hold on tight enough, it would slip through my hands. I hated the insecurity the sensation stewed inside of me. Perhaps I could dismiss it as a consequence of being blindsided by Andrew's death, but it seemed like more than that.

He ran his fingers restlessly through his already disorderly hair. "We're not. Forget what I said.

Thinking about him pisses me off for a lot of reasons that don't make sense. We should make the whole subject off limits."

As silly as it sounded, the little girl inside of me beamed at the thought that he might be jealous. "I'm not opposed to that."

He laughed, the sound rich and deep, and it made my belly flutter. I lifted up on my toes, and kissed him.

"I like it when you laugh."

Chapter Forty

After I charged my phone for ten minutes, I listened to my voicemails and read my texts. It quickly became evident that my disappearance hadn't gone unnoticed by Nora. Her messages started out quizzical, then became increasing frantic last night. Then, apparently she'd tracked down Brock and he'd left a barrage of messages. About thirty minutes ago, he said he was planning to drive to my house within the hour to check on me.

"What a colossal mess," I murmured to no one in particular as I called him.

He picked up the call on the first ring. "Jesus, Emma. Where in the hell are you?"

"Tybee Island with a friend, and before you go off on me, I'm sorry I didn't tell you or Nora. It was a last-minute thing."

Silence greeted me.

"Brock, are you there?"

"Yeah. Yeah. Sorry. Nora had me so worked up." He chuckled. "She can be really intense, if you know what I mean."

"I do." I'd been on the receiving end of her tirades more than once during my marriage, and I could go a lifetime without hearing another one. It was part of the reason I called Brock first rather than her. Maybe if I sweet talked him, he'd call her with the happy news that he found me and I could put off the confrontation with her for another day.

"So, what's up with the sudden trip? You finally realize that big ol' house is creepy as fuck?"

"Honestly." I perched on the end of the counter stool and tapped one foot nervously on the floor. "I needed a break. And you're right. It gives me the creeps, sitting there in the old house. At first, I thought it was beautiful. Romantic even. Now…"

"Now?" he prodded.

I thought of Elizabeth for the first time in days. "I'm not so sure I want to go back there. Ever."

"Shit. I'm sorry. You know, I was just kidding about the bad karma thing, right? I didn't mean to put ideas in your head. I just wanted you to think about coming home for a while."

"God, Brock, I don't think you were that far off base." I glanced out the window, watching the long seagrasses sway in the breeze. "But enough talk about me. What's new with you?"

"Emma," he drew out my name with caution. "You can't drop a bomb like that and change the subject. Don't try to hide shit from me. You know I won't stop until you tell me what's going on."

I groaned. Brock was worse than Nora when he wanted to be. As a kid, Mom never paid attention to me, but if Brock sensed something was up he was relentless. I knew from experience that it'd be less painful if I just gave in.

"Fine, but don't try to check me into a mental hospital because if this wasn't happening to me, I wouldn't believe it."

I spilled every last detail. He peppered me with a few questions, but mostly he stayed silent. I ended with my fear for Elizabeth and her impending forced marriage to a sadistic asshole. "So that's the whole sad story. Do you think I'm crazy?"

"No, but I think I should come home for a while. I have room in my house and Mom is barely there. I don't like the idea of you being alone and going through this."

"That's not necessary. Caleb is staying with me." The instant the admission left my lips, I wanted to scoop it up and shove it away.

"Who the hell is he?"

"He rents the converted barn and we're kind of together."

He snorted. "Nora's gonna shit. She pretends she wants you to move on, but I think she secretly hopes you spend the rest of your life grieving her piece of shit son."

"Brock," I warned.

"Yeah. Yeah. You don't want to talk about him. Tell me about the new guy. What does he think of this flashback thing?"

"You know, he's been oddly supportive. In fact, I think he really believes this is happening. I mean, the minute I said I needed to get out of there because I couldn't take it, he drove me out to his house here. No questions asked."

I heard his chair squeak as he shifted, and I

prepared myself for all sorts of recriminations. Brock wasn't a trusting person by nature, so he was probably organizing his thoughts to present me with hundreds of reasons why I shouldn't depend on Caleb.

"Have you ever wondered if all these people Elizabeth encounters in these flashbacks are people who've been reincarnated and are now a part of your life?"

"Maybe. I don't know. Honestly, I haven't spent a lot of time trying to put the pieces of the puzzle together. I kind of chalked it up to Elizabeth having a story to tell. Anything bigger seemed too crazy."

"Think about it. You're obviously Elizabeth. Who's Charles and Henry? Maybe Elizabeth had unfinished business with these people and you're—"

"Supposed to tie up the loose ends with them in this life," I finished.

"Somethin' like that," he agreed.

"That would make sense," I mumbled, my mind spinning with possibilities. I'd been so caught up in the pending tragedy of her life that I hadn't stopped to consider what it could mean in the context of my life. If there were some sort of correlation between my life and hers, I should stop avoiding everything and face the music.

The lock on the front door jingled and it swung open. I whirled around to find Caleb standing at the entrance, two coffees and a bag of pastries in hand.

I lifted a hand in greeting. "Are you coming in?"

"I can wait outside if you're still talking on the phone."

I patted the empty stool next to me. "Brock, I've gotta run. Caleb's back."

"Yeah. Okay. Don't be a stranger and keep me posted."

"I will." I paused for a second. "So, um, can you call Nora for me?"

He barked out a half-laugh, half-scoff. "I'd rather lick a cactus."

"Please, Brock. I can't deal with her right now. I really need a break from everything and that includes her. Talking to her will stress me out even more, and I don't need that. Just tell her I'm out of town and I'll call her when I get back."

"Fine. You suck," he grumbled.

I giggled. "Love you too, bye."

I disconnected the call and turned my attention to Caleb. He hovered uncertainly near the now closed front door. "That was my brother. He and Andrew's mom were worried because I hadn't returned their phone calls in a couple of days."

He gazed at me quietly. "Did you get everything sorted out?"

I nodded slowly. "I think I'm ready to go back," I said, not even realizing that I'd made the decision to return until it came out of my mouth.

"Why's that?"

"I'm ready to face everything, and Brock brought up a good point."

He moved closer to me. "What's that?"

"Elizabeth's life or the people in it might be connected to me somehow. Maybe I or we have unfinished business."

His eyes darkened, and he stroked the back of his

265

hand gently down the side of my neck, looking almost expectant. "When do you want to go?"

"Is this afternoon too soon?"

He scooped me up as though I weighed no more than a feather, and I looped my arms around his neck as he carried me the short distance to the bedroom.

"What about my coffee?" I asked as he lowered me onto the bed.

With his body braced above mine, his eyes were like molten lava. "It'll keep."

Chapter Forty-One

Sunday morning, Caleb and I found ourselves driving to meet Addison at church. I had to use blackmail to get him to accompany me. Well, not really, but he was strongly opposed to going. In the grand scheme of things, it probably was better if he stayed home. Our trip to Tybee Island had put him even further behind on his commissioned paintings. Even more disconcerting, this town wasn't a bustling metropolis by any stretch of the imagination. Like any small southern town, no one and nothing escaped scrutiny. Showing up together would make us the subject of some serious gossip.

I considered myself immune to the gossip. Except for Addison and Josh, I hadn't made any other connections in the community. I'd been too busy chasing ghosts and getting to know Caleb. It was surreal how my life had transformed since I'd moved here and not only because of all of the supernatural things I'd experienced. Caleb changed everything too. Being with him felt as natural as taking my next breath, and in some moments, my life before him seemed so distant it almost felt like a dream.

The second we pulled into the parking lot, a wave of uneasiness rolled through me. "Okay. It's official. I think this might be the last place I want to be right now."

"Told you so." He scanned the parking lot. A steady stream of people made their way inside the building. It had white lap siding with high gothic windows and a tall front steeple. "It's not too late to turn around."

I rubbed my temples. "Addison would kill me."

"Suit yourself." He turned off the ignition and I begrudgingly climbed out of the car.

We entered through a cornflower blue painted wood door and took a seat in the back wooden pew. I studied the brightly colored stained glass windows that lined the walls on either side of the church. Up front was a simple wooden table and a podium with a microphone.

Less than a minute later, Addison slid into the pew next to me. "Josh is sitting up front with his mama, but I'll stay back here with you two."

"I can't believe you talked me into this." I hadn't stepped foot in a church in a long time. We hadn't been very religious growing up. Mama dragged us to church on holidays when we were younger. After my dad died and she let her addiction take over her life, she stopped bothering with anything that took effort.

She patted my leg. "Don't worry. The new minister won't go over forty minutes. It's kind of like the drive through of churches."

"Hmm." I refrained from commenting because even forty minutes felt long with all the gazes in the church surreptitiously darting in our direction before snapping forward again. "How old is this place anyway?"

"The church was founded around 1840, but I think this particular structure was built in the 1920's. The old church is still standing. It's around back surrounded by the cemetery. They only open it for services on Christmas and Easter. You should go poke around, though. It's kind of interesting if you like that sort of stuff."

I smiled. Andrew had taken me on a tour of historic churches in Georgia when I started my Master's program. Given the history of this place, I was surprised this spot didn't make his list. "Yeah, I do. I think I'll take a look while you're trying to get Josh's attention."

Like Addison said, the service didn't last long and in under an hour, the three of us were filing out of the church. Instead of piling into their cars, everyone congregated in the parking lot. Addison threaded her arm through mine and introduced Caleb and me to dozens of people before we were in striking distance of Josh and his mother. Caleb excused himself, pointing to his phone. I nodded and turned my attention back to Addison.

"It's now or never," I whispered in her ear.

"I don't know. Do you think I'm being too forward?"

I rolled my eyes. "Exactly how long have you and Josh been circling around each other?"

"Since high school, but I thought we'd finally

put it all behind us." She lowered her voice. "His mama hates me. I have no clue why, though I secretly suspect she doesn't want anyone to take her son away from her. Look at the way she clings to him."

I shot a glance in Josh's direction. Addison was right. His mother had a cane in one hand and she clutched Josh's arm with her other hand. "What's her deal?"

"Other than being an overbearing bitch," she rolled her eyes, "I don't have a clue. Her husband left her when Josh was barely two, and she's clung to him with both hands ever since. I should probably write him off. He'll never have a normal relationship. At least not while she's still alive."

I winced. "That's harsh."

"It's true."

"So, what's the plan?"

"I don't have one." Her shoulders sagged. "God, he sucks. I don't know why I keep thinking things will change. I mean, he finally moved out of her house three months ago and we started dating for real. Then she showed up when I was over there and he's gone radio silent."

"You know what? I think you should ignore him. Let him do the chasing for a while."

She kicked a pebble with her black flats. "And if he doesn't bother?"

"Then fuck him. He doesn't deserve you." And I truly believed that. While Nora had been controlling in the beginning, she wasn't even in this woman's league. "Trust me, my mother-in-law had those tendencies and it wasn't fun. My husband was always scrambling to placate both of us and it didn't always work. I came out the loser more often than not."

Caleb materialized behind me, placing a hand at the small of his back. "You ready to go?"

I glanced at Addison. "Yeah."

Addison cast one last longing look at Josh. "I'm gonna head out too."

"Wait? You're really not gonna talk to him?"

"No. You're right." She pulled her phone out of her brown leather hobo bag. "Besides, I told my dad I'd pick up an afternoon shift. Thanks for coming. It really helped me."

I studied her vulnerable expression. "Hey, my friend Lainey owns a few restaurants in Atlanta. I'm sure you could get a job at one of them for a few months if you want to get out of here for a while."

"My dad would freak."

"It doesn't have to be a permanent move. The change of scenery might help you work through the Josh thing without having to worry about running into him all of the time. You might meet someone new or your absence might force Josh to make a decision one way or another."

She chewed on her lower lip for a second. "You know what, I think that might be exactly what I need."

"I'll talk to Lainey and text you the details. I might even be able to find a place for you to live short term."

Nora had a small apartment over her detached garage. She'd let Addison stay there if I asked her.

"Thanks." She hugged me, then started walking

backward, a big grin on her face. "See y'all."

"What was that about?" Caleb asked.

"I told her to stop chasing Josh and let him come to her for once."

"Ah." He threaded his hand through mind. "You ready to go?"

"I want to take a look at the old church over there before we go."

He frowned. "Why?"

I exhaled a large breath "Before Andrew got sick, I was working on my Masters in history. Things like old churches are my jam, and I feel like I need to see it for some reason. Come on. It won't take long. I don't think we can go inside."

"Are you sure you don't want to save it for another day?" he asked tentatively.

"I'm sure."

My low heels squished into the sodden grass as we made our way toward the old white church. The quaint structure sat underneath a large grove of trees, keeping it permanently in the shade. It had small, pointed windows and doors and a curved roof. Nestled in the shadow of the churchyard wall, there was a small well-kept garden full of vibrant purple flowers.

We halted near the cherry red front doors, and I twirled in a circle. Then a strange sensation swirled through me. I gripped the iron handrail, anxiety and panic colliding in my chest when I realized what was happening. It'd been nearly a week since my last flashback and I had initiated those.

"No, no, no," I pleaded, locking eyes with Caleb, my mind racing uncontrollably. I dropped to my knees and squeezed my eyelids shut, praying it would stop.

I felt Caleb's hands fall on my shoulders. "Emma. Emma. Emma."

His voice morphed into an agonizing buzzing noise that reverberated through my entire body. Then nearly as quickly as it started it came to a stop, and I opened my eyes. I was standing on the steps in front of the old church except now it seemed relatively new and the front doors were a deep mahogany rather than red.

Chapter Forty-Two

I turned around and the vibrant green lawn stretched out before me. The church where the morning service was conducted was replaced with a smattering of people. The women wore varying shades of hoop skirts embellished with bows and lace and carried coordinating parasols. The men dressed in simple grays and blacks with high stovepipe hats, and long frock coats with puffy cravats.

Ignoring the gathering outside of the church, I slipped around the side of the building. I'd seen Henry walk back here followed by Anna ten minutes ago. Every time I thought about her, my stomach pitched. By most standards, she would be considered beautiful with her dark hair and pale as moonlight skin. I, on the other hand, had been on the receiving end of her wicked barbs enough times that I could no longer see her appeal.

I spotted them standing beneath one of the spreading branches of a tree. Immediately, I regretted following them here. Wishing I were invisible, I pressed my back against the wall of the church, tucking my body tightly into the tangled branches of the angel trumpets shrub. The pendulous flowers hung like bells, slightly obscuring my view. I said a silent prayer that someone in my family wouldn't find me here, spying on Henry.

Anna twirled her parasol and tipped up her chin to laugh. I longed to inch closer so I could hear what Henry was saying. I groaned inwardly. My obsession with Henry wasn't healthy. While our families had a tentative agreement that we would marry at some point, I was nineteen years old and he and Anna were twenty-two. Right now, those years seemed insurmountable.

Sighing, I pushed away from the wall and inched toward the small garden on the opposite side of the church. Trying to eavesdrop on them wouldn't do me any good, and while Henry tolerated my habit of following him around, I doubted it would endear him to me if he caught me right now.

Henry's dad, Thomas, came around the corner accompanied by my father, waving to Henry. I ducked behind the half wall enclosing the garden, my heart beating like a drum. The wide yellow lace ribbon at the bottom of my hoop skirt fell into a puddle of muddy water. If Axie couldn't repair it Mama would have a conniption fit. Speaking of Mama, hopefully she wouldn't notice my absence. I hated making small talk after church. I'd rather be out riding my horse through the cotton fields.

Behind me, I heard the crunching of footsteps and I smelled the sweet scent of cigars. I curled into

275

a tighter ball, cursing my stupid skirt. If I could get away with it, I'd wear trousers every single day.

"Henry, those people didn't appreciate your words," Thomas said.

"They're dangerous notions, for sure," my father added.

"I wasn't the only one with reservations about the arrangement under which our family has lived for five generations," Henry countered, a sharp edge to his voice.

"You shouldn't bite the hand that feeds you. Our way of life has allowed us to prosper," Thomas barked and tapped his cane against the stone wall I hid behind. My breathing accelerated and I covered my mouth with my hand to stifle the noise. Pa didn't approve of me interfering in men's business.

"Even Elizabeth flaunts my rules about the house slaves. She's always following them around and rambling on about this and that, treating them like her friends. The younger generation doesn't respect the system."

"Excuse me for doubting the wisdom of having nearly half of the population of Georgia enslaved. Those numbers alone are reason for concern, and don't get me started on the horrors of the whole institution," Henry countered.

"We aren't Haiti. There isn't going to be a rebellion," Thomas said, referring to the attempted slave uprising of 1822. It had been thwarted, but the memory of it influenced the decisions of most Georgians, or at least that's what I heard Pa say on more than one occasion.

"It's not only the number of slaves, but here in

Georgia we stubbornly cling to the past. Every year we lose influence at the national level, and with good reason. The last time we made the trip to the North, there were factories everywhere. We're falling behind. They think we're backward and I'm inclined to agree. We can't continue to build our future on the backs of others. It's not sustainable. You're both too hardheaded to see what's right in front of you. The institution of slavery will end with or without our consent."

Pa scoffed. "You're as bad as my niece in New Hampshire. She's always writing letters to Elizabeth, planting abolitionist ideas in her head. But we have our own way of doing things down here. They should respect that instead of looking down their noses at us. In fact, Georgia should follow South Carolina and secede with all due haste. It's only a matter of time before this all comes to a head. No use beating around the bush."

"Amen," Thomas grumbled.

"Current political circumstances don't call for drastic action. We need to modernize. Look at the railroad. They're making money. We need to think forward, not backward. Heck, in the recent election, the city of Atlanta voted for pro-union candidates. It'll be tough to convince them to go along with such a drastic solution."

"They'll fall in line. Come on," Pa said, "let's head back before the women come looking for us."

My muscles relaxed. Thank goodness, they were leaving. Now, if only I could get home without Mama noticing the dirt on my skirt. I didn't need another lecture from her today. Pa avoided her so she took out all of her frustration on me.

Thomas laughed. "I think I see them looking this way."

"You can come out and stop eavesdropping. They're gone," Henry drawled less than thirty seconds later.

Chapter Forty-Three

"Dash it all. You scared me half to death," I blurted out, jumping to my feet and brushing off the loose debris. "And I wasn't eavesdropping. I was just taking a stroll around the church."

Henry laughed as he straightened his hat, looking even more handsome as he shook his head. "Pshaw, nonsense. Even hidden beside that bush I saw you watching Anna and me."

"Ugh, Anna," I grumbled. "I don't know why you talk to her. I've got a mind to row her up Salt River. She's awful."

"She's harmless."

"No. She's the devil. You should hear the unkind things she says to me, and if you're really my friend, you wouldn't wander off with her. The more time she spends with you, the meaner she is to me."

She bore a deep enmity for me and the feelings were mutual. I couldn't count the number of times she mocked my hair or clothing. She even said snide things about me to Mama, and Lord knew, Mama didn't need any encouragement to find fault with me.

His eyebrows snapped together. "She's hurt your feelings?"

I glanced down at the ground, feeling out of sorts from the heat of his stare. "Yes. She's always making nasty remarks about me, but it doesn't matter."

He snatched my hand and guided me out from behind the garden wall. "Well then, I think it's time we put a stop to this."

"Henry!" I whined, trying to wrest his long fingers from mine. "Let me go! What will everyone say if they see us?"

"I don't give a damn what anybody says about us. You're important to me, Elizabeth, and I don't like anyone thinking they can talk badly about you."

We were still hand and hand as we neared the gathering of people socializing outside the church. A few people paused to stare at us, and I lifted my chin and smiled, refusing to act guilty, but my stomach rolled like I'd lose the contents any second. By the time we reached Anna, I was winded from trying to keep pace with him.

"Anna, you're acquainted with Lizzy, right?" Henry said, his jaw clenched.

"Why, yes. She's your little neighbor. She's so cute, always trailing after you like a lost puppy. It must be vexing, though, to have a shadow around-the-clock," she answered, a toothless smile on her face.

She wouldn't think I was so cute when I stabbed her with the tip of my parasol. I opened my mouth to respond, but Henry squeezed my hand to silence me.

"Now, Anna, tell me why you care?" he ground out.

"Oh, please, everyone knows she's pathetically infatuated with you. It's quite embarrassing, actually. Bless her heart."

Just a few words from her sharp tongue and I wanted to die, swoon, or anything that would allow me to disappear. While I followed Henry on occasion, he sought me out too. It wasn't one-sided by any stretch of my imagination.

He lifted one brow. "Who do you mean when you say everyone?"

"Well," she chuckled, "I don't want to mention names, but we all sympathize with your predicament. I imagine you're compelled to hold your tongue around her because your families are friendly and have joint business interests. You're ever the gentleman not to scold her or lose your patience."

Henry stared at her for a prolonged moment, his face unreadable, and then began to articulate his next words very clearly. "Listen closely to what I say. I won't tolerate you or anyone else being rude to Elizabeth. If you think our family's connection is the only reason for my kindness toward Lizzy, then you don't know me very well. She is one of the most important people in my life. Now hear this. You are well aware our parents intend for us to marry. Whether or not that happens, know that from this moment forward, you will treat her with respect or I'll make sure you regret it."

Her chin quivered and she glanced to the side. "I don't appreciate your threatening manner, Henry. I

*was under the misconception that we were friends
as well, but I understand your position very clearly.
I reckon you don't need to worry about it happening
again. Have a good day."*

*Anna narrowed her eyes at me before whirling
around, fleeing in the direction of her family's
buggy. Some small part of me felt bad for her. I
noticed the way her eyes followed Henry
everywhere. Clearly, she liked him and she had
hoped he returned the sentiment. Until today, he
hadn't done anything to discourage her, and even I
knew while our parents had entertained a marriage
between the two of us, it wasn't inevitable. He could
fall in love with someone else, and I wouldn't have
a claim on him other than in his memories.*

*In fact, I'd overheard my parents discussing the
matter not less than a month ago. Mama felt with
me turning twenty in a couple of months, Pa should
put pressure on Henry to propose. Pa quickly put
her in her place, explaining in no uncertain terms
that Henry wouldn't marry me unless he wanted to
and trying to force his hand would have the
opposite effect.*

*"You didn't have to do that. I didn't tell you any
of that so you'd interfere. I'm just frustrated with
her. Nothing more," I mumbled.*

"I wanted to set her straight."

*"I feel bad," I said, not meeting his eyes and
instead scanning the area for Mama. I'd already
been away from her side for too long. She always
assumed I'd get into some sort of mischief when I
disappeared, but listening to her tiresome
conversations and chiming in when appropriate*

bored me to tears.

His mouth went rigid. "She'll get over it. Why don't you ride back with me today?"

"Oh, I couldn't. Mama wouldn't permit it. You know how she is."

"They can follow behind us."

I really wanted to join him. Unless we ran into each other, we were rarely allowed time alone anymore, and I missed him. Missed our conversations. Missed his gaze on me. Missed the way he was always there rooting me on no matter what.

I nodded. "As long as my parents don't protest."

Less than five minutes later, I was seated next to Henry in his buggy. He lifted the reins and the horse's high-heeled trot lengthened to a leisurely pace. The breeze offered a welcoming respite from the humid air. A smile slid across my face. Being in the fresh air away from all of the expectations of society and Mama brightened my spirits.

Henry glanced at me. "You like this?"

I laughed and tipped my face to the sun, loving the feel of it warming my skin. "You know I do. I despise being stuck inside the confines of my house or trailing after Mama making polite conversation. You don't know how lucky you are. You can go wherever you want with whomever you want. What I wouldn't give to be free like that."

"Where would you go?" He wrapped an arm around me and the smell of his soap and skin made me feel like nothing else existed except the two of us.

I nibbled on the inside of my cheek as I gathered

my thoughts. "I'd get on my horse and wander for hours. I love the feel of the wind hitting me in the face and I wouldn't worry about the leaves or twigs in my hair. I'd ride as fast and far as my horse would let me."

"Oh, really." Henry turned his head to me, his eyes half-mast, and slapped the reins, coaxing his horse to go faster.

The buggy jolted forward. My body bounced up and down and I squeezed my eyes closed, laughing.

"Mama is gonna have a fit."

"She'll get over it and you look like you need to have some fun. Besides, I like seeing you smile," he answered with a devilish grin.

The thunder of hooves and the clatter of wheels over the dirt trail became louder and louder until I could feel it deep in my bones. Then it suddenly stopped.

When I opened my eyes, I found myself sitting in Caleb's lap on the steps of the old church.

"Emma, are you okay?"

I smiled. "I am."

It was the unvarnished truth. The memory of the way Henry defended Elizabeth and indulged her warmed something deep inside of me. It was so unlike the more recent flashbacks that seemed like a harbinger of doom. This one felt harmless, like a gift that weakened my resistance to experiencing the next part of Elizabeth's life.

Every person's life had good and bad chapters. If someone had plopped down in my life the instant of Andrew's diagnosis, it would give them the impression my life was tragedy. While I felt exactly that when I watched him suffer, we had beautiful moments I wouldn't take back for anything, and now, with Caleb, I had new reasons to believe in my future. My heart squeezed with hope and anticipation.

Caleb wrapped his arm around my shoulder and that feeling inside of me grew even more. "Let's go."

Hand in hand, we made our way to the parking lot. I felt grateful for whatever twist in fate that had brought Caleb to me. He was the perfect person to support me during this time. He never pressed me for information or pushed me to explain. He didn't laugh or doubt me. He accepted everything at face value.

"Thanks for being here for me," I said, resting my head against his shoulder.

Chapter Forty-Four

The next day came with a renewed sense of determination. Cowering wasn't an option any longer. I had to find out what happened to Elizabeth. By the time I made my way downstairs, Caleb had a breakfast of eggs, bacon, and fruit on the counter.

"Are you working today?" I asked as he handed me a cup of coffee.

"Kind of. I need to do an inventory of the paintings in the loft."

I loaded up my plate with the food and popped a blueberry into my mouth. "Why?"

"I cut ties with the Savannah gallery, and I need to take pictures of what I have laying around for my website."

I hid a smile, happy that I wouldn't have to cross paths with that awful woman again. "Are you looking for a new gallery?"

"I will when the timing is right." He took a sip of his coffee and rubbed the back of his neck. "Are you going to try to force another flashback?"

"Yeah. I'm ready to find out what happened to Elizabeth. I couldn't stop thinking about her yesterday. And truthfully, I think I'd slip into her life today regardless of what I did or didn't do. I can feel a weird energy building inside of me, pulling me back there. I need to know the whole story. It's time."

He glanced at the wall over my head, his thoughts unreadable. "Just promise me you won't lose touch with what's happening between us."

I scrunched up my eyebrows, not understanding where he was going with that comment. "What did or didn't happen with Elizabeth has nothing to do with us."

"I hope you're right, Emma." He kissed the tip of my nose, then my lips. He took a step toward the door before hauling me into his arms like he was afraid to let me go. "I'll bring dinner with me tonight, but if you need me, I'll be around."

I snagged his arm as he moved to leave. I studied his golden-brown eyes, trying to understand what he was getting at. "Hey. Is something bothering you?

He blew out a breath. "No. Have a good day and don't wear yourself out chasing the past."

"Okay." I gave him one last hug and watched him leave.

After cleaning up breakfast, I found a candle and a book of matches and settled onto the chair near the fireplace in my bedroom. It seemed like the most logical place to force a flashback if I wanted the story to start exactly where it left off.

I lit the candle and the yellow flame danced in a circle on the darkened wick. I replayed every detail of the day Elizabeth ended up a prisoner in her bedroom, preparing for her marriage to Henry's brother, Brett. Her mother rivaled mine for the title of worst parent. While I couldn't comprehend the full breadth of her mother's despair over losing a husband and not hearing from her son for years, I couldn't believe she'd force her daughter to marry someone so callous, especially when she had to realize he'd mistreat Elizabeth.

After a while, my eyes became heavy as I slid into a hypnagogic state. The colors in my room softened and blurred. My body pulsed and swayed. The world went black.

"Elizabeth." A knock sounded at the door, and I rolled on my side, refusing to respond. The sun had come up less than an hour ago and I couldn't even bring myself to enjoy the beautiful display of colors. Somehow the pink and orange had morphed into something sinister. Then again, nearly everything had felt that way since I said goodbye to Henry. If I could go back in time, I'd tie him up and take him far away from this mess, so we could get the life this war had stolen from us.

"Elizabeth, it's Lydia, dear. Are you awake? Can I come in?"

Lydia, Henry and Brett's mom, had always been wonderful to me. My stomach dipped when I came to the realization that she likely had a hand in plotting my marriage to Brett. She'd always seemed so gentle, kind, and supportive—the complete opposite of Mama. Maybe I read her wrong. I shuddered at the thought of facing another critical person, yet I answered her, knowing ignoring her or anyone else wouldn't matter. Come hell or highwater, by the end of the day, I'd be married to Brett.

"I'm awake," I answered, my voice flat.

The key rattled in the lock and the door creaked open. I sat up, my bare feet dangling off the side of the bed. Lydia stood in the doorway, an ivory dress draped over one arm and a gentle smile on her face. Her eyes were so much like Henry's that my stomach clenched.

"So, um." She paused. "Henry had this dress made for you before he left. I know he'd want you to wear it today." She swallowed and looked down at her feet as if only now realizing how horrible her words sounded.

I cleared my throat. "I don't think it would be appropriate to wear it given the circumstances. My marriage to Henry would have been sacred. What's happening today is a travesty. I could not wear that dress in good conscience. It makes me sick merely thinking about it."

Her lips turned down. "I know you don't see the wisdom in marrying Brett, but I believe the marriage will be good for both of you. While he may seem harder than Henry, he's a good man deep down. If you give him a chance, you won't regret it."

I tightened my hands into fists to hold back the stream of unkind words I wanted to say about her son. He wasn't merely hard, he was cruel. I hated him with every fiber of my being. "I reckon there's no point in having this discussion. Brett won't change his mind and Mama refuses to see reason. Apparently, you agree with them, so there's nothing to debate."

She sighed. "I suppose not, but I truly believe you two will be a good match once things settle down."

"We have nothing in common."

"You both loved Henry. You've both lost a lot over the past few years. You're both in pain."

"Those things are superficial."

"It's a start."

She lifted the dress, holding it in front of her like a peace offering. It was made of a decadent silk. Ribbon, flowers, pearls, and lace decorated the bodice. The wide skirt had layer after layer of lace, bows, and flowers with a wide similarly outfitted train on the back.

"Henry insisted on adding the flowers." She spread out the dress on my bed and brushed her hand lovingly over one of the silk blooms. "You don't think they're took much, do you?"

I bit my lower lip to keep from dissolving into tears. So many emotions rushed through my head at once, I didn't know whether I wanted to smile, laugh, or weep. I stuffed my fist inside of my mouth to stifle the animalistic sound that crept up from deep in my gut. My limbs were like jelly, and I reached out to steady myself on the post of the bed. The ability to respond escaped me.

My Lord, I couldn't have conceived of a more perfect dress. And the flowers—of course, Henry wouldn't forget the flowers. He'd been tucking them behind my ear since I was a kid. My lungs squeezed so tight at the thought of wearing this dress to marry someone other than Henry, especially his brother.

"I can't," I finally pushed out, the words shaky. "Please take it away."

Lydia wrapped her arms around me, and I was engulfed in the familiar scent of bergamot and lemon. "I know this hurts right now, but think of it as a gift from Henry. A blessing, if you will. You and Brett haven't had the most auspicious beginning and maybe this will help bring light into something that feels so dire. Please wear the dress. Don't let his efforts be in vain."

"Brett wants me to wear a dress his brother partially designed."

"He doesn't know, and it should stay that way. It'd be a shame to waste such a beautiful gown."

I shivered at the thought of stroking Brett's temper. "I don't think it's a good idea. I can find something else suitable."

"Elizabeth," Mama hollered from the door and my trembling increased. I stepped out of Lydia's embrace and stared at Mama. Her arms were crossed and her lips were pressed together so hard they were nonexistent. "I know you have a hard time behaving yourself, but for the sake of your future family, do attempt to portray yourself as gracious and mannerly. Accept the gift and stop whining. And be quick about it, we don't have much time."

I swiped at the tears streaming down my face and lifted my chin. While a part of me longed to rip the dress to pieces, I wouldn't do it. It was Henry's *final gift to me, and the beauty and sentiment of it alone stifled some of the rage brewing inside of me, urging me to rebel.*

Lydia squeezed my hand. "Brett left at sunrise to retrieve the reverend. Everything should be ready by noon. I'll see you then."

When her footsteps no longer could be heard, Mama said, "I'll send Axie in to help you dress."

After Axie had poured no less than five buckets of water into the copper tub in my bathing chamber, I dismissed her and poured the rose-scented oils she had set on a small table nearby into the water. I climbed inside carefully, still sore from Brett's assault. I cleaned every inch of my skin, inspecting the bruises and scratches that marked my body. When my fingertips wrinkled, I dried off and rubbed lotion into my skin. Finally, I brushed my blonde tresses gently, wincing when I touched a particularly tender spot. To an outsider, it might appear as if I were painstakingly preparing for my upcoming nuptials, but in reality I was stalling, praying for some sort of divine intervention.

When none came, I moved to my bedroom and rested on the edge of chair and rolled on the knee-length silk stockings I found lying to next to the dress on my bed. I eased on my corset. Unable to tie the corset myself, I opened my door to call for Axie, only to find her waiting for me. Without murmuring a word, she laced my corset, her gaze intentionally eluding mine. I wondered if it was the circumstances or all of the bruises on my body that made her avoid studying me too closely.

"Sit, Miz Elizabeth. I need to fix yer hair." Axie

pointed to the bench in front of a small dressing table.

While she crafted a roll of hair at my nape and twisted two plaits around it, I dusted my face with rice powder and swiped a clear pomade of beeswax on my lips. When everything was in order, she helped me into my petticoats and the dress.

"Lordy, me!" Axie exclaimed, taking a few steps back. "You is pretty as a flower, chile."

"Thank you." I forced out the words as I stared at my reflection in the small oval mirror. Objectively, I did look nice, beautiful even, but it was hard to revel in the thought when I knew Mama would fetch me within the hour to marry Brett. Even worse, I felt positively nauseous at the thought of wearing the dress Henry had commissioned for me. "I have something for you."

When her brows scrunched together, I ignored the question in her eyes and ran to my bureau. Hidden in a pouch at the bottom was a few gold coins Pa gave me years ago. I stuffed an old letter from my cousin in New Hampshire inside. Between the war and my pending marriage to a madman, I didn't know what would happen to Axie. This was my way of offering her some security, and she deserved it and more. I knew there was a time when she might need the information.

I pressed the pouch into her hand. "Take these coins. You'll need them when you leave."

Her eyes widened and she shook her head. "I can't take those."

"We don't know what the future holds, and this might help you with whatever comes next. My

cousin's address is on the letter. She will help you if you make it that far north. Her husband is an abolitionist. They've been sheltering people since before the war." I swallowed hard. This didn't come close to repaying her for her kindness and love, and yet it was all I had. "Please take it. It's the very least I could do."

"Thank you." She closed her hand around the pouch. "Yer mammy will fetch you at noon."

Seconds later, she disappeared, locking the door behind her. From my room, I could hear footsteps rushing about the house, preparing for the ceremony, not that it would be the grand party Mama had envisioned when I planned to marry Henry. I found it more than a little ironic that she refused to move up my wedding because she wanted to turn it into an event society wouldn't forget and now I was getting married to someone else with only Mama and Brett's parents present.

Regret rolled through me. Henry was right. I should've defied my parents and married him before he left. Right now, I would be a widow with my own household and Mama wouldn't have any say in my future.

I thought of the keepsakes I'd kept in the floorboards. I still hadn't got around to reading the letter from Henry. I pried open the flooring again and fingered the envelope from Henry. I desperately wanted to read it, but I stopped myself. Dwelling on the past wouldn't help me survive the future. I replaced the letter where I found it. After a few seconds, I slipped off the bracelet Henry gave me and added it to the pile of mementos before wrapping it up in the oiled cloth and putting the floorboards back. Maybe one day when I could recall the memories without crying myself silly, I'd come back and collect them along with the bracelet. But for now, they'd stay where I left them, a shrine of sorts to happier times.

Chapter Forty-Five

Around ten in the morning, the banging and stomping in the house escalated until I couldn't ignore the commotion any longer. It sounded like they were tearing down the house rather than preparing for a wedding. The faint acrid scent of smoke reached the inside of my room and my heart skipped a beat.

I wiggled my doorknob and it wouldn't budge. so, I banged on the door. "Mama? Axie? What's going on?"

No one answered.

"Let me out," I yelled over and over, banging with both fists.

After nearly twenty minutes, the door flung open and Mama stood in front of me, her face deathly white and her hair disheveled. "Sherman's army is nearly here."

"What?" I hissed.

"You heard me."

"But how?"

"Brett rode into town this morning and it was all

everyone was talking about. He said between the soldiers, wagons, and animals, the march stretched two to three miles. He nearly ran his horse into the ground to get back here to warn us in time."

"It's probably a foraging party," I said, not believing it myself. I ran to my window, searching for any sign of the impending invasion, and I gasped in horror. In the distance, the garish flames of burning structures lit up the heavens and I could just make out the army. It looked like thousands of ants lined up as far as I could see.

"Mama. They're almost here. We have to run."

She rushed to my side, sunk to her knees, and squeezed her eyes closed as if she couldn't bear to look at the sight in front of us. She whispered, "For whosoever shall call upon the name of the Lord shall be saved."

"Mama. Mama." I shook her arm, but she ignored me and continued praying.

As I darted around my room, stuffing clothes and every small piece of jewelry I had into a valise, I yelled for Axie. I needed her to help me out of this dress so I could breathe.

"She's gone," Mama said from behind me, her voice frail.

I swiveled around and she was still on her knees. With her shoulders hunched and her clothes smudged with dirt, she looked like a shell of her former self. Even when she'd dipped into Pa's whiskey she seemed so formidable.

"What do you mean she's gone?"

"I told her to move the food to the cellar, then go up and unlock the door for you while I hid the

silver, Pa's watch, and my jewelry in the garden. When I came back, I couldn't find her anywhere."

"I reckon that makes sense." She had been a steady presence in my life for as long as I could remember and it killed me to think I'd never see her beautiful smile again. I sat back on my bed, missing her already. She'd really done it. For some reason, I thought she'd wait until after my marriage, but with the Yankees closing in and gold in her pocket, there wasn't a better time. *"Sam and his son are gone too?"*

"As far as I can tell. I was caught up in marriage preparation and then everything fell apart so quickly. I haven't been thinking clearly, but I don't think she'd leave them behind."

Rage built inside of my chest. I couldn't believe Mama didn't come to get me the second she heard the news. She'd spent her morning preparing for some stupid wedding when we should have been getting ready for the impending invasion. She'd said it herself yesterday. The Union army was in the vicinity, and she'd done nothing except strip me of my dignity and abuse me until I bowed to her wishes.

"Get up, Mama. We need to go."

She shook her head. *"Brett, Lydia, and Thomas are coming here. We're going to stand together so we aren't two women confronting those devils alone, and whatever happens, we must bear it as best we can."*

As though it been timed perfectly, I heard Brett's family come in the front door, and Lydia called out to us. My eyes narrowed on Mama. In that instant I *knew our dire circumstance hadn't altered her plans. She fully intended me to marry Brett as soon as humanly feasible regardless of our fate after we faced the Yankees. Part of me was too numb to care either way.*

"Go down and talk to them. I'm going to change out of this dress."

When she left, I slowly removed the gown and the petticoats and put on one of my soft muslin dresses. Rather than joining the Cadwells, I pushed my chair closer to the window and watched the enemy close in on us. For a second, I wondered if Charles would be with them and somehow convince his fellow soldiers to spare us and then I wondered why I cared. Life as I'd known it had changed so drastically over the past few years. Being stripped of everything seemed like a fitting end to it all.

After a half an hour, I could see the muzzle of the enemy's guns and hear the steady clops of hooves, groaning axles, and crunching wheels. Still, I didn't make any move to join Mama and the Cadwells in the parlor and no one called out to me either. Not fifteen minutes later, the army had surrounded my house and a pounding sounded at the front door.

Fear made my legs unusable and muted my voice. My heart pumped at twice its normal rate. My mind scrambled, and I couldn't decide what to do. In the absence of any direction, I sat motionless in the chair.

Mama's screams echoed up the stairs and into my bedroom. Booted feet clomped through the house, and I ran out of my room to watch the commotion from the railing overlooking the foyer.

Soldiers stormed the house, going in every direction. I watched from the hall as they entered the bedrooms only to slice open the mattresses and pillows, scattering feathers and cotton everywhere. It looked like a snowstorm in the rooms and the hallway.

They filled their satchels with whatever objects they fancied. Laughter, shouts, and banging collided, creating a symphony of terror and chaos I'd never forget. Broken chairs, plates, grits, and flour covered the hardwood floors below. After what seemed like days but was likely no more than an hour, the soldiers abandoned the inside of the house altogether, leaving it in ruins. From the railing, I could see Mama with her back pressed to the foyer wall, tears spilling down her face.

"Mama," I called out to her, but she didn't respond. It was almost as if she were frozen in a trance.

"Mama," I yelled, louder this time. Instead of answering, she collapsed onto her knees.

I would have gone to her, but the stench of fire hit my nose and I hurried to my room to look out the window. At first I stared in disbelief, as if it were a dream, then it changed to horror when reality set in.

Outside, red flames swallowed the gin house. Soldiers stood outside the barn, systematically slaughtering what little remained of our livestock. Chickens and hogs bled out on the dirt. They escorted our few remaining horses and mules out of the barn, and I suspected that'd be the last time I'd see them. When I could no longer take in the destruction of my home, I closed my eyes and rested my forehead against the window. The cold from the winter day seeped through the glass and into my skin, and I shivered. At this point, I just hoped they would have enough decency to spare our lives.

"We should have run when we had the chance," I whispered to myself.

Chapter Forty-Six

"Elizabeth! Elizabeth!" I heard a man yell, snapping me out of my numbness.

"Go away. She's not here."

Yelling and the sound of things breaking filled my ears. My stomach tilted, and I sprinted down the hallway, nearly colliding with Brett. He stood on the top step of the stairs, a gun raised, pointing at someone or something below. In the foyer, a man hidden by his hat, held a gun to Thomas' head. When I joined Brett at the stop of the stairs, the Yankee turned and I gasped.

"Charles? What are you doing here?"

My heart skipped a beat when I realized he was alive and Axie hadn't lied about patching him up. Then my chest squeezed tight as I fully comprehended the stand-off in front of me. This wouldn't end well. Brett was unreasonable on a good day and Charles, well, he had reason to seek retribution.

Charles' hard eyes swiveled to mine. "Elizabeth, go back to your room. I'll come for you after I settle things here."

I looked back and forth between the two men, the room crackling with energy. I took a step back, intending to do exactly that, but I halted in my tracks. Despite what they'd done to me, I couldn't abandon Mama or the Cadwells.

"Charles, don't hurt them."

He didn't spare me a glance. "It's over. Put down your gun."

"This is disgraceful," Mama shouted. "I won't allow this. You and your friends have torn apart my home and now you're threating my dear friends. Why, if I had known you would treat us like this after my daughter—"

Charles cocked his gun, the noise as loud as cannon fire and Mama froze midsentence. "I'll give you one more chance. Put away your gun."

"You're a cussed fool if you think I'll listen to you," Brett snarled.

"You're a fool if you don't. If you shoot me, the rest of the soldiers will be in here straightaway." Charles pointed his gun at Brett's missing hand. "I think you already know they're always happy to spill Rebel blood."

Brett's hand shook, then after what felt like an hour he lowered his gun, and stuffed it into his holster inside his coat. My muscles relaxed. I couldn't believe he had actually backed down.

I put a hand on his shoulder, and I whispered so only he could hear, "Thank you, Brett. I know that was hard for you."

He hooked his left arm around my neck and grabbed his gun again with his right hand. "You move and I'll kill her."

"No!" Mama screeched and Lydia covered her face as if she couldn't bear to witness the events unfolding in front of her for another minute.

"Please, Brett. You don't need to do this. I'll marry you. I'll do whatever you want," I pleaded.

"'First Corinthians 15:33, 'Be not deceived: evil communications corrupt good manners.' This is particularly instructional right now. You brought this hell upon my family by inviting the enemy into our life. I don't want anything to do with you," Brett sneered.

The front door flew open and three Yankees filed inside, laughing. They quickly halted when they saw the guns drawn. One of the Yankees pulled out his gun and aimed it at Brett and me. The world paused for a second, cementing the moment in my brain for all eternity.

The frozen expression on everyone's face. The flat light of the cloudy day mixed with plumes of smoke. The shouts of revelry that carried on outside heedless of what was occurring in my house. The ivory feathers stuck to the hem of my skirt. The smell of the burning gin house. The way Brett's arm tightened fractionally around my neck. The brush of the wool of his jacket against my throat.

"No!" Charles yelled, but it was too late.

The Yankee pulled the trigger. A loud bang filled the air, and I screamed, the force of it shredding my throat. Brett jerked and tumbled to his knees, taking me with him. I flew face forward. I stretched my arms out in front of me, trying to brace my fall. The heel of my hand slapped the wooden step, sending a stinging shock up my wrist, but it failed to stop my descent. My head hit next, and I somersaulted, my vision a blur of the ceiling and then the floor again.

Brett's body hit mine and for a millisecond our eyes met. His were blank and glassy and blood dripped down his face from a hole in the center of his head. I didn't have time to process what it meant because my shoulder struck the wooden spindles, and I heard a crack.

My muscles bellowed. My back hummed like I'd endured a hundred lashes of a whip. Nausea swirled in my belly. Tears swallowed my eyes and I kept sliding downward. The back of my skull smashed against the floor foyer. Pain exploded inside of my head.

Mama's face swam in front of me and I felt her hand curl around mine. "I'm so sorry, Lizzy. This is all my fault. We should have run. We should have joined your brother. Please forgive me."

"I can't move," I whispered, except the words were so faint, I wasn't sure if she could hear them.

"Please don't leave me, Lizzy. I'll do better. I'll be better. You don't have to get married if you don't want and I promise not to say a word about those trousers you like to wear or the freckles from the sun."

No longer caring, I tuned out her rambling lists of promises and regrets. I had no idea how much time had elapsed as I drifted in and out of consciousness, wishing I could disappear altogether. Wishing it were Henry holding my hand rather than my mother. Wishing Henry and I had run away together and escaped the wrath of the war. If only...

Booted feet shook the floor beneath me and I winced. Shouts, screams, and cries echoed in my ears, but they were quickly eclipsed by the ringing in my ears from my crushing headache. The noise became louder and louder until it blotted out the dreadful radiating pain in my body. A bright light flashed, and I gasped. Then my vision dimmed, the edges darkening inch by inch until everything was black.

Chapter Forty-Seven

I opened my eyes and I found myself sitting on the bottom step in the entryway of my home. Tears stained my face. I glanced down at the hole in the knee of my jeans, and I breathed out a sigh of relief. I was Emma again. I scrubbed a hand over my face, trying to comprehend what had happened to Elizabeth, and the only thing I could come up with was that she died.

Holy shit. She died.

Or maybe I just experienced how I'd died in a prior life. Whatever happened to her, I knew deep down in my gut that the journeys back to Elizabeth's life had come to an end. I saw whatever I needed to see. The only remaining question was whether I'd learned something relevant to my current life or if it were just a story that I experienced by being in the right place at the right time.

Tempted to call Caleb to unload on him or maybe even my brother, I slid my phone from my pocket and stared at the screen for a moment before setting it on the step next to my thigh. I wasn't ready to talk to anyone, and truthfully, I was drained.

Needing time to process everything, I climbed the stairs and went back to bed. For over an hour I lay there, staring at the ceiling, yet my mind refused to quiet. The last day of Elizabeth's life played over and over in my head like a loop bent on torturing me. I felt the grief, betrayal, the acceptance of her fate when she took off Henry's bracelet, and the physical pain had been so vivid.

The memory of the bracelet had me scrambling to my feet and across the room. On all fours, I ran my hand along the floorboards where Elizabeth stored her memories. Could they still be here after all of this time? Everything seemed to be undisturbed until I came to an area where a few planks had been top nailed beneath a chair. I slid it aside and I knew I'd hit the jackpot.

Butterflies flipped crazily inside my stomach and it took all of my strength to move my body from the spot where I sat, almost as if I had somehow grown roots. My heart thundered loudly inside my ears as I weighed my options. While part of me wanted to let the story end with Elizabeth, I couldn't do it. I'd relived her life for a reason. I'd seen her place things right there more than once and I took that as a sign.

It didn't take me longer than a few minutes to grab the tool kit from the kitchen drawer and return to my bedroom. I hooked the claw of the hammer under the wood planks and pried it back with all of my weight. The boards cracked in half and a musty plume of dust filled the air.

I reached inside the hole, my hand blindly circling the space. Then I felt it—the oiled cloth, brittle with age. I recognized the faded blue ribbon from my flashbacks tied around the outside. My hand shook as I tugged on one end and carefully unfolded the fabric.

"Holy shit," I breathed, blinking a few times to make sure it was real.

On top of a stack of papers was the bracelet Henry gave Elizbeth. I picked it up and dusted it with the hem of my t-shirt. Before I could think better of it, I unclasped it and put it on my wrist. I held it up to the afternoon sunlight that spilled into my window, and smiled. For some reason, I loved it as much as Elizabeth did the moment Henry presented it to her.

One by one, I unfolded the fragile sketches. There were a few depictions of the Civil War camp and the country exactly as I had seen them through Elizabeth's eyes. A lump formed in my throat when I came to the drawings of Elizabeth in dozens of poses. Sitting at a formal dinner. One of her standing in profile with a magnolia in her hair. Another sitting on the tree swing. Her leaning against the railing of the front porch of this exact house with a fan in her hand. It was strange how the house had changed, but was still instantly recognizable. The last was a drawing of Henry and Elizabeth sitting side by side in the countryside.

Then I came to the unopened letter from Henry, and a lump welled up inside my throat, making it nearly impossible to swallow. It felt like an invasion of privacy to read it. My finger traced Elizabeth's name on the envelope, and I closed my eyes, letting my heart guide me. Decision made, I slowly opened the flap. The seal was weakened from age.

My darling Lizzy,

I write to let you know that I was badly wounded during a battle. When we pushed forward, a bullet hit my left arm and passed clear through it. As the charge continued, a shell exploded and shattered my right leg and killed one of my comrades.

I was taken to a field hospital and that same afternoon they took my arm. They gave me chloroform so I had no knowledge of the operation, but it has been painful. Over the last few days I've been feeling feverish, and I fear the worst.

While I know these words will cause you much grief, I beg you not to have any regrets about us. Have faith, for if I never meet you again in this life, I know we will meet each other in heaven or in the next life. And in that next stage of existence, whatever it may be, I will remember you and I will find you because in all of the universe, there is no soul that will fit me like yours. Tell me I'm not being presumptuous for believing you feel the same.

Yours now and for eternity,
Henry
P.S. Our time will come.

Sitting right there, surrounded by broken floor planks, letters, sketches of another era, wearing Elizabeth's bracelet, I fell apart.

I cried for their lost love.

I cried because I wanted them to find each other again, no matter how improbable it seemed.

I cried because fate had steered me here and I'd found someone who filled my heart more than I'd ever thought possible after Andrew had died.

I cried because I didn't know if I would change the events that led me to this moment in my life even if I could. Just as he'd said in his letter, I had to have faith that things would work out the way they were supposed to be.

After my tears had dried up, I emptied my purse and carefully tucked the letters and drawings inside. I had to share them with Caleb. After the past few weeks, I'd only offered bits and pieces of what was happening, yet he'd been incredibly understanding and supportive, never pushing me for details, never questioning my sanity. He'd deserved to hear Elizabeth's story. Elizabeth would want people to know what happened to her.

Chapter Forty-Eight

My purse dangling from my shoulder, I jogged to the barn. Despite knowing he was sensitive about people seeing his work, I pushed open the door and walked into the open space of his home.

"Caleb. Caleb," I yelled, searching for him.

His bed was neatly made. A cup of water sat on the kitchen counter next to an empty glass plate. My stomach rumbled, admonishing me for not eating since breakfast. The door to the bathroom was open and he wasn't inside.

Left with no other options, I made my way up the winding metal staircase to the loft area. I paused at the top of the stairs. He was crouching in front of a row of canvases, his ears covered with headphones.

I tapped him on his shoulder, and he straightened. He pulled the headphones from his head and set them on a table beside him.

"What are you doing here? I didn't think I'd hear from you for hours."

"It's over," I said absently, my attention on the

paintings behind him.

He framed my face with his hands, sending a jolt of awareness through me. "What do you mean it's over? Let's go downstairs so we can sit down and talk."

I stepped out of his hold and inched toward the paintings, needing to get a closer look. When I saw them, my heart stalled for a beat. Bewildered, I turned to face him, looking for some indication of what he was thinking behind his impassive façade. "You painted these?"

"I did."

The familiar scenes came into focus and my mind whirled. The resemblance to some of the sketches inside of my purse had me sliding my hand inside to check they were real. The painting of a woman so like Elizabeth sitting on a swing hanging from an oak tree. Other than having color, they were eerily similar. There were others too. Elizabeth standing on the porch. Elizabeth outside the historic church except the church was as I'd seen it in my flashback rather than in person.

"I don't understand. You painted these…and it's her and…how did you, and I and…" Over the course of the last few minutes, I'd lost the ability to form coherent sentences.

Caleb leaned in close to me, his front brushing along the length of my back. "The images have been stuck in my head for a while. I wanted to paint them before I forgot, though it doesn't seem possible."

"I see," I mumbled, not sure how to comprehend what he was saying or what I was seeing.

"You aren't going to ask why I painted what I did?"

My blood roaring in my ears, I closed my eyes. He was confusing me. Okay, not just him, everything. "No. I'm not sure I'm ready."

"You said it was over. We need to talk."

"I don't know where to start."

"Do you like them? Are they how you remember it?" he persisted.

I nodded, keeping my eyes closed.

"You aren't even looking at them."

I whirled around and faced him. "No. I need to look at you. The man who painted them."

"And what do you see when you're looking at me, Emma?"

"I don't know."

"Look with your soul, not your eyes."

How did I explain? I was dumbfounded, ecstatic, perplexed, and freaked out all at once. It was as if he had reached inside my head and pulled out memories from my time as Elizabeth. I sighed, and looked at the worn wood planks beneath my white sneakers, afraid to believe what my soul was telling me. What it'd been telling me for a while now, but I'd refused to listen.

For a prolonged moment, I couldn't say the words. They were beyond ridiculous. Then he lifted my chin with two fingers and stepped back so I could see the full length of him. His ochre eyes locked on mine, and in the quietness of the loft, I saw destiny more than a century in the making.

"Oh my God," I choked out.

"Do you see it now?" he inquired, tenderly.

"You're Henry, and I'm Elizabeth."

His shoulders dropped like a hundred years of tension had been lifted off him. "Finally."

"You experienced all of this madness too?"

"Yes. I mean, it ended years ago, but it hit me out of nowhere. I took a ghost tour with some friends as a joke when we were passing through on a road trip. This house was the third stop. Unable to stop myself, I wandered off, and well, you know what it's like when the first flashback hits. Afterwards, I convinced myself I'd had too much to drink. That night someone in town mentioned the Claytons were looking for a caretaker for the property. I called the next day. Once I moved in here, the flashbacks kept coming and I felt like I was lost between two worlds.

"Then I met Andrew in person when he came to check on the property. He wanted one of the paintings of you, I mean, of Elizabeth on the swing. When I refused, he showed me your picture to try and convince me, and I lost my mind. Somehow, I knew you were her."

"And you stayed?"

His gaze slid to the side. "I don't know why I didn't give up. You'd married someone else. He seemed to adore you. I tried to move on, to date, to find a new place to live. Nothing helped, so I made a life here. My gut told me you'd show up at some point, and I'd know then whether there was any point in holding out hope."

"I don't get it. Why were you so mean to me when I met you?"

He considered me for a moment, slanting his

head to the side. "I didn't realize it at the time, but I think I was mad at you for marrying someone else and living your life while I'd been sitting in this town, waiting for you. Then I realized you hadn't experienced what I had, and I didn't have the right to resent you for things you didn't understand. Instead of being mad, I decided to support you during this because I didn't have anyone to help me, and I'd nearly checked myself into the hospital a half of a dozen times."

"That must've been hard."

"Yes." He heaved out a breath. "The worst part was not knowing what happened to Elizabeth after…"

"Henry died," I finished, my voice a mere whisper.

He ran a hand through his dark hair. "Yeah. The story ended there, and it left me with this hole that nothing could fill. I tried to research Elizabeth's life, and all I found was the grave telling me she died in 1865, not long after Henry."

I thought of all the things I could explain. Brett. Charles. Elizabeth's mother. Her death, and I decided none of them mattered. It was finally in the past. "I don't want to talk about that."

He nodded, his eyes full of understanding. "Maybe someday."

"Yeah." I swallowed the lump gathering in my throat, remembering her final days. "You knew I was going crazy. If I'd known the same thing happened to you, it might have been easier. You should've said something."

"Trust me, it's been torture waiting for you

figure it out. You don't know how many times I wanted to confess everything, but I couldn't do it. I even tried to stop our relationship from becoming too physical because it felt like cheating. I wanted you to find your way without interfering so you could decide whether this," he motioned us between us, "is what you wanted. Then this morning, when you were determined to see it to the end, I wanted to press the pause button because things were going so well. The past had become less and less relevant with every moment we'd spent together. We'd found each other again and that's all that mattered. Later, I realized it wasn't my call. I had to trust the process, fate, or whatever you want to call it."

I fished out Henry's final letter to Elizabeth from my purse and held it out to him. "I don't think Henry was being presumptuous with what he wrote in here."

He grasped it from my hand, scanned it, lifted his eyes to mine, and read the last few lines aloud. *"And in that next stage of existence, whatever it may be, I will remember you and I will find you because in all of the universe, there is no soul that will fit me like yours. Tell me I'm not being presumptuous for believing you feel the same."*

"I feel the same. Don't you?"

For a drawn-out moment in time he stared down at me, his gaze tender and his parted lips soft. And in his eyes, I could see his answer as clear as if he voiced the words aloud. He grinned and kissed the tip of my nose. "This is our time, Emma Clayton."

Epilogue

Six months later

"Are you ready for this?" Caleb asked, studying my reflection in the mirror as he leaned against the doorjamb to my bedroom.

He looked incredible in his indigo blue tuxedo with the ivory bow tie. Of course, he had a magnolia boutonniere pinned to his jacket. I took a second to commit this moment to memory. After all, it had been more than a century in the making.

"You look even more beautiful than I'd imagined in that dress," he said, his voice thick with all the emotions of our journey.

I rolled my eyes. "You did have a hand in designing it so you don't have to act surprised."

I had described the dress Henry had created for Elizabeth, and while I didn't want something so ornate given this was my second marriage, we tried to stay true to the concept. Like the original, my dress had flowers, tiny pearls, and hints of lace. However, this version was strapless and had a high slit up to my right thigh. I'd styled my long blonde hair with loose curls that covered my bare shoulders and I'd kept my makeup relatively light.

When the music began to play, I peeked out my window. Addison, Josh, Brock, Lainey, Noah, and few faces I didn't recognize, but knew were Caleb's close friends and family sat on white folding chairs beneath Henry and Elizabeth's tree.

Addison had been living in Atlanta in the apartment over Nora's garage and working in one of Lainey's restaurants. After she'd been gone for a month, Josh finally reached out to her. She took a few weeks to get back to him, and when she did, she told him not to bother if he intended to flake on her again. So far, things had been going well, and he'd been driving there every weekend to visit. Addison was over the moon with happiness, but I was still skeptical. Time would tell.

We decided not to have a big wedding out of respect for Andrew's memory. And truthfully, Caleb and I got married at the courthouse near his house a week after I found Henry's letters. Without a doubt, our friends and family would be hurt if they discovered the truth, but neither of us wanted to give destiny the opportunity to get in the way again.

A knock sounded at the door. "That'll be Nora," I said, picking up my bouquet of magnolias tied with an ivory satin ribbon.

Even though Caleb and Nora didn't have the best relationship, he didn't complain about her. When I told her we were getting married, she cried and hung up on me. The next day, she asked me if she could walk me down the aisle. I accepted because I understood how she felt, and although she wasn't perfect, I knew she loved me and I loved her. Elizabeth's story taught me life was too short to hold grudges. I had even invited my mom to the wedding. She didn't respond, but maybe one day she'd turn things around and want to be a part of our life.

Caleb kissed my nose, my cheek, and finally my lips. In his kiss, I tasted all of our yesterdays and all of our tomorrows, saw our future children, felt lifetimes of passion and commitment. The promise I sensed during our first kiss in the barn finally made sense.

"See you in a few minutes," he whispered when he pulled back.

With Nora's arm linked with mine I walked down the aisle, keeping my gaze glued to Caleb the entire time. He stood beneath our tree. The glass lanterns dangling from its branches swayed in the breeze. The sweet scent of flowers filled the air, and the music from the string quartet swelled around me, inside of me, filling my soul with love.

In this moment, I knew the circle of Elizabeth and Henry's life had finally closed. But I also knew my relationship with Caleb was about more than a past connection. We shared laughter, unconditional love, loyalty, and the deep peace that came with knowing we found each other this time around and we'd find each other again in the next life.

About the Author

After spending years practicing law and running a real estate development company with her husband, Lisa decided to pursue her dream of becoming a writer and she must confess that inventing characters is so much more fun than writing contracts and legal briefs. A native of Colorado, she lives with her husband and three children in Denver. When she isn't managing the chaos of raising three children and owning her own business, she can be found reading or writing a book or tinkering in her garden.

Social Media Links

Facebook:
https://www.facebook.com/lcardiff11

Twitter:
https://twitter.com/lcardiff_author

Goodreads:
https://www.goodreads.com/author/show/7692079.Lisa_Cardiff

Website:
https://lisacardiff.wordpress.com

Join our Reader Group on Facebook and don't miss out on meeting our authors and entering epic giveaways!

Limitless Reading

Where reading a book
is your first step to becoming
limitless...

LIMITLESS PUBLISHING *Reader Group*

Join today! *"Where reading a book is your first step to becoming limitless..."*

https://www.facebook.com/groups/LimitlessReading/